SAVAGE BLOW

Boone Logan's eyes went absolutely black. He said, and his tone was as thin and toneless as a shift of cold wind: "Get aside, McClure. I won't warn you again."

Buzz, going a trifle white around the lips, for he knew what was coming, said: "No."

Quick as a pouncing wolf, Boone Logan rolled his shoulder and hit him. The blow was solid, savage. It landed with a *crunch* and snapped Buzz's head back and would have knocked him down, had not the bar caught Buzz across the shoulders and held him up. Buzz weaved a little, but spread his feet and stayed erect. His lips were mashed and bleeding and a queer hurt shone deeply in his blue eyes. But he kept his place.

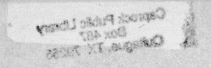

RIVER RANGE
A Western Trio

L. P. Holmes

LEISURE BOOKS NEW YORK CITY

A LEISURE BOOK®

February 2008

Published by special arrangement with Golden West Literary Agency.

Dorchester Publishing Co., Inc.
200 Madison Avenue
New York, NY 10016

"The Buzzard's Brethren" first appeared in *Action Stories* (8/41). Copyright © 1941 by Fiction House, Inc. Copyright © renewed 1969 by L. P. Holmes. Copyright © 2006 by Golden West Literary Agency for restored material.

"Horse Thief Trail" first appeared under the title "Make Way for a Maverick" in *Western Trails* (7/42). Copyright © 1942 by Periodical House, Inc. Copyright © renewed 1970 by L. P. Holmes. Copyright © 2006 by Golden West Literary Agency for restored material.

"River Range" first appeared in *Ranch Romances* (2nd May number = May 17, 1946). Copyright © 1946 by Warner Publications, Inc. Copyright © renewed 1974 by L. P. Holmes. Copyright © 2006 by Golden West Literary Agency for restored material.

ISBN 10: 0-8439-6031-0
ISBN 13: 978-0-8439-6031-0

The name "Leisure Books" and the stylized "L" with design are trademarks of Dorchester Publishing Co., Inc.

Printed in the United States of America.

10 9 8 7 6 5 4 3 2 1

Visit us on the web at www.dorchesterpub.com.

RIVER RANGE
A Western Trio

TABLE OF CONTENTS

The Buzzard's Brethren

L. P. Holmes completed this story, which he titled "War of the High Plains," in late December 1940, and sent the manuscript to his agent, August Lenniger. Lenniger sent it on to Malcolm Reiss, general manager at Fiction House, who bought it on April 11, 1941. It was retitled "The Buzzard's Brethren" prior to publication in *Action Stories* (8/41). For its appearance here, the magazine title has been retained.

I

Perhaps a superman might have stood up under the punishment of the lash without an outcry. But Slip Hankins was no superman. And when the cruel, hissing length of the bullwhip wrapped about his thin, shrinking shoulders and body, Slip Hankins shrieked his agony.

Cass Denio was a big, burly, powerful man and he had put every ounce of strength he owned into the blow of that bullwhip. And when the lash, after clinging a moment like some venomous snake, fell away, a dark stripe of crimson leaped to take its place on Slip Hankins's thin, faded shirt. That shriek of mortal fear and pain carried a long way in the hot afternoon air that overlay the little cow town of Rocky Pass.

At his bench in the rear of his saddle shop, old Joe Kirby was twisting a final wax end to finish his repair job on the saddle before him. His gnarled, wax-stained fingers grew still and his shaggy, grizzled head swung to an attitude of strained listening.

"What the devil was that?" he growled.

Perched on the end of the tool- and leather-littered

bench, Rick Dalton slid lithely to the floor. "I'll go look," he said.

From the door of the shop the scene lay stark and plain and brutal. The long, white, dusty length of the street, and the figure of Cass Denio standing over the cringing Slip Hankins. Even as Rick watched, Denio flung the lash back over his shoulder, gathered himself, and flung another savage blow. And again, as the lash *crackled* about him, Slip Hankins shrieked.

The afternoon before, Shawnee O'Day, the stage driver, had brought his whip to the saddle shop to have a new rawhide lash braided to the tip of it. Joe Kirby had completed the job and the whip now stood just inside the door, waiting for O'Day to call for it.

Rick Dalton grabbed that whip and sped along the street, full of lean, wolfish speed despite the encumbrance of chaps and spurs. In the rugged planes and angles of his sun-blackened face and in the cold depths of his gray eyes, Rick showed a dark and dangerous anger. The knuckles of the hand that gripped Shawnee O'Day's whip were knotted to whiteness.

This whip had not the thick and brutal weight of the one Cass Denio was wielding. But in the hands of a man who knew how to use it, that six-foot length of worn, tough hickory and the twelve-foot lash of hard, braided leather was no puny weapon. Rick shook the lash clear as he ran.

The brute lay strong in Cass Denio. He was enjoying this job and he wanted to savor it to the full. The first blow had shaken the thin frailty of Slip Hankins like a tempest. The second had brought him nearly to his knees. He was weaving on his feet now, a sick, stark horror filming his eyes. And Cass Denio, big, white teeth bared and snarling, was figuring on bringing his victim flat in the dust with the third blow. He had the lash flung out behind him and the muscles of his burly shoulders were bunching for the effort.

Cass Denio never delivered that blow. A sharp *hissing* filled his ears. And then a slender line of fire cut fully across his face and wound about his throat, half blinding him and filling him with an agony that jerked from his throat in a bawl like a wounded animal.

Denio clawed at his face, tore at the lash encircling his throat, and the slender, hard, braided lash burned his hand as it was jerked away from him. Denio spun instinctively to face the source of this sudden, unexpected attack. He saw Rick Dalton, spat a curse, then gave his wounded animal bawl as the merciless lash took him a second time around the face and neck.

"That's right . . . yell!" rapped out Rick Dalton, his tone as thin and merciless as the lash he wielded. "Open your lungs, you big hawg, and let the world know you're suffering. Not so nice when you have to take it, is it? Two for Slip Hankins . . . now two for you. Ah! No you don't . . . !"

Cass Denio had dropped his bullwhip and in instinctive and blind defense had gone for his gun. He had it just clear of the leather when the licking lash of Rick Dalton's whip closed around his wrist in a band of fire, and the sudden pull Rick gave to the whip, before the lash could unwind, jerked the weapon from Denio's fist.

The gun fell in the dust some ten feet in front of Denio, and he dived for it, clawing and scrabbling in the dust. By the time Denio got hold of the weapon again, Rick had closed in. "If that's the way you want to play . . . ," he gritted. And Rick flipped out his own gun and hammered Denio solidly across the head with the heavy barrel. Denio grunted and went flat and motionless. Rick picked up Denio's gun, tossed it across the street where it skidded from view under the board sidewalk. Then he moved over to Slip Hankins, took him by the arm.

"Come on, you poor devil," he said.

Rick led Hankins over to the swinging doors of the Buffalo House, where a silent group of men opened up to let them through. "Pour him a double shot of bourbon," Rick ordered of the bartender brusquely. "Then trot out some of that healing oil you're always bragging about."

The bartender shook a bullet head obdurately. "No whiskey or anything else over this bar for any damn' High Plains man," he blurted sullenly.

"Listen, Caraway," crackled Rick, "I just bent my gun over Cass Denio's thick skull. You can have exactly the same medicine if you want. You heard what I ordered."

Hob Caraway tried to meet the cold intensity burning in Rick's eyes, failed, shrugged, pushed over bottle and glass. Rick poured the liquor, held it out to Slip Hankins, who gulped it down. Rick then led his man to a chair, while speaking over his shoulder. "A bucket of clean water and a couple of towels along with that healing oil, Caraway."

The bartender shrugged again, brought the required articles. That heavy jolt of liquor had brought back some measure of strength to Slip Hankins and cleared the shock from his dazed brain. He sat up straight now, and said no word as Rick carefully pulled his shirt over his head. At sight of Hankins's shoulders and back, Rick's lips pulled to a thin, white line.

"I should have shot Denio's black heart out," he growled. "I would have, too, if I hadn't known he was acting under the orders of somebody else. Hang on to yourself, Slip. This is going to hurt like hell for a minute or two, but it'll be a lot better when I'm finally done."

"Go ahead, Rick," said Hankins thickly. "Nothing could be as bad as . . . as that was."

Rick washed the blood from the livid, savage welts, then smeared on healing oil, which gave off the rich, unguent odor of balsam. Then he eased Hankins's shirt back on.

"There," he said. "That's going to help a heap. Want another jolt of liquor?"

Hankins shook his head. "Thanks a lot, Rick. You're the one white man left in this lower valley range."

"You're wrong there, Slip. There's a heap of white men along the lower valley. All they need is waking up. Well, you better grab your buckboard and get before the word gets out and Matt Iberg comes riding in with more of his bullies. No . . . I don't want any thanks. It was a supreme pleasure to work over Cass Denio. Get going."

A number of men had come into the Buffalo House while Rick had been caring for Hankins. Most of them were cowboys, a few citizens of Rocky Pass. Now, as Slip Hankins started for the door, a rider, one Howdy Orleans, barred his way. Three other riders moved in as though to back up Orleans.

"Not so fast, not so fast, Hankins," said Howdy Orleans thinly. "The Box I ain't done with you yet. Had you stood up and took the licking Cass Denio was givin' you, then you could have gone your way as a good example that it doesn't pay to beef Box I strays. As it is, we ain't done with you."

"I never beefed any Box I stray," quavered Hankins. "You know that as well as I do, Orleans."

"All I know," bit out Howdy Orleans harshly, "is that a fresh hide was found spread on your corral fence and that hide carried a Box I brand. And in your meat house was the carcass of a fresh-beefed two-year-old. Which is plenty good evidence for Matt Iberg, Cass Denio, and the rest of us Box I boys."

"The hide I hung on my corral carried my own brand, Lazy H," argued Hankins. "The beef in my meat house carried that hide. Somebody must have taken that hide and put the Box I hide in its place. Why should I beef a Box I critter when I got cattle of my own? That's a fair question."

Howdy Orleans grinned crookedly. "Yeah . . . and why should a hold-up rob a stage or a bank when he's got ten dollars in his jeans? Same thing, Hankins, and makes just as much sense. It won't do at all. What we're going to with you is. . . ."

"Get out of the way and let him go." Rick Dalton had listened to the interplay of words. Now he moved forward beside Hankins. "Move out, Orleans," he growled. "Get out of the way."

Howdy Orleans's eyes flickered. It was one thing to bully and threaten Slip Hankins. It was something else again to stand up before Rick Dalton. But Orleans tried.

"I reckon the boss will have plenty to say to you,

too," he blurted. "I know that for a long time Matt Iberg hasn't liked the way you play in with the High Plains crowd. Today you went over the line a little too far when you butted in and gun-whipped Cass Denio. What you trying to do, anyhow . . . take the part of a cow thief?"

Rick's lips curled. "Orleans, the shinamaroo that Iberg and all the rest of you Box I gents are trying to put over on this range is a little too thick in some spots and a little too thin in others. About that hide you claim you found on Slip Hankins's corral . . . well, that reminds me of the Box I horse that Iberg claimed he found in old Bob Shelly's corral. So he lynched Bob Shelly as a horse thief. Oh, he was righteous as hell about it all, Matt Iberg was. He whined about how he hated to do it and all that, and that he only did it because law and order had to be preserved and horse thieves discouraged and more of that guff.

"Now all that happened near three years ago and I guess a lot of skulls hereabouts have forgotten about it. I haven't. Because I notice now that the Six Springs water hole, which used to be Bob Shelly's water, is now watering Box I cattle. So, from now on, when any Box I jigger starts yelping around about what he's found in somebody else's corral, or on the fence of it, why I'm going to hold my nose and yell . . . 'Boo.'" Rick Dalton's voice had been dripping with sarcasm. Now it took on that crackling chill once more. "Back away, Orleans. You're cluttering up the trail."

Howdy Orleans and two of the others who had moved as though to back him up shuffled sullenly aside. But the last of the quartet held his ground. He was tall and lank, with a hatchet face seamed with hard, wild living. His eyes were little and pale and no deeper than mere surface. He was a new man to the Rocky Pass range, and, as far as Rick knew, he had never seen the fellow before. He noticed one thing. The man wore a pair of guns, tied low, butts flaring. And now he spoke, after throwing a glance of sneering contempt at Orleans and the other two.

"Judging from the way some of these shorthorns knuckle under, you must rate as a woolly wolf in these parts, mister. But from where I come, we know that a wolf ain't far removed from a coyote. Lots of time he's all coyote, once you get under his bluff and bully puss. So right now, I aim to find out the real color of your liver. Maybe it's white, or yellow. Maybe. . . ."

"Yeah," cut in Rick harshly, "maybe."

And then his right fist was whistling. It came in with slashing speed, caught the fellow squarely on the point of his hatchet jaw. And the doubter spun around, crossed his feet, and crashed.

"The answer was a lulu, Rick," drawled an amused voice in the crowd. "No question . . . when you hit 'em right, they shore drop. Scat Kelly talkin', Rick. Go your way, boy. I'll watch your back for you."

"Thanks, Scat," said Rick, blowing on his knuckles. "Come on, Slip . . . we're wasting time."

Nobody else tried to stop them from leaving the Buffalo House after that. They hit the sidewalk and clattered along the loose, warped boards to where Hankins had tethered his buckboard in front of John App's store.

"You roll right along home, Slip," cautioned Rick. "And was I you, I'd sleep a little light for the next week or two. I might not even sleep in the cabin. Fact is, I'd roll my blankets back in the sage a little way and I'd take me a rifle to bed with me. And if Iberg or any of his Box I bullies come prowling, I'd shoot first and ask questions after."

Hankins nodded as he picked up the reins. "They'll kill me before they ever lay another whip on me," he said somberly. "Matt Iberg better steer plenty wide of me from here on out. And I won't forget what you've done for me, Rick. Neither will anybody else up on the High Plains range."

"Forget it." Rick shrugged. "You High Plains folks got a right to live, just as much as Matt Iberg has. *Adiós*, Slip . . . and good luck."

Rick watched the buckboard out of sight, then turned back toward the street. Somebody had helped Cass Denio out of the dust and over to the shade of a building, where he sat, holding his head in his hands, staring at nothing with numbed, befuddled eyes. He glared at Rick as Rick passed, but said nothing. And Rick gathered up the borrowed whip from the street and returned it to Joe Kirby's saddle shop.

The old saddle maker frowned at Rick from under shaggy, grizzled brows. "Your pappy all over again . . . that's what you are, Rick Dalton," he growled. "Quick, sudden, and plumb complete, that's you. Which means that few folks will ever feel halfway about you. Either they'll hate you everlasting and complete, or they'll swear by you and stick with you through hellfire and then some. You made some enemies today, boy."

"You mean I brought 'em out in the open, Joe. They've always been against me. While I'm at it, how do you feel about what I did just now?"

The old saddle maker tamped tobacco into the bowl of a black, stubby pipe with a methodical forefinger. "Wal," he mumbled, "I jest finished fixin' a saddle . . . for nothin'. And it's your saddle. I guess that's answer enough. But don't ever forget for a minute, son . . . Matt Iberg has made a strong man of himself in this section. He's going to have a lot of followers and folks who'll back his hand toward the High Plains ranchers. Some of them Iberg backers will surprise you who they are."

II

It had been Rick Dalton's original idea that he would head back to his own little spread along the headwaters of Chinquapin Creek as soon as Joe Kirby finished repairing his saddle. That was about all that had brought Rick to Rocky Pass in the first place. Subsequent things that had happened had not been in his original calculations at all. Now he couldn't very well head for home without some people drawing the wrong conclusions. It would look as if he was running away, trying to avoid meeting Matt Iberg, after he had horsewhipped and pistol-whipped Iberg's most favored and trusted lieutenant, Cass Denio, had made another of Iberg's riders, Howdy Orleans, back down, and had topped off the whole thing by knocking still a third of Iberg's cohorts stiff with a good solid right to the jaw.

Rick well knew that word of all this would reach Iberg's ear and that Iberg would be heading for town to see about it. And Rick's self-respect demanded that he be here when Iberg showed up. It was one of those things. You couldn't help but see it that way, especially when you were just twenty-seven years young and the vigorous blood of youth overrode the caution that more mature years generally brought to a man. So Rick prepared to kill time around town until Iberg showed.

He went back to the Buffalo House where he found Scat Kelly lounging just outside the door. Scat Kelly was a big, raw-boned, red-headed Irish cowpuncher with a wide and infectious grin and reckless blue eyes. Scat was a good rider, a good hand on any outfit, but he was a restless cuss, too restless to stay put very long. Consequently Scat was without a job half the time. But Scat didn't seem to mind. Tomorrow, in Scat's philosophy, would always take care of itself.

"A wise man, in your boots," Scat observed, "would shag it out of town before Iberg shows up. But you ain't wise, Rick, old son. You're just a hellity-larrup chunk of dynamite that explodes whenever the notion strikes you. Maybe that's why I kinda like you and why I'm going to trail around behind you for a time and see that nobody sneaks up on you when you ain't lookin'. I hope you realize that Cass Denio and that lantern-jawed jigger you knocked for a loop ain't going to be maudlin with love of you from here on out."

Rick grinned. "I realize it, all right . . . but I ain't worrying none. Where are those gents right now?"

"Dunno. They snuck out of sight somewhere to sort of lick their wounds."

"Then there ain't a thing to keep you and me from going in and having a drink, is there?"

"Nothin' except you'll have to pay for it. Right now I'm flatter than a stepped-on flapjack."

So they went in to the Buffalo House, two lean, brown, spur-clashing sons of the saddle, strangely alike with their reckless grins and cool, alert eyes. Hob Caraway, behind the bar, showed little enthusiasm at sight of them, but he pushed bottle and glasses across the bar. They poured and drank, and Rick spun a coin across the mahogany in payment. Caraway, as soon as he had dropped the coin in the till, shuffled to the far end of the bar and made out he was reading a grimy, two-weeks-old newspaper.

"Hospitable joint, this," remarked Rick drawlingly. "Ever notice how they go out of their way to make you feel welcome, Scat?"

"Yeah," said Scat, "and the way the house sets up the drinks is little short of amazing."

Hob Caraway's ears and thick neck burned crimson, but he did not look up until Rick and Scat had sauntered out into the street again. Then he stared at the swinging doors with a quick, hot hatred gleaming in his glance.

Upstreet in front of John App's store a buckboard had just spun to a halt. Two people got out of it. One was a burly, round-faced young fellow of thirty-five. The other was a slim, feminine figure in divided skirts and gray wool blouse, with a bared dark head glinting in the sun.

Scat Kelly saw the quick, leaping eagerness in Rick Dalton's eyes, and chuckled. "Go ahead, if you want to talk to her. Don't mind me. I'm above such childish foolishness. I don't mind adding that in my book Kit Rowan assays clear thoroughbred. But you can have that clunk-headed half-brother of hers."

"I want to see you again, Scat . . . before I leave town," said Rick. "Don't forget."

Katherine Rowan, about to follow her half-brother George into the store, glimpsed the approaching figure of Rick Dalton, and waited for him, a musing half smile pulling at the tender curve of her red lips. Rick stopped a couple of paces from her, dragged off his hat, and looked at her with an intensity that brought a soft flush creeping up her throat and into her cheeks.

"Gentlemen," she said with a slight toss of her head, "don't stare."

"Can't help it, Kit," said Rick. "Got to make shore I wasn't dreaming. Last time I saw you and talked with you, reckon I wasn't. You're real. That's something I never get over marveling about."

The color in her cheeks deepened, her laugh was soft and low. "The same old blarney, Rick Dalton. Why can't you ever talk of sensible things, like the weather, cattle, chances of an early rain, or something of the sort?"

"Who cares about them things? They're just commonplace. You're not. You're something to make a man think of sunrise and sunset, of wild violets with the dew on 'em, of spring grass waving in the sun."

"Heavens! The man is a poet. Next he'll be telling me I've a neck like a swan and with wild roses in my cheeks, eyes full of stars, and all that other tommyrot. If you please, Mister Dalton, you'll come down to earth and talk sense, or I'll go into the store and talk over the price of laundry soap with John App."

Rick chuckled. "*Whew!* Am I that bad? Well, let it pass, my lovely one. But I still say you can change Rocky Pass from a grubby little town into a thing of beauty, just by appearing in it. With that off my mind, we'll come down to earth. When you going to make up your mind to marry me?"

Again that little toss of a gleaming dark head. "Never, sir . . . positively never. Men are only half-civilized brutes, and I want nothing to do with any of them. Always fighting and brawling."

Rick rubbed the lean angle of his jaw. "*Hum!* You've been hearing things again. Young woman, you shouldn't go listening to all the old gabby mouths in creation. Forget all that. Take me just as I am now, begging for a smile, ready to go out and knock a mountain down if you say so."

Her tone and glance became a trifle severe. "Your biggest fault, my friend, is your lust for knocking mountains down. No woman would care to spend a lifetime with a continuous explosion of dynamite."

"Now," mourned Rick disconsolately, "she's cussin' me. And me fair burned to a crisp with love of her."

"*Bosh!*" exploded Kit Rowan. "*Bosh* and *pish* and *tusk* and . . . and rats! I'm going in and talk to John App. He at least is sensible."

She would have gone, too, had not at that moment a fast-riding group of men come spurring in from the open range, chopping a cloud of dust from the street as they clattered up. Apparently they were headed for the Buffalo House, but, as the leader of the group glimpsed the two figures standing just outside the store door, he set back on the reins and spun his mount to a halt at the hitch rail out front.

Matt Iberg was a big man, thick-shouldered, with an air of domination about him. His rather handsome features were a trifle on the heavy side, marked by a bold and masterful nose. In his slightly pale eyes was a poorly veiled arrogance. And no man could read deeper than that veil of arrogance.

Iberg spoke a low word to his companions and they headed on for the Buffalo House, while Iberg ducked under the hitch rail and *clanked* up to Rick and Kit Rowan. He touched his hat briefly.

"Hello, Kit," he said.

Kit Rowan was not only an exceedingly personable young woman, but a very clever one besides. Long had she realized that between Rick Dalton and Matt Iberg existed a mutual dislike and ever-present antagonism. And she was too inherently honest and clear-minded not to know that there was more to this antipathy than competition for her smiles and favors, although no doubt this had some bearing on the matter. In the main, however, the true cause was deeper, more fundamental, more instinctive. It was as though, in the scheme of mortal things, these two men were created to hate each other. And sometimes, when she thought it all over, she knew a deep fear of what this hate must inevitably lead to. She sensed that cold, watchful bristling now and was searching a little frantically for something to say that might carry off the situation gracefully.

But she was too late. Iberg turned on Rick Dalton with out-thrust jaw and spread feet.

"You moved into some of my business again today, Dalton," charged Iberg. "I'm getting powerful fed up."

A cool, twisted, vastly remote smile lay on Rick Dalton's lips. "Feed up and choke, for all I care. This is still a free country, Iberg. There may be some people on this range ready to accept you as the lord high mogul of all creation. But I'm not one of them. Maybe you figure yourself so big and heavy you can order one of your bully-puss riders to publicly use a bullwhip on a decent, inoffensive citizen. But I differ with you on that point, complete."

"Slip Hankins is a cow thief," rapped Iberg angrily. "He beefed one of my two-year-olds. I got the proof. I know. . . ."

"Slip differs on that point, Iberg," cut in Rick coolly. "He says he beefed one of his own critters and that somebody switched hides on him. As I see it, Slip Hankins's word is as good as yours, maybe better. I'm not forgetting, Iberg, that after you have one of your so righteous outbursts of law and order, and work out on some poor helpless devil, it all ends up with some direct benefit to you. Like the Six Springs water, which used to belong to old Bob Shelly, before your outfit lynched him on the claim he was a horse thief. Your big mistake, Iberg, is in figuring that everybody is as thick-skulled as you'd like 'em to be. Well, they ain't."

Iberg's scowl grew blacker and his heavy fists, hanging at his sides, knotted. "Dalton," he gritted, "the day ain't far away when you and me are going to the mat for a showdown, final and complete."

There was a world of contempt and scorn in Rick Dalton's shrug. "You can make that time right now, Iberg . . . if that's what you want. Right now!"

The air was taut with the imminence of hovering conflict. Somehow Kit Rowan sensed that these two men had entirely forgotten her presence, so caught up were they in mutual hatred. And in her fear of what might break, she instinctively appealed to Rick Dalton.

"Rick," she cried, "drop this foolishness!"

She saw his lean head shake slowly, while his cool glance never left Iberg's face. "Just about anything else you'd ask of me, I'd be proud and happy to do, Kit," he said quietly. "But not even for you would I back down before this blustering four-flusher."

That set it off. Matt Iberg, with something of a whine of animal fury in his throat, hunched his right shoulder and drove a powerful blow at Rick's face. Rick, swaying easily at the hips, let the blow slide harmlessly over his left shoulder. And then, with an uncoiling rush of power that started clear down in his heels, Rick knocked Matt Iberg flat with a thunderous wallop on the jaw.

For a moment Iberg lay where he had fallen. Any man of less thick, vicious vitality would have been knocked cold by that blow. But Matt Iberg was a tremendously powerful man, almost impervious to shock. He rose to one elbow, shaking his head. Then he came to his knees, and finally to his feet, where he stood, swaying slightly, his head thrust forward, lips peeled back, eyes red with mad fury.

Rick Dalton watched him with the alertness of a hawk, while his fingesrs sought the buckle of his gun belt. "This is it, Iberg," he said frostily. "Something we've both been looking forward to. Shall we take off the guns and make it man to man, or don't your nerve reach that far?"

Matt Iberg spat a curse, ripped his gun belt off, tossed it and holstered weapon aside. With a quick twitch, Rick did the same. And then Iberg, with the silent, deadly rush of a maddened grizzly, came at him.

III

It was the most savage, brutal, relentless, no-quarter fight that the town of Rocky Pass ever witnessed. Word spread like wildfire and men came running from every direction until the two fighters were ringed by a solid mass of cursing, feverish-eyed men. Here was the thing that every man present knew was bound to happen, sooner or later. It was in the books, such a meeting as this between Rick Dalton and Matt Iberg. And now that it was taking place, no man wanted to miss a single move, a single blow.

Matt Iberg was the heavier of the two, Rick Dalton the faster. It was the massive broadsword against the flexible, relentless rapier. Kit Rowan, at first indignant, then angry, and finally frightened, from the added height of the store doorstep could look down over the seething crowd to the whirling center which was the fight. Although, as the thudding impact of blows given and received carried clearly to her ears and the faces of the fighters turned to blood-smeared masks to make her feel weak and deathly sick, she found she could not tear herself away from the terrible fascination of it all.

Her half-brother George, charging out of the store when the fight first started, shouted at her, tried to push her inside. But the moment he left her and joined the wild crowd for a closer view, she regained her point of vantage and watched, while cold tears ran down her white cheeks and her dark eyes grew wide and stricken.

It did not take Rick Dalton long to find out he

had the fight of his life on his hands. He hit Matt Iberg harder than he'd ever hit any man before, but Iberg seemed impervious to punishment. Even when Rick knocked him down again and again, Iberg came right back, seemingly more powerful than ever.

Rick hit the dirt himself more than once. Behind Iberg's fists lay a deadening, brutal power that hurt a man all through when they landed. Yet there was an unquenchable flame in Rick which burned, bright and clear and remorseless, regardless of punishment.

They swung punches at long range; they fought in close; they stood toe to toe and swapped blows. They wrestled back and forth, with clawing, ripping fingers. Iberg got a handhold on Rick's shirt and with one savage drag ripped it clearly off his back, and the steely muscled torso gleamed, white one moment, the next smeared and spattered with the blood of both men.

Kit Rowan whimpered like a hurt child. "It's horrible," she moaned. "Can't someone . . . won't someone stop them?"

But there was no stopping this thing, no more than the chance of stopping the hurricane, the tornado, the lightning and thunder of a storm-tossed sky. And no man in the swirling crowd wanted to stop it. For this thing was epic.

It seemed to Rick Dalton that he had been fighting for æons. Breath burned and rasped in his swollen throat, and the salt taste of blood half choked him. Yet his sinewy arms lashed out again and again and the fists at the end of them were like chunks of lead tipping withes of whalebone.

A thunderous blow caught Rick on the side of

the head and he went down in the dust again. For a terrible moment he thought he was going to lose the grip on his senses. But that unquenchable flame still burned in him and he lunged to his feet once more and nailed the charging Iberg with two crashing blows, a left and right to the jaw. It seemed that finally Rick had softened his man up, that shock at length was working on the nerve centers of Iberg's brain. For, under the impact of those two blows, Iberg tottered backward, jaw sagging, eyes rolling.

"Now you got him, Rick!" yelled Scat Kelly's voice. "Go in and finish him, boy!"

It wasn't that cry of encouragement that sent Rick leaping forward, for he never even heard it. Instead, it was an instinctive realization that at last he had really hurt Iberg—hurt him badly. So he piled in, galvanized to a new strength and battered his man with relentless, savage blows. Iberg could not regain his balance. He kept staggering back and back, his arms flailing wildly, uselessly. Finally he was up against the hitch rail before John App's store, and could retreat no farther. There Rick Dalton chopped his man down in one final surge of fighting fury that was as resistless as it was completely remorseless.

Matt Iberg's arms began to drop lower and lower, until they dangled uselessly at his sides. He reeled back and forth, back and forth as Rick's punches lashed him from this side and that. Iberg's knees began to cave, his head dropped forward, and then he fell, face down and motionless in the dust.

The fight was over.

It was over, right before Kit Rowan's eyes. The

Scat executed a few steps of a jig and departed in high glee.

"I'll feel better about you myself, knowing Scat's hanging around," admitted Joe Kirby thoughtfully. "You bit yourself off a chunk of something today, Rick, that's li'ble to end up in blood and hell. So watch yourself."

Scat was soon back and there was a hard, sober look in his blue eyes. "You used to have a big old double-barreled, eight-gauge Greener shotgun around here, Joe," he said. "Still got it?"

"Shore have. Why?"

"Well, down around the lower end of the street, where Rick and me'll be riding, there's Howdy Orleans, that skinny jigger you whopped on the jaw in the Buffalo House, Rick, and couple, three more of the Box I crowd. They jest seem to be hanging around, waiting for something to drop. It might be you. So, forewarned, forearmed, say I. Trot that buckshot-spreader out, Joe."

Old Joe produced the big weapon, along with a handful of buckshot shells. Scat broke the weapon, glanced through the huge barrels, slid a brace of shells into the gaping chambers, and *clicked* the breech shut. He pocketed the rest of the shells. "Bring 'er back next time I come to town, Joe. OK, Rick . . . let's ride. And if any of them junipers want to take a chance on facing this cannon, then I say they ain't got the sense the Lord give a fish worm."

Rick pulled his hat low over his battered face as he stepped out into the street. The waning glare of the afternoon sun hurt his eyes and he squinted painfully up- and downstreet. He saw the little group of men at the lower end of the street and he was more than glad Scat was along. For right now he did not feel up to any more ruckus of any kind. And for the first time he remembered about his belt and gun, so he took his bronc's rein and walked over to the store, leading the animal.

"How come?" asked Scat.

"Going to get my belt and gun. Be right with you, cowboy."

Rick thought the store empty of all except John App, until he was well inside and his eyes adjusted to the gloom. Then he saw her, perched in a somewhat disconsolate-looking little bundle on the far end of the counter. John App, tall and gaunt and bearded, moved toward him.

"Yeah?" he said, his voice harsh and none too friendly. "What you want, Dalton?"

"My belt and gun," answered Rick curtly. "I figured you might have picked them up."

"I did," said App. "Here they are."

Rick took them, buckled the belt around his waist, pulled out the gun, and spun the cylinder to make sure it was loaded. Then, re-holstering the weapon, he walked slowly over beside Kit Rowan. "I reckon," he said a little diffidently, "I look like something the cat dragged in. But it's still me, Rick Dalton, Kit. Somehow I feel I'm owing you an apology, so I'm offering it."

Her face seemed a little wooden as she looked at him. "You owe me neither an apology . . . nor anything else, Rick Dalton." Her voice was low and tense. "I hope you realize that I can recognize a thorough brute when I see one. Does that mean anything to you?"

Rick stood very still for a long moment. "It means aplenty," he said stoically. "My mistake. Sorry."

He turned and walked out, battered head high.

As they started out of town, Scat Kelly deliberately placed his mount between Rick and the group of riders lounging in too studied carelessness at the lower end of the street. As they came even with the group, Scat dropped the big shotgun over the crook of his left arm and threaded a gnarled forefinger through the trigger guard. The enormous twin bores of the gun seemed to take in all that side of the street and a restlessness ran through the group. Scat grinned thinly.

"Don't like the looks of it, do you?" he murmured, as though to himself. "You're wise, gents . . . very wise. Was I to slap down on you and let both barrels go, this son-of-a-cannon would likely kick me plumb out of my boots, but what it would do to you would be downright scandalous. So . . . think it over . . . think it over."

Apparently they did, and thought the better of any previous intentions, for, aside from sullen stares of hatred, the group did nothing. Presently Rick and Scat were well beyond town and whipping along through the gray sage.

Rick was so silent that Scat bent a look of inquiry upon him, made a swift deduction, and grinned. "Don't let it get you down, cowboy," he drawled. "You ain't the first man in the world to wonder why a woman's mind works like it does, and not find the answer. Give her time and she'll get over it. After all, you know, you *did* lick him. She'll remember that."

"I guess it was a pretty rough brawl," growled Rick. "And, of course, Kit would have to see the whole thing. But dog-gone it, Iberg made the first pass at me. What did she expect me to do, stand there and let him knock the daylights out of me? Had I done so, I bet she'd be twice as sore at me."

"Right!" affirmed Scat emphatically. "What she's mainly mad about is that the affair upset her and at the moment she's blaming you. Was Iberg to show up and try and talk to her, she'd singe him a lot worse than she did you. Only Iberg ain't in shape, and won't be for a week, to show up anywhere. Thinking back, you gave him one whale of a licking, Rick."

Rick was feeling a little better. Scat's reasoning might have been erroneous, but it was comforting, so Rick accepted it. "I ain't what you'd call a lovely lily myself," he said. "Darned if I don't feel all pushed and pulled lopsided. I feel like I was moving along sideways, like a hog going to war."

Behind them, Rocky Pass was soon lost to sight. On all sides the gray sage ran away, giving the effect of a world covered with powder-blue dust. Out ahead, to the east, this world washed up against the base of the Choctaw Rim, which lifted its rocky flanks in sheer abruptness, softened now by the warm haze of a rapidly westering sun. Beyond the Choctaw Rim lay the High Plains country. From the base of the rim, spreading west clear to the hostile wilderness of the Cedar Brakes country, lay the valley range, more fertile and fat than that above the rim.

As they neared the rim, Rick turned to the north where finally he and Scat hit the narrow little watercourse known as Chinquapin Creek and up this they rode to arrive finally, just at dusk, at Rick's cabin, set close under the shadow of the rim and just below where the rim split into a funneling gorge that let down the foaming waters of Chinquapin Creek from the heights beyond the rim.

Since starting his little spread, Rick Dalton had

run it as a one-man outfit. But he knew that in time he would have to pick up a hand somewhere to help him. So, when he built his cabin, he had installed a spare bunk, which Scat Kelly could now occupy. They turned their broncos into the pole corral behind the cabin, a corral with the rear end fenced by the sheer wall of the rim. Inside, Rick made a light, and then, at Scat's insistence, took it easy on his bunk while Scat threw together a frugal supper.

"Ever try and figure," drawled Scat easily, "the real reason behind Matt Iberg's rawhiding the High Plains ranchers?"

Rick flashed a quick glance at the redhead. "Some. What's your answer?"

"Spring and summer range," stated Scat emphatically. "So far, the valley range has been holding up to the amount of cattle grazing it. But the valley grass won't stand any more increase of cattle. Howsomever, if the valley ranchers could throw their herds on the High Plains range for a few months of late spring and early summer feeding, a few outfits could maybe figure on as high as a fifty percent increase in the size of their herds. Matt Iberg, for one, is hipped on the idea. I heard him and Bosco Scarlett talking over the idea one time. So me, I figure the moves Iberg has made against High Plains folks like Bob Shelly and Slip Hankins as the first steps toward running all the High Plains ranchers plumb out of the country and taking over their range himself. Maybe I'm wrong, but that's the way it shapes up in my book."

Rick nodded in grim thoughtfulness. "I've had the same hunch. By rubbing out Bob Shelly, Iberg got control of the Six Springs water. Slip Hankins's spread controls the upper end of the Bottle Rock

Chute, which provides the only road up over the rim for a wagon. If a man wanted to move a sizable herd of cattle up to the High Plains or back down off it, he'd just naturally take 'em by way of Bottle Rock Chute. I ain't the smartest guy in the world, but I can see the outline of a pattern there. Yet, Iberg ain't big enough and strong enough to whip the High Plains ranchers single-handed."

"That's just it," declared Scat. "My hunch is he knows he can figure on the backing of some of the valley outfits in the steal. Bosco Scarlett for one, and probably more. You've noticed, maybe, that there ain't been a single one of them who've let out one single squeak of protest against anything that Iberg does. You're the lone valley cattle owner who's made any attempt to tell Iberg off. The rest just stand around and let him pull his meanness. Did any of 'em except you rise up and holler when the Box I outfit lynched old Bob Shelly? They did not! Yet a child would know that no man would steal a bronc' and then leave it stand around in his own cavvy corral for all the world to see."

Rick smiled crookedly. "You don't seem to have a very high opinion of the valley ranchers, Scat."

Scat shrugged. "I've rode for all of 'em at one time or another and I ain't seen wings sproutin' on ary one of 'em. I ain't afraid to take a long-time bet on my ideas about 'em. You mark my words, cowboy, there'll come a day when red hell will ride the High Plains range."

For the next ten days, Rick Dalton stuck strictly to his own knitting. There was a multitude of things to be done, things Rick had been putting off until he had someone to help him. Now, with Scat Kelly

later. My first port of call is the Rocking R. I aim to find out where George Rowan stands in relation to Iberg."

"If I was plumb shore you wouldn't spring a brain storm and go rammin' right in at the Box I . . . ," began Scat.

"I'm not that clunk-headed," said Rick impatiently. "I yearn to keep my health as well as the next guy. Here, I'll make you a promise, you big red-headed ape. Should I ever go on the shoot for the Box I, you'll be riding stirrup to stirrup with me. Satisfied?"

Scat grinned. "Plumb. On your way, cowboy."

The Rocking R headquarters lay some five miles south of Rick's own ranch, buildings and corrals making the most of one of the few groves of cottonwoods standing in the valley. The rear of the house was to the north and Rick, just before he turned the corner of the building, was startled at the number of saddled broncos lining the corral fence. But the moment he cleared the corner, so he could see along the wide, shady verandah of the ranch house, he understood. Nearly a dozen men were grouped on that verandah and with his first glance he recognized not only George Rowan, but Matt Iberg, Cass Denio, and Bosco Scarlett. His second glance identified Stooly Maxwell, Frank Orland, and old man Guest. Here, in one group, were practically all of the cattlemen of the valley.

Rick hid his surprise behind a lean, inscrutable mask as he swung his bronco over to a handy cottonwood, dismounted, and looped the reins loosely about the gnarled trunk. Then, with studied carelessness, he climbed the steps, spur chains *clanking*.

"Must be something in the wind," he drawled, "with all these heavy minds sitting in. What's the gathering all about?"

Rick needed no more than a glance or two to realize that he definitely wasn't welcome. Frank Orland alone, a spare, cool-eyed man, who as a rule kept pretty much to himself, gave Rick a nod. The rest, including George Rowan, wore scowls.

Rick's tone took on a combative crispness. "You guys must have been plotting against the whites. Go ahead, keep on talking. Don't let me spoil the party."

Bosco Scarlett, a big, untidy, swarthy man, who could, on occasion, exude an oily joviality, was the first to recover. His grin was forced, but his tone was suave and smooth.

"You come along just in time, Dalton. We were just figuring on what we should do to protect ourselves from the threat of that bunch of outlaws up on the High Plains."

Rick built a cigarette, his eyebrows lifted. "News to me . . . two ways," he drawled. "That the High Plains people were outlaws, or that they were offering any threat to anybody. I know those folks up there pretty well and I ain't met an outlaw among 'em. And so far I ain't seen 'em threatening ary soul down here in the valley. Shore you ain't got your rope tangled, Scarlett?"

Bosco Scarlett's somewhat muddy eyes veiled warily. "You heard me. If you want to sit in on the confab, say so."

Matt Iberg spat harshly. "He don't. He's more High Plains than he is valley, anyhow. We don't want him in on this at all."

Rick turned, looked Iberg up and down. Iberg

still carried very discernible effects of the fight about his face. "You aiming on speaking for all these gents, Iberg?" asked Rick gently.

"No! But where you're concerned. . . ."

"Wait a minute, Matt . . . wait a minute." It was George Rowan. His round, blunt features were set in stubborn lines, and his eyes showed a tendency to a somewhat choleric temper. Rick had often mused over the vast difference between Kit and George Rowan. Even though they were but half-sister and half-brother, it was reasonable to expect some likeness in appearance or disposition or personality. But Rick had never been able to recognize any such likeness. They were as different as two people possibly could be. For Kit possessed a slim, dark, vibrant grace and an alert, sparkling mind. While George Rowan was stodgy, none too swift in the wits, and tending too easily to a sulky, sullen manner. His hair had a bleached rustiness to it, his eyes full of a balky mule glint. His voice harshened as he faced Rick.

"You can sit in on this confab, Dalton . . . on two conditions," he growled. "First, you got to get that chip off your shoulder where Matt Iberg is concerned. Second, you got to be willing to follow, instead of trying always to lead the parade. If that suits you, you're welcome. If not. . . ." George Rowan shrugged.

Rick looked at him with hardening eyes. "Conditions declined," he said curtly. "Especially the first one. You're wrong about the second. The only parade I've ever insisted on leading is my own. I aim to keep on that way. I came over here today, George, to have a little private talk with you. I can see now I don't need to. I already got my answer.

Yet, if I were you, I'd think it over a long time before I tied in with Iberg. It may lead you places you don't want to go. And whatever name you gents are giving this thing you're cooking up, the real name of it is thievery, plain and simple. I thought better of some of you, but I see I was wrong. You're all tarred with the same brush."

George Rowan bristled furiously: "You aim to stand on my porch and call me a thief . . . call all my friends thieves! Why you . . . !"

"Cut it fine . . . cut it fine," broke in Rick. "Ask yourselves the answer and let your consciences, if you've got any, make honest answer."

Cass Denio lunged to his feet. "Before we do anything else," he bawled, "the best thing we can do is run this jasper plumb out of the country! He's too wise for his own good. He. . . ."

"Shut up, Cass," cut in Matt Iberg. "I'm passing up the insinuations and remarks you just made, Dalton . . . out of respect for George here, and his sister. But you don't want to go circulating lies about me. It won't be healthy."

Rick smiled thinly. "You got a great act there, Iberg. Only it gets tiresome." He whirled to face some of the others, such men as Stooly Maxwell, Frank Orland, and old man Guest. "I wonder if you fellows happened to hear of a dry-gulching that took place this morning, up on the High Plains? There was one. Jim Prentiss was murdered, shot in the back by some creeping rat that walks like a man. Jim Prentiss . . . and no finer man ever breathed. Dry-gulched! Get that! And not by anybody who belongs on the High Plains range. Up there he was everybody's friend. He was my friend. I only hope that someday I get the chance to look through smoke at the whelp who did it. And if there is anybody in this crowd the shoe fits, let him step out and say so. Or any two of you." Rick's scathing glance took in Matt Iberg and Cass Denio with pointed emphasis.

Neither met his eyes. Rick spat, turned, and *clanked* down the steps, crossed to his horse, and rode away.

Frank Orland stood up. "I don't like the smell around here," he said curtly. "Too much like a buzzard's roost. But I like that guy, Rick Dalton. Yes, I like him. He's got guts . . . and a heart."

Without another word, Frank Orland strode off toward his horse at the corrals.

There was a long, long moment of silence. Then Cass Denio stirred restlessly. "Let him go," he croaked. "Let him go."

V

From the Rocking R, Rick Dalton headed straight for town, although without any particular purpose except that he had told Scat Kelly he'd meet him there. Rick had hoped, more than he dared admit, that he would be able to convince other valley cattlemen of the fallacy of following Matt Iberg any longer. For the High Plains cattlemen, although they might be outnumbered, would never be outfought. Before they bowed to the range-grabbing idea that was plainly apparent behind Iberg's acts, they would indeed stage the red hell Scat Kelly had prophesied.

Iberg was just clever enough to see that the other valley cattlemen would take the brunt of the inevitable punishment. As far as he was able, Iberg would see to it that someone else dragged the chestnuts out of the fire for him. And this could easily mean ruin for some of them—George Rowan, perhaps. Which, in turn, would be a bitter blow to Kit Rowan. And that was one thing that Rick did not want to see happen. No more than he wanted to see the High Plains people dispossessed, men folks killed, families broken up, stunned and desolate women and kids left without a husband and father and provider. And it all came back to the greed and unscrupulous plotting and cunning of Matt Iberg.

Silently Rick cursed the man. Strange how he had had Iberg ticketed, right from the first, how he had sensed the ruthless, scheming make-up of the fellow. He found himself wishing that instead of fists it had been guns, that other day. It would have solved things pretty well; either he himself would not now be here to anticipate and see the inevitable misery ahead, or Iberg would have been down and done for and his infamous scheming with him.

To seek Iberg out now, force him to a draw, then gun him, might help and might not. For by this time Iberg had plainly infected the minds of the other valley cattlemen with his own greed. To fight Iberg now, he would have to fight the whole bunch of them, George Rowan among the rest. And Rick didn't want to fight George Rowan. Because of Kit Rowan. Because of slim, vibrant, dark-eyed Kit, the one woman in his life Rick had ever given a second thought to. Kit who set his heart to singing and filled his whole world with roseate color whenever he was near her and talking to her. For, if Rick fought George Rowan, he knew that Kit Rowan would be as far from him as the poles of the earth were apart.

Yet it seemed that he was being driven by some relentless destiny to this very thing. He *had* to fight Iberg. Which meant he had to fight George Rowan. For he couldn't sit by in a thing like this. He couldn't sit by and see those good folks of the High Plains harassed and punished and dispossessed of range and cattle, home and life. He couldn't sit by and see injustice done. It just wasn't in him to be that sort. No matter what the cost to him personally, he knew he would be in this thing up to his ears.

Strangely enough, now that he had brought this conviction right out into the open and had definitely committed himself to it, regardless of what it cost him, he felt better. After all, a man had to play the game the way he saw the rules.

Rick had been riding instinctively, chin sunk on his chest, in the depths of his thoughts. Now, abruptly, his jogging pony stopped. Rick's head jerked up, his right hand darting to his holstered gun. But immediately his hand fell away again. Out there in front of him, her horse barring the trail, sat Kit Rowan, a faint smile on her face, her dark eyes unreadable.

"My," she said lightly, "I don't believe I ever saw anyone so deeply sunk in thought. And not pleasant thoughts, either, judging by the man's face. Why all the gloom, Mister Dalton?"

Rick looked at her soberly. Kit Rowan was just as good to look at on a horse as off one. She rode with that easy grace that only a lifetime in the saddle could give. And her big white Stetson was pushed back so that it hung between her shoulders, held there by the beaded throatlatch that encircled her slender neck. Which left the sun free to work its sheening magic on her sleek, dark head. Rick felt a strange twist of pain run through him. He'd never be able to forget this girl—never! And the course fate was pushing him into meant that he would lose her just as surely as there was a sun overhead this moment.

Rick tried to answer in a tone as light as her own. "You can't ever please 'em. Last time I talked to the lady she as much as told me I was as empty-headed as a sage wren. Now, when I'm full of heavy thoughts, she jibes at me, just the same. For that matter, if I remember right, she as much as told me I was no darn' good, that I was a brute and a savage, and that she never wanted to see me again."

Kit colored slightly. "At the time I didn't," she admitted candidly. "I was a very upset person, and, when I'm upset, I often say things I don't mean. I didn't mean that, Rick. I've been hoping to meet you so I could tell you that. After all, you were no more to blame than . . . than he was, and I suppose I should be thankful you chose to settle your differences with your fists instead of with guns. But I do hope you've both got it out of your systems."

She was pretty wonderful, thought Rick disconsolately. Honest and generous enough to admit she was wrong and sorry for her attitude in the store, the day of the fight. And now he had to dash the hope she had just expressed.

He shook his head slowly. "There can never be any peace between Matt Iberg and me, Kit. Less chance of that now than ever before. Shore, I'm sorry."

She bit her lip slightly, staring at him intently. "Even if I asked it of you, Rick? Remember, you said the other day that you'd go out and . . . and knock a mountain down if I wanted you to."

"I meant that." Rick nodded. "And it holds good now. Except for this one thing."

She frowned. "Isn't that being a little bit stupid?" she asked impatiently. "After all, you should be satisfied. You won that fight. And surely you, as victor, should be as big and broad about it as the man you whipped, Matt Iberg. Matt told me he was willing to forget and forgive."

Rick stared at her. Then his lips twisted in that hard, reckless grin. "Matt Iberg told you that? And you believe him?"

"Yes . . . and . . . yes. I see no reason why he should have lied to me."

"I do," said Rick grimly. "Yeah, I do. I wonder just why it is."

"Why . . . what?"

"Why he's so darned transparent to me and not to others!" Rick exploded. "The way that jigger can pull the wool over the eyes of other folks is a caution. But me, I can read him like a book. He knows it, too. That's why he hates me as bad as I hate him. Because I know he's a scheming crook, and he knows I know it. Seems to me that ought to answer one of your questions, Kit."

"It doesn't answer a thing," she flared. "It just sounds ridiculous to me, that a grown man should persist in acting like a child. I don't understand you, Rick Dalton."

Rick could see she was growing angry with him again. He decided to give her the truth before she rode away in a huff. He built a cigarette, lighted it, inhaled deeply. "You've met Jim Prentiss, I reckon?"

"Why . . . yes, I have. His wife, too. What of it?"

"She's not a wife any more. She's a widow. Jim Prentiss was killed this morning. Murdered. Shot in the back by a dry-gulcher."

Kit went slowly white, her dark eyes shocked and wide. But she did not miss the inference in the way Rick said it. "That . . . that's terrible," she stammered. "But you act as though you had the blame for it already fixed on someone."

"I have. Matt Iberg. Oh, it's hardly possible that he did it himself. He doesn't work that way. But he had it done. I'd stake my life on that."

"That's a dreadful accusation, Rick Dalton. I . . . I don't believe it. Matt isn't that sort. He's rough and ready . . . and . . . masterful. But . . . he isn't a . . . a murderer."

Rick shrugged. "I just came from the Rocking R, Kit. I found there, talking with George, Matt Iberg, Cass Denio, Stooly Maxwell, Frank Orland, old man Guest. Know what they were talking about? I can guess, and you ask George when you get home. They were fixing up a scheme to run the High Plains ranchers out of the country. Just a plain dirty steal. Iberg's had his sights fixed on the High Plains country for spring and summer range for a long time. He's got the rest seeing things his way now. And you know what that means. Scat Kelly has it right. It means red hell along the Choctaw Rim. The lynching of Bob Shelly, the attempted bullwhipping of Slip Hankins, and now the killing of Jim Prentiss are all preliminary moves of Iberg toward that steal."

"You're absolutely insane, Rick Dalton!" stormed the girl. "You don't know what you are saying. Do you realize that you just charged George, my brother, with being an intended thief and murderer? I refuse to listen to you any longer."

Before she could whirl her pony away, Rick had hold of her rein. "Just a minute, Kit," he said a little wearily. "Long as I've started, I'm going to say it all. George Rowan is only your half-brother. You're not alike in any other way but the name . . . Rowan. George has got a streak in him. Maybe it's not bad, but it's weak. He's letting Matt Iberg talk him into this thing. And once Iberg gets him in, he'll use him and ruin him. And if the Rocking R goes under, you go under, too. I'd like to agree with you, Kit . . . honest I would. I don't want to argue with you, fight with you. But a thing is so, or it isn't so."

Kit had lifted her quirt from the saddle horn. Now she gripped it so tightly the knuckles of her slim, brown right hand showed white. "I refuse to listen to such utter, utter tommyrot," she gritted. "I don't see how I could ever have thought you a sane, normal human being, Rick Dalton. Just because you blindly hate Matt Iberg, you are deliberately maligning all those who still like him and consider him a friend. Well, you might as well malign me, too . . . because I like Matt Iberg and he is my friend, my very good friend. Now, will you let go of that rein, or do I have to use this quirt on you?"

"Yes," said Rick simply, "I'll let go, after I say one more thing. I love you, Kit. I've always loved

you. I always will. I've told you that before . . . I tell
it to you again. And someday, when your whole
world comes tumbling down around your ears, remember that, will you, please? I love you. Good
bye, Kit."

She had swung the quirt up, ready to lash at
him. But she didn't. Instead, as Rick dropped her
rein and pulled his bronco off the trail, she used
the quirt on her pony and sped away up the trail in
a flurry of dust. For a moment Rick stared after her.
When he turned to face townward again, his face
looked old and seamed and bitter. There, he told
himself harshly, went the finest dream of his life.
Left were only the harsher, sterner duties. Taut energy gripped him. He found himself hungering for
combat, for the last big showdown.

When Kit Rowan reached home on a foaming, indignant pony, she saw Stooly Maxwell, Bosco Scarlett, old man Guest, Cass Denio, and several others
swinging into their saddles, ready to leave. On the
ranch house porch were her brother George and
Matt Iberg, talking. Kit ignored the others and sped
straight to the house. Both Iberg and George
seemed a little startled at her abrupt appearance
and the sight of her white face.

Kit wasted no time. "I want the truth of this meeting," she demanded. "I met Rick Dalton down the
trail toward town. He told me his version of what
was going on here. Now, I want to hear yours."

A sulky look came over George Rowan, but, before he could speak, Matt Iberg was laughing care-
lessly. "I can imagine what he told you, Kit.
Probably what he accused us of when he was here.
Some wild, harebrained idea about we valley cat-

tlemen ganging up to drive the High Plains crowd plumb off the earth. That guy is loco, if you ask me. He sees bugaboos behind every sage bush."

"What about the killing of Jim Prentiss?" demanded Kit.

Iberg shrugged, spread his hands. "I know no more about that than you do, my dear. Dalton broke that bit of news, practically accused us of it. Too bad, if it's true. Jim Prentiss was one of the few honest men above the rim, in my book. I'm mighty sorry to hear about it."

Kit bit her lip. "Then, just what was this meeting for?"

"Nothing for anybody to get excited about," explained Iberg glibly. "Just a little measure of self-protection. Here is the setup, as I see it, Kit. Our valley range is a lot fatter than that above the rim. Here and there over the past couple of years I've heard talk, seen signs begin to grow. The High Plains cattlemen would like nothing better than to edge down into this valley. I'm convinced they've already made up their minds to something of the sort and are ready to try it at 'most any time. They could get away with it, too, if they could catch us and pick us off, one by one. My idea has been that all of us get together and organize to protect the whole valley from an encroachment. And there is the answer to your question. That's what this meeting was all about."

Kit shot a swift glance at her half-brother. "That right, George?"

He nodded sullenly. "Yeah, that's right. And for the Lord's sake, don't go listening to any more pipe dreams from that juniper, Dalton . . . and then come tearing home ready to take everybody apart.

Seems to me you'd have Dalton figured by this time."

Kit seemed suddenly very weary. "I'm sorry. I . . . I guess maybe I was upset, hearing about Jim Prentiss. You'll stay to dinner, of course, Matt?"

"I hadn't figured on it, beautiful." He smiled. "But seeing as it's you who asked me, I'll be glad to."

Kit went into the house, with Matt Iberg's voice ringing in her ears. But somehow there seemed to be another voice in the background saying—"I love you, Kit. I've always loved you."

VI

Scat Kelly was hunkered on his heels in the shade of the livery corrals, where he could accost Rick Dalton as soon as Rick hit town. As Rick came jogging in, Scat stood up and beckoned him over.

"Remember that lantern-jawed wahoo you slapped down in the Buffalo House the day him and Howdy Orleans weren't going to let Slip Hankins leave? Well, he's in there now, hitting the bottle and acting ugly as sin. I heard Caraway call him by name. It's Granger. And I'm wondering if he can be the Spike Granger we heard about sometime back, the Spike Granger who was the big boss gun-thrower who shot hell out of everybody for the Delta Cattle Company when that outfit moved in and stole the Antelope Basin range down south. If he is, maybe that's why Iberg has hired him, aiming to use him on the High Plains folks."

"We can easy find out," growled Rick. "We'll go ask him . . . now!"

"Hey!" cried Scat. "Wait a minute . . . wait a minute. Not so fast. If he is *the* Spike Granger, he's pretty sudden medicine to go asking personal questions."

"He won't be near sudden enough," gritted Rick. "Scat, I'm going all out on this thing. I owe it to you to let you know that. And I won't blame you a bit if you cut loose from me. But I ain't sitting around no more, looking wise, while Iberg and the rest of the coyotes in this valley get set to hit. Me, I'm going to hit first. Now you know."

"You ain't had time to contact everybody," said Scat. "Something's happened."

Rick nodded, and told him about the gathering at the Rocking R. "They're set, Scat," he ended. "Set to go right now. There's only one thing to do. They've organized down here. I got to organize the High Plains ranchers. Meet fire with fire. But it's asking too much of you to expect you to ride along with me."

"I'll be the maddest man this side of hell in a minute," snarled Scat, his blue eyes blazing. "You trying to insult me? Dog-gone it, cowboy . . . when I side up to ride a trail, I ride it, regardless. Don't you make any more cracks like that."

Rick met Scat's blazing eyes, smiled grimly, gripped Scat's big, muscular arm. "OK, partner. That's the way it will be. Come on. The first chore is to run this Granger *hombre* out of the country . . . or kill him."

Scat gulped and swallowed. "You don't believe in ridin' 'em bareback, do you? Well, if you say so, that's how it stacks up."

Rick left his bronco at the corral fence and headed for the Buffalo House. Before he and Scat could get there, however, another rider came swiftly into town, passed them, dismounted, and tied before the Buffalo House and went in. It was Frank Orland.

"Well, well," murmured Scat, "you said Orland was at the Rocking R with the rest of that gang. Maybe this means we'll have to push him out of the way, too."

"If we have to, we will," said Rick harshly.

Orland was just pouring a drink when Rick and Scat came through the swinging doors of the saloon. At the far end of the bar, bottle before him, talon fingers wrapped around a glass of whiskey, stood the lantern-jawed gunfighter. He stirred slightly at sight of Rick and Scat, but gave no further sign of their presence. Frank Orland, however, hunched a beckoning shoulder. "Hi, boys. Step up and have one."

Rick looked at him with level, contemptuous eyes. "No, thanks. We don't drink with coyotes."

At which Hob Caraway gulped and licked his lips, the look upon him of expecting a bolt of lightning to strike. But Frank Orland, far from taking offense, merely shrugged and smiled slightly. He had the air of a man enjoying a secret of his own.

Rick went right by him, stopping a couple of paces from the lantern-jawed Granger. Granger moved a little farther from the bar, his lead-colored eyes taking on a murky, set stare.

"Your name Granger?" spat Rick.

"If it is, so what?" was the toneless answer.

"Spike Granger?"

This question seemed to hang in the air a moment, during which Frank Orland turned swiftly, as though startled by the name.

Granger nodded slowly. "Yeah . . . Spike Granger."

"*The* Spike Granger . . . from Antelope Basin?"

The gunman was set now. He had both thumbs hooked in his gun belts, just in front of the splayed, black gun butts flaring there. His thin upper lip lifted in a sort of mocking snarl. He seemed to be relishing some prospect.

"Yeah," he said again, his voice slightly hissing, "*the* Spike Granger. And now I'm asking a question. Which way do you want to die, Dalton . . . quick or slow? Because you're going to . . . one way or the other."

"Get out of the country," rasped Rick, almost as though he hadn't heard what Granger had said. "Light a shuck and get out . . . and don't hit this valley again. From now on it's going to be open season on any and all of Matt Iberg's hired gun-throwers and killers. You're getting your last chance. Move on, Granger. You're not wanted around here."

The room went so still the *buzz* of a bluebottle fly sounded plainly. Then Granger laughed and in it was the sound of rattling bones. "Rich!" he gasped. "Richest thing I ever ran across. A guy like you trying to give Spike Granger a floater. Well, I don't float. I kill! Like this!"

The last four words snapped out like pistol shots and Granger had both guns out and lifting level. And then Rick's gun blasted flat thunder, once— twice—the crimson flame of it reaching almost across the interval.

Spike Granger froze, just as he was, while a look of vast, incredulous astonishment spread across his graying face. Then his chin dropped, his eyes fluttered, and he pitched forward on his face.

Rick Dalton stood for a moment, looking down on the man he had just killed. His face was wooden, his voice empty. "You had two chances," he said. "You took the wrong one."

Then Rick turned and left the place, with Scat Kelly scuffing along behind, a stunned incredulousness about him. Behind, Hob Caraway stood, hands flat on the bar, leaning over to stare at the man on the floor. Caraway's beefy, sweat-greased face was white, his eyes bugged. He licked his lips, grabbed a bottle, and took a drag at it.

"*The* Spike Granger," he mumbled finally. "And Dalton let him get his guns out first and then smoked him down as calm as you please. . . . I can't figure it."

"I can," said Frank Orland crisply. "There is always a better man. A certain *hombre* in this valley is due to find that out."

Then Orland left, leaving Hob Caraway with his jumbled thoughts, and the dead man on the floor.

Outside, Rick Dalton went straight back to his horse, swung into the saddle, and headed out of town. Scat Kelly sent his horse hurrying up to even pace with Rick. Scat wanted to say a lot of things, but he held them all back except one brief question. "Where to now, Rick?"

"The High Plains," was the terse answer. "To tell those folks what is in the wind and to get them organized."

Rick went straight home, paused only long enough to catch and saddle a fresh bronco, a move emulated by Scat Kelly, then headed up the gorge trail to the country beyond the rim. Here the world ran back in vast flats from the rim, to lift finally into a backbone of broken, tangled low hills, furred with sage and cat-claw and yellow oaks, stabbed through by bald flanks and jagged outcroppings of weathered rock. The flats were scabbed by broad stretches of so-called dry lakes, areas where the soil lay paper-thin and where the grass withered and died as soon as the first summer sun sucked the scanty moisture from shallow roots. A hard country, this, hard on cattle, hard on men, but a great toughener of both.

The first port of call was Charley Curtiss's C Over C spread. A buckboard was just pulling into the yard. Driving it was Charley Curtiss. On the seat beside him was his sister Sarah Prentiss, widow of the murdered Jim Prentiss. Charley Curtiss nodded gravely to Rick and Scat, then turned gently to help his bereaved sister from the buckboard. Her face was set and masklike, her eyes dull and stunned and fixed in a straight-ahead stare. Rick and Scat took off their hats as she passed them on her way to the house. She showed no sign of seeing them, of being aware of their presence in any way. The chill in Rick's eyes deepened, the lines about his mouth and jaw more taut and grimly set. This was the sort of thing the greed of a man like Matt Iberg could do to the women of the High Plains.

Scat Kelly mumbled a curse, slapped a clenched fist down on his saddle horn. "I yearn," said Scat harshly, "to knock hell outta something or somebody. And I hope I don't have to wait too long."

"You won't," said Rick tersely, building a smoke.

Charley Curtiss came back from the house. "Well," he growled, "that's that. I've watched my own sister's heart break." And then he voiced Scat

Kelly's exact words. "I want to knock hell out of something or somebody."

"You'll get the chance, Charley," said Rick. "Listen to this."

And then Rick told him of the meeting he had observed taking place at the Rocking R and gave his terse opinion of what lay behind it. "So," he ended, "I want you to ride a circle and see all of the High Plains ranchers. Tell 'em what's in the wind, what they got to do if they want to keep from being wiped off the earth, from being robbed blind. They got to organize, too . . . every man jack of them. They got to make these High Plains an armed camp. They got to maintain an armed patrol, day and night, along the rim, so as to be able to warn against the attack that's shore to come. They got to cook up some kind of signals so they can throw a defending force at any necessary point along the rim. This is life and death with you men, Charley. You won't get a second chance. Iberg is figuring on overrunning the High Plains at one stroke."

Curtiss nodded grimly. "We'll be ready," he promised. "I'd been figuring on something along that line myself. But," he added bitterly, "while I can understand such slickery ones as Bosco Scarlett, Stooly Maxwell, and old man Guest tying in with Iberg's unholy schemes, I can't figure Frank Orland or those two Rowan kids joining in with him. I thought they were a different kind of people."

"Frank Orland has always been a hard man to figure," said Rick. "Sometimes I've figured him pretty white. Other times, I wasn't so shore. He's such a lone wolf, distant sort. About the Rowans . . . don't blame Kit. She doesn't realize what this is all about. She's naturally loyal to her half-brother, refuses to believe he'd do anything dirty or underhanded. She's going to suffer plenty when she gets her eyes opened, as she inevitably will. But George Rowan . . . well, he ain't a bit like his sister. He's a sulky, sullen sort, none too fast between the ears. By flattering him and petting his fur with the grain, Matt Iberg can do just about what he wants with him. I wouldn't say that George Rowan is as bad as he is stupid. But I'm not trying to hold anything away from him. What he gets, he'll deserve. All I want to do is just keep Kit Rowan from being hurt too bad. But that's aside from the point. You start in organizing as quick as you can, Charley. You ain't got no time to waste."

"I'd sort of figured on trying to track down the dry-gulcher who did for Jim Prentiss," said Curtiss. "But I reckon this other is more important now."

"You leave it up to Scat and me to track that *hombre* down," asserted Rick. "We'll do it, too . . . if it's humanly possible. And the trail, if we do pick it up, is bound to lead down into the valley, where we can follow it better than you could. Should you start rambling back and forth in the valley, chances are strong you'd run into the same thing Jim Prentiss did. All we want you to do is give us some idea of where Jim's body was found."

Charley Curtiss squatted on his heels and with the palm of his hand smoothed a place in the dust. Then with a match he drew lines and indicated directions, while Rick and Scat leaned forward in their saddles to miss no item of information.

"Here is the ranch house," said Curtiss. "Over here . . . that's west . . . is that long backbone of rock that cuts halfway through the lower pasture. Over here . . . about three hundred yards beyond the far end of the ridge . . . is a thicket of yellow oak. And the spring Jim was working at is right alongside the thicket. You can't miss it." Curtiss got up, dusted his hands together, and looked at Rick with deep, gleaming eyes. "Should you have luck, Rick, and come up with the rat who did that killing, say to yourself when you pull down on him . . . 'This is for Jim and Sarah Prentiss . . . and for Charley Curtiss.' Will you do that?"

"Glad to," said Rick. "Now you go get together your organization. Much as we can, Scat and I will keep you notified of the way things are going down in the valley. But it's up to you to make these High Plains folks realize they're going to have to fight for everything they possess, not the least of which is their lives. Good luck, Charley."

VII

"Here's where Jim Prentiss must have been layin'," said Scat Kelly, pointing to a dark, caked stain on the earth. "There's a flock of them green death flies buzzin' around."

Scat and Rick Dalton were dismounted, their broncos ground-reined nearby. Rick glanced at the indicated spot on the earth, nodded, then turned and looked over all the country surrounding. The chances were strong, as Rick reasoned it, that the dry-gulcher had been hid out somewhere between the spring and the rim. Across one of the interminable dry lakes, where acrid dust fingers curled and crept under the slightest stir of air, a tongue of yellow oak reached out to a point about 200 yards from the spring. Farther south, about 300 yards distant, a little rocky knoll lifted.

"You take a look through that tongue of brush yonder, Scat," Rick ordered. "I'll mosey around that pile of rock over south. Make a good search. Sign ain't going to be easy to read in this kind of country."

They separated, each to his selected spot. Rick left his saddle again and circled the knoll on foot, eyes centered and busy. Most of the upward slope to the crest of the knoll was barren, flinty rock, over which a thousand men could have traveled without leaving a trace. So Rick climbed up through the broken stuff toward the summit of the knoll. And about halfway up he struck his first encouraging sign. There, on a little shelf of rock, lay the thick, repulsive coils of a rattlesnake. A dead rattlesnake, its head crushed flat. The reptile had not been long killed, not more than a few hours, perhaps that morning. The time checked about right.

Rick studied the snake carefully, especially that crushed head. A few inches to either side of the head the rock was scarified slightly, as though it had been jabbed with some hard instrument. And suddenly Rick understood. He straightened up and waved his hat until he caught Scat's eye, then beckoned, and Scat came riding swiftly.

Rick pointed to the dead snake. "Get it? See where the rock is scarred, both sides of the head? Well, the two ends of a steel butt plate of a rifle did that. This jigger is climbing up to the top of these rocks to do his dirty work. He runs across this rattler and smashes its head with the butt plate of his gun. He must have left his bronc' back yonder somewhere toward the rim. You go see. I'm taking a look at the top of this knoll."

Within fifteen minutes, both found more sign, Scat where the dry-gulcher had left his bronco, Rick the exact spot from which the fatal shot was fired. He found the dead butt of a cigarette and the empty shell of the cartridge used. This was a regular .30-30, which meant nothing, for practically every saddle gun carried in that country was of the same caliber. Scat's discovery was the more important of the two. And Rick studied that horse sign long and carefully.

He worked back from where the animal had been tied in a brush thicket and finally on one piece of scant, bare earth found reasonably clear tracks of all four hoofs. A moment of study of these made his eyes gleam. For while the sign showed that both forehoofs and the near hind one wore smooth and worn shoes, the off hind print showed a relatively new shoe, the calks of which still bit in sharply and deeply.

Rick and Scat had a smoke over this momentous discovery. "That dry-gulching rat might's well stuck up a sign with his name on it," exulted Scat. "All we got to find now is a *hombre* riding a bronc' with smooth shoes on three hoofs and a new one on the off hind and a Thirty-Thirty saddle gun with a butt plate jabbed up from pounding on rock. Yes, sir, this ought to be easy."

"Unless he cuts that bronc' back into a cavvy corral somewhere and leaves it there while doing his riding on a different one," cautioned Rick. "But we got a lot more to work on than I hoped we'd have. Let's go!"

Back at the Rocking R spread, Kit Rowan, her half-brother George, and Matt Iberg had finished their meal, and Iberg was making ready to leave. Throughout the meal, George Rowan had been a little more silent and stodgy-appearing than usual, but Iberg had bubbled with geniality.

There was one thing Kit Rowan had been aware of for a long time. And that was that Matt Iberg entertained serious thoughts about her. In his lighter moments the man was far from unattractive. Many women would have found his powerful physique and bold, aggressive features fascinating. But there was an imperious ruthlessness, an arrogance about him that Kit found disquieting and vaguely offensive to some finer strain in her make-up. Consequently, despite the fervor of his approach, she always cloaked herself in a cool aloofness that fended him off and kept him at his distance. Which plainly irritated him.

And then there was Rick Dalton. Rick, with his lithe, clean-cut, sinewy physique, the lean brownness of his face, his clear reckless eyes, his ready, boyish grin, and the magic of a silver tongue. That was the old Rick, the one before this dreadful blight of hostility and suspicion and combat had settled over the valley. Rick who, with his laughing eyes and silver tongue, could set her heart to fluttering strangely and her pulses to singing. But that Rick had disappeared. In his stead was a man who seemed older, whose eyes and lips no longer laughed so easily, but instead were cold and alert, grim and set.

No one could doubt the capacity for terrible conflict in Rick Dalton, once he was aroused. She herself had seen that, the day of that brutal, bloody fight, when he had beaten Matt Iberg into senselessness against all the odds of superior weight and brute strength. For Rick Dalton had a flame in him that nothing, it seemed, could extinguish.

But the old Rick was the one who had become more dear to Kit's heart than she cared to admit, even to herself. And he wasn't in the valley any longer. And the new Rick she could not understand. Somehow the new Rick frightened her. And thinking of all this, Kit knew she had not been the most gracious hostess in the world throughout the meal they had just finished.

She wished she was more sure of herself, that her emotions weren't so jumbled, pulling her this way and that. Life, it seemed, with its new and strange and frightening currents, was stampeding her. By all rights she should be completely done with Rick Dalton. He had made dreadful, impossible accusations against her friends, against her own half-brother. Yes, she should be all done with Rick Dalton. In his hate of Matt Iberg he was out trying to poison the minds of everyone against not only Iberg, but even against her half-brother. Which indirectly, she somehow felt, was against her, also. She couldn't understand the man. He must have lost his mind. She had to forget him, to give her favors a little more generously to a man who was definitely a friend of the Rocking R. Matt Iberg, for instance.

So, as Iberg and George walked down to the corrals where Iberg's bronco was tethered, Kit walked with them. And she gave Matt Iberg her hand as he was about to mount.

"I'm afraid I wasn't the best of company at dinner, Matt," she said. "But all this hovering threat and animosity in the valley has me pretty disturbed. In happier, quieter times, perhaps I can act more myself."

Iberg pressed her hand warmly. "I've no kick with you ever, Kit," he assured her. "Regardless of what your mood is. In my eyes, you're always perfect. And those better times will come, you'll see."

Iberg might have said more, had not George Rowan broken in: "Rider dusting the trail from town, Matt. Looks like Howdy Orleans. And he ain't letting any grass grow under him. Acts like he was packing some pretty urgent news."

Howdy Orleans it was, using spurs and quirt and his mount was foaming as he set it up in a cloud of dust. Iberg strode over to him. "What's up, Howdy?" he growled. "You ain't half killed that bronc' for nothin'. What's wrong?"

"Spike Granger is done for. That damned Rick Dalton killed him, 'long about ten o'clock this morning, in the Buffalo House."

For a moment Iberg was motionless. "Dalton . . . killed Spike Granger? Gunfight, you mean?"

"I reckon. Shot Granger twice. But according to Hob Caraway, Dalton never gave Granger any show to draw his gun. Just walked into the Buffalo House, pulled a gun, let Granger have it, then walked out again. Scat Kelly was with Dalton."

Iberg's face twisted into a mask of black, bitter rage and hate. He had to bite his lips to keep from breaking into a fury of cursing. But he kept his back to Kit and George Rowan until he had somewhat mastered himself. Then he jerked his head briefly. "All right, Howdy," he growled. "You get along home. I'll be following in a minute or two."

Orleans turned and rode away and Iberg watched him go, giving himself more time to master the surface effects of the rage burning in him. For even in his fury the man was clever. When he finally faced Kit and George Rowan again, he had himself pretty much under control and particularly he watched Kit's face to read her reaction to this sinister bit of news.

"Well," said Iberg, "there it is. I always said that one of these days Dalton would go off the deep end. He's got that streak in him. His father, from what I've heard some people say, had that same killer streak, too. Sooner or later it breaks loose in them that have it. Dalton has gone all wolf now."

Kit was very white, her lips trembling. "I . . . I can hardly believe that of . . . of Rick," she stammered. "Not that he'd shoot a man down, without some cause."

"A killer can always figure out some cause to slake his devilish blood hunger," rapped Iberg sharply. "How about it, George?"

George Rowan nodded somewhat dazedly. "I . . . I guess you're right, Matt."

Iberg went into his saddle. "He'll have to be stopped," he said. "Lord knows where he'll strike next, if he ain't. I'll get in touch with the other boys, George, and see what they think should be done. And something will have to be done. We can't afford to have a killer running around loose, shooting down inoffensive riders. I suppose what me and the other boys decide will be all right with you, George?"

Again George Rowan nodded in that stupid way of his. "Shore, Matt . . . shore. Whatever is decided on will suit me."

"Good! I'll see you folks later."

As Matt Iberg spurred away, a savage, exultant smile was pulling at his lips. *For a long time I been waiting for this,* he told himself. *A real reason to close in on Dalton, the one man in this valley who might have been able to tie a knot in my future plans. Now I got him. Before I get through with him, he'll be open game for any man who can line a pair of sights on him. I could have used Granger. But it is worth losing him to get Dalton where I want him. Best of all, Miss Kit Rowan was there herself to hear Howdy's report of the killing. Before you're done, old boy, you'll have just about everything you want in this world.*

Back at the corrals, George Rowan turned to the white-faced, tragic-eyed Kit. "Well," he growled, "I guess that ought to cross off Dalton as far as you're concerned. He's gone all bad."

Kit gulped, said nothing, and she was turning away a little blindly when two riders showed, coming in from the east, from the country toward the rim. One of them was Scat Kelly, the other Rick Dalton. They cut quickly around the barns and feed sheds, drew to a halt beside the corrals. Rick was stony-faced and grim, Scat alert and watchful.

By a supreme effort, Kit managed to face them with some show of composure, while George Rowan faced them with a surly truculence. "What do you want?" he demanded. "You might know, after all that's happened, that you ain't noways welcome around this spread any more, Dalton. And that goes for you, too, Kelly."

"Yes," echoed Kit a little numbly, "what do you want?"

"Just a look at the ground along this corral fence," said Rick harshly. "It won't take long."

"It'll take too long, far as I'm concerned," said George Rowan. "On your way, both of you."

In answer to this, Rick dismounted. George Rowan spat a curse and stepped forward threateningly, but stopped under the flaming impact of Rick's glance. "Don't act any dumber than the Lord made you, Rowan," crackled Rick. "I'm looking over the ground. Watch him, Scat."

"With pleasure," drawled Scat. "Go ahead, cowboy."

And then, as though neither Kit nor George existed, Rick prowled along the corral fence, eyes flickering back and forth across the trampled dust. Presently he stopped, got down on one knee, stared at the dust with pursed lips. His lean head jerked in a nod, as though in conviction of something. Then he got up and went back to his horse.

"Any luck?" asked Scat.

"Yeah. That guy was here. I'll have to try and remember them that I saw."

Rick swung into the saddle. As he lifted the reins, he looked at Kit and George Rowan. "Too bad your father isn't alive. He'd take you both into the woodshed and teach you manners, and maybe a couple of grains of savvy."

George's florid face flamed a deeper shade. "Kit and me don't need any advice from any dirty killer, Dalton. You see, we just heard about you chopping one of Iberg's riders down, without giving him a chance to go for his gun. Granger, the guy's name was. And nobody hates a killer worse than we do."

Rick's eyebrows lifted slightly, a mirthless smile on his tight lips. "I can't believe that, Rowan . . . not with both of you so fond of Matt Iberg. You ain't consistent. Come on, Scat."

Rick spurred away, but Scat lingered just a moment, and, when he spoke, it was mainly to Kit Rowan. "I was there when it happened," said Scat. "I was right behind Rick. This Granger happened to be a certain Spike Granger, a pretty well-known gunfighter who hires his guns out, like he did to Iberg. And whoever says that Granger had no chance for his draw lies. He had his guns out of the leather before Rick made a move. That happens to be the real truth, because, not giving a plugged dime whether you believe me or not, I'd have no reason to lie about it. The guy with the real forked tongue on this range ain't Rick Dalton, or me. It's your dear friend, Matt Iberg."

Scat lit out after the departing Rick, leaving Kit and George Rowan more confused and uncertain than ever.

VIII

The freshness of a new day lay over the world. Shortly after sunup, shifting dust clouds showed riders on the move here and there throughout the valley, and these dust clouds all converged upon the town of Rocky Pass. Matt Iberg, shrewd and calculating always, was staging this meeting in the very place where Spike Granger had come to an

abrupt end of an infamous career. But Granger
would not be what he truly had been, by the time
Iberg got through talking. By then, Granger would
be a poor inoffensive rider, who had been ruthlessly
shot down by that arch-enemy of every other man
in the valley, Rick Dalton. Iberg had already re-
hearsed his speech to himself, and now, as he jogged
toward town at the head of half a dozen riders, he
was still playing over the highlights in his mind.

Where another trail converged with the one he
was riding, a few miles from town, Iberg was a trifle disturbed to see Kit Rowan riding along with
her half-brother George. Iberg had sent word to
George Rowan about the meeting, but hadn't expected Kit would be in town, also. However, he
smoothed the first touch of scowl from his features
as he greeted them.

Kit wasn't the same as when he had parted from
her the day before. Some of that old aloofness, that
untouchable dignity was mantling her again. She
answered his greeting with a brief nod, her face
pale and unsmiling.

When they reached town, they found a number
of other riders already there and lounging about in
the morning sunshine. Stooly Maxwell was there,
with old man Guest. And Bosco Scarlett. Each of
them had brought at least two riders with them.

Kit Rowan reined in before John App's store. She
spoke for the first time, looking at George Rowan.
"Don't jump to any hasty conclusions, George,"
she said. "Remember, there are generally two sides
to everything."

Matt Iberg didn't like the sound of that, and, as
he and George Rowan dismounted in front of the
Buffalo House, he pulled George aside.

"What's got into Kit this morning?" Iberg asked gruffly. "She still trying to defend that damned killer, Dalton?"

George shrugged. "Dalton and Scat Kelly hit the ranch right after you left yesterday. I braced Dalton about being a killer and told him to get off the ranch and stay off. I told him why. Dalton pulled out, but Scat Kelly stayed long enough to give Kit and me a line of guff about Dalton giving Spike Granger a chance to get his guns plumb out of the leather before he smoked him down. Apparently that left Kit not quite able to make up her mind. But it didn't fool me none. I've heard all about Spike Granger. There wasn't nobody could give that jigger first bite and then beat him to it. Don't worry about Kit. She'll get over it."

With a show of heartiness, Iberg slapped George Rowan on the shoulder. "Ain't nobody fooling you, is there, George?"

They went into the Buffalo House and every other rider crowded in behind them, not wanting to miss a word of what was to take place. The street was empty, except for the line of ponies tied to various hitch rails.

Kit Rowan lingered under the overhang of the store, moody eyes fixed on the street, but seeing none of it until two figures stepped from the door of Joe Kirby's saddle shop. Then Kit stiffened, one slim hand creeping to her throat, the other going out to steady herself against the front of the store. For those two figures were Rick Dalton and Scat Kelly.

Kit wanted to cry out in alarm. Wasn't there any limit to the careless audacity of Rick Dalton? Didn't he know that all of those men in the Buffalo

House would soon be his sworn enemies, ready to do their best to ride down and shoot him to death?

She watched, fascinated, unable to move, as Rick and Scat separated, one on either side of the street, whence they started moving along the lines of cow ponies, apparently examining the butts of the saddle guns slung to various kaks.

She saw Rick Dalton move in dangerously close to the Buffalo House, to examine the saddles of the ponies tied to that hitch rail. He moved past two of those horses, stopped at the third, examined the saddle gun it carried carefully, then stooped, lifted each of the animal's hoofs in turn, looking apparently at the shoes the horse was wearing.

He straightened, waved to Scat, who hurried over and went through the same moves Rick had done. They talked for a moment, then went back into Joe Kirby's place.

Behind Kit sounded a soft chuckle. "Wonder what those two scalawags are up to now?" came a drawling voice.

Kit turned to behold Frank Orland standing beside her. Kit knew Frank Orland, but he was as big a puzzle to her as he was to everyone else in the valley.

"G-good morning, Mister Orland," stammered the startled Kit. "Why is it you're not down at the Buffalo House with the others?"

Orland shrugged. "Because I want no part of their dirty scheming," he said coolly. "I reckon there's only about half a dozen people in this valley Matt Iberg ain't completely fooling. I happen to be one of them. Rick Dalton and Scat Kelly are a couple of others. I'd still like to know why they were so interested in that blue gelding that Bat Tulane always rides."

He moved as though to go down the street, but Kit caught him by the arm. "Please, Mister Orland. I want to talk to you. What you just said . . . about dirty scheming going on? What did you mean by that?"

Frank Orland looked at her with those cold blue eyes of his. "Mean to tell me you don't know? About what Iberg is hatching up to do to those High Plains people?"

"Only . . . only that he thinks the valley cattlemen should organize to keep the High Plains ranchers from coming down and hogging our valley range."

Orland threw back his head and laughed noiselessly. "The guy must he good," he gasped. "Yes, sir, he shore must be good, if he's got a level-headed youngster like you believing all that hogwash. The truth is, child . . . Matt Iberg is organizing the valley ranchers to go up and run the High Plains people plumb off the earth. Iberg, Maxwell, Bosco Scarlett, old man Guest . . . they all figure they could use the High Plains for a spring and summer range, which would give them enough extra grass to enlarge their present herds past the mark which valley grass alone could stand. From the looks of things, Iberg has your brother George sold on the same idea. They wanted me to sit in with their rotten steal. But while I make no claims at being a saint, there are some things I draw a line at. Robbing honest men is one of them, fighting women and kids is another, backing a polecat who orders decent men drygulched, lynched, bull-whipped is another. And Matt Iberg is that polecat."

Kit Rowan couldn't explain the tears that filled her eyes. Maybe it was the terrific relief that flooded her. What Frank Orland was telling her meant that Rick Dalton was right—that he had been right all the time! And if Iberg had lied in that manner, maybe this other thing was a lie, too—about Rick shooting down a man without giving him a chance.

"What . . . what do you know about that . . . that killing, in the Buffalo House yesterday, Mister Orland?"

"I know all about it. I was there. This Spike Granger, a no-good, murdering whelp if there ever was one, was in there working himself up with whiskey for a trick of meanness of some sort. Rick Dalton and Scat Kelly came in. Rick faced Granger, told him he knew he was just a dirty gunfighter that Iberg had brought in to help him with this range-hog scheme. And Rick told Granger to fork leather and get plumb out of the country. Granger went for his guns instead. I thought Rick was a goner, shore. For Granger had his guns plumb out and free before Rick moved. Yet Rick got him, with the fastest draw I ever saw. That feller, Rick Dalton, is plenty of man in lots of ways. More power to him. With a little luck he'll bust Matt Iberg wide open yet. Now I'm going down to the saddle shop and warn Rick and Scat out of town. Maybe they don't realize that every man jack now in the Buffalo House will come out honing to get 'em over gun sights. Which is another smooth little trick Mister Iberg is cooking up. Yep, I'm going to warn those two rascals."

Frank Orland strode off. Kit Rowan looked after him, whispering through her tears: "Yes . . . yes, warn them . . . warn him! Oh, Rick . . . I'm sorry. I've had you wrong all the time. And my heart kept telling me so. . . ."

But Rick and Scat weren't in the saddle shop. They had slipped out the back way. And Joe Kirby faced Frank Orland with open antagonism. "You and the rest of Iberg's crowd won't get any line on those two boys," growled old Joe. "Not through me, anyhow."

Again Frank Orland gave that silent laugh of his. "You got me wrong, Joe," he said. "I got no more use for Iberg than you have."

"You were out to the Rocking R yesterday with the rest when Iberg cooked up his scheme of razing the High Plains country," charged Kirby. "I know. Rick told me you were. And that, as far as I'm concerned, writes you off, Orland."

"I was there," admitted Orland. "But if Rick had bothered to look back after he left, he'd have seen me pulling out, too. I want no part of Iberg and his schemes and he knows it. I went to the Rocking R just to see how smooth Iberg could really be. That's the truth, Joe. Rick don't know it, but I'm backing him all the way."

Orland's eyes were level and cold—and truthful. Joe Kirby let his bristles down. "I'm glad to hear that, Frank . . . damned glad. Rick's out to fight a mighty tough proposition, and every friend he can scrape will help. Him and Scat got something under their hats now, but the consarned hyenas wouldn't let me in on it. I dunno where they went to. That's a fact. They had their bronc's out back and they took 'em when they left. Only . . . Scat did borrow my old eight-gauge Greener shotgun again."

"The day's yet a pup," drawled Orland. "Suppose we just kind of wait around and see if anything breaks."

Orland squatted in Joe Kirby's doorway, built a cigarette, and let his eyes play lazily up and down the street.

The meeting in the Buffalo House didn't last very long. Men began to appear, getting their broncos, and riding out of town. Stooly Maxwell and old man Guest showed with their riders and pulled out. Bosco Scarlett and his men left a little later. And finally Matt Iberg and his contingent of Box I riders sought their broncos and prepared to leave. Iberg talked with George Rowan a moment and George headed for the store, where he had left Kit.

Iberg and his men were leisurely as they jogged past the store. The smugness on Iberg's face reflected the fact that he had put over another scheme. But the smugness left his face very abruptly when Scat Kelly stepped into view beyond the far corner of the store, a big, double-barreled shotgun at his shoulder, the gaping muzzles taking in every man jack of the Box I crowd as they swung slowly back and forth in a menacing arc.

"Lift 'em!" rapped Scat. "Lift 'em high . . . and quick! Get 'em up!"

That big shotgun was a deadly persuader. Hands shot skywards and Iberg's were the first up, a tinge of pallor showing under the slight swarthiness of his skin. At that moment Rick Dalton showed at the other corner of the store, a pair of six-guns stabbing level in his fists. The Box I crowd was caught cold.

Matt Iberg licked his lips. "What is this?" he croaked. "Gone in for hold-up work as well as killin', Dalton?"

"Rat hunting," rapped Rick harshly. "Roundin' up a dry-gulcher. All right, Bat Tulane, you can knee your bronc' over this way."

Bat Tulane was a round-headed, high-shouldered rider, with a pair of flaring ears that had given him his sobriquet. His pale eyes turned shifty, fear-laden.

"Wh-what you want me for?" he blurted.

"For dry-gulching Jim Prentiss, that's what for. Don't bother to argue. We know you did it. Come over here! I ain't saying it again!"

Bat Tulane looked helplessly around. But if he was expecting any backing from his companions, he was wrong. That shotgun Scat Kelly held had them mesmerized. Tulane was whimpering as he obediently kneed his bronco over to Rick. "What I did, I did at orders. And. . . ."

Tulane jammed home the spurs, lifted his bronco straight at Rick with a savage lunge, at the same time dropping low over his bronco's neck and stabbing his hands to his guns.

The wild, desperate gleam in Tulane's eyes was all that saved Rick Dalton. Rick saw that gleam flash into being, just before Tulane used the spurs, and Rick managed to side-step the plunging horse by a fraction.

Tulane had a gun out as he sped past Rick and he flung a desperate, stabbing shot back and down, which churned up the dust right between Rick's feet. Spinning his horse in a crazy circle, Bat Tulane flung two more shots, but his haste and the action of his horse kept them wide. And then, before he could shoot again, Rick flung a shot of his own, followed it up with another, and then a third. An invisible force jerked Tulane back in his saddle, where he hung a moment before toppling to the ground. He fell, limp and dead, right in front of George Rowan, who was leading his horse on his way to the store.

As soon as he saw Tulane down, Rick spun back to watch Iberg and the others, expecting Tulane's desperate try to set them off, also. But the spell of the big shotgun still held them, although Cass Denio was mumbling and cursing with growing rage. And Rick saw something else. He saw Kit Rowan in the doorway of the store, watching him with that dazed, white-faced look that had been so much a part of her lately.

George Rowan stood for a moment, staring down at the dead Bat Tulane, while his face grew darker and darker with quick rage. Then his eyes lifted and stabbed at Rick Dalton, who appeared to be unconscious of his presence, who had eyes only for Iberg and the others. George Rowan started to draw a gun. But a cold voice behind him stopped him. Frank Orland's voice.

"Wouldn't, was I you, Rowan. You'll bust your brains first thing you know, if you keep on playing the fool. This is Dalton's and Kelly's play. Let's you and me keep out of it."

George Rowan let go of the gun.

Rick Dalton was speaking, his voice harsh and ringing. "Just to keep the record straight, Iberg . . . though you know it as well as I do . . . Scat and me wanted Tulane because he dry-gulched Jim Prentiss. We've had the deadwood on him, complete . . . and he admitted it just now before he took that wild chance to get away. Any bronc' with three smooth shoes and one with new calks can't help but leave a pretty fair trail. That blue bronc' of Tulane's is shod that way. He should have thought of that . . . or you should. Then, if you use your saddle gun to smash a rattlesnake's head, you're liable to batter up the points of the butt plate a heap, besides have some bloodstains left on it. Well, Tulane's saddle gun shows those marks. Yeah, we had him dead to rights. We aimed to take him up to the High Plains, where those folks could lynch him, all right and proper. I'd rather it had ended that way. But . . . he took his chance. Only thing, by rights you should be in his shoes. For I reckon you put him up to it. As it is . . . git! Let 'em on their way, Scat."

Scat waved the shotgun. "You heard what the old boy said. Rattle your hocks!"

They didn't argue. They went on their way. And when they were fifty yards distant, Rick said crisply: "All right, Scat . . . let's go."

Scat darted down one side of the store, Rick down the other. And Kit Rowan heard the fading tattoo of hoofs as they sped away from town, taking to the sage for cover.

Frank Orland moved around in front of the sullen-eyed George Cowan. "You see, Rowan," he drawled. "If you had butted in there, you'd've been all wrong. You ought to thank me for keeping you out of it."

George Rowan snarled. "Don't ever move in on me again, Orland. It'll be your neck if you do."

Orland looked him up an down. "You pore damn' fool," he said. Then he turned on his heel, and walked off.

IX

Out in the shelter of the sage, Rick Dalton's thoughts were bitter as he and Scat sped along. *She was there*, he mused to himself. *She saw me kill him. That winds it all up, I reckon. She'll never have a bit of use for me again . . . never!*

Rick Dalton had no illusions as to what the future probably held in store for him now. Matt Iberg and all the other cattlemen behind Iberg would be after him with a vengeance. With the forces of the valley, he felt himself completely outlawed. Scat Kelly was in the same boat with him and he felt badly about that, although he knew Scat wouldn't have it any other way. He had made good his promise to Charley Curtiss to round up the dry-gulcher who had killed Jim Prentiss. It hadn't come out the way Rick had planned and hoped it might, but at least Prentiss was fully avenged. That was history to be forgotten, and Rick probably could have forgotten it had he not remembered the white, shocked face of Kit Rowan staring at him from the doorway of the store.

As to the ruckus with Spike Granger, Rick had confidently felt that sooner or later Kit must hear the full truth, which in all fairness would have exonerated him. But this last smoke out! She had seen the whole thing, right before her eyes. It seemed she was always seeing him at some disadvantage. Like the day he had whipped Iberg with his bare hands. Always Kit saw him in moments of conflict, never in any softer light. And he knew how fine and tender and true the real Kit Rowan was. To such a nature as hers, the conflict he was always in, in her eyes, must have damned him forever and ever. He groaned in disgust. How damnable the way fate could chuck a man around sometimes!

A shout by Scat Kelly broke sharply through the consuming bitterness of Rick's thoughts. He jerked his head up and followed Scat's pointing arm. Out there was a scudding dust cloud, paralleling but slightly behind their own course. When Rick narrowed his eyes to a straining intensity, he saw under that dust the scudding shapes of riders, driving full out through the sage.

"If there's any more run in these bronc's of ours, we better get it out of 'em!" yelled Scat. "Those *hombres* out yonder are aiming to head us off and cut our strings. Iberg and his gang, I reckon."

Scat was right. It would be Iberg. Once beyond the immediate threat of Scat's shotgun and Rick's revolvers, Iberg was quick to seize the advantage that lay in the longer range of the saddle guns his men carried. As Rick and Scat had fled town, Iberg had set up a chase to bring them in range and cut them down with those threatening rifles.

This getaway wasn't going to be as simple as Rick had figured. Iberg's men, farther to the east, had a good chance of keeping Rick and Scat from an escape over the rim into the High Plains country, unless the fugitives' broncos had enough speed and bottom to outrun their pursuers. Rick settled himself in the saddle and, with Scat spurring beside him, settled down to a ride for life.

This was going to be close; Rick could see that. The outcome might lie in the right or wrong judgment of when to use speed and when not to. Rick measured the distance and the angle and made his decision. He reined down his speeding bronco slightly, and Scat, guessing Rick's intent, did likewise.

They had the advantage of a slight head start. On the other hand, theirs was the longer angle to ride to reach the rim. One about balanced the other. Yes, it was going to be close.

The broncos, pulled down from an all-out pace, ran more easily now. Rick knew from long experience that there was a speed at which a horse could run for miles and still have a little left for a final burst. But forcing the animal a little beyond that first speed would set it to laboring and it would burn itself out in a few hundred yards. His task of judgment now was to maintain the one and avoid the other. In their fury over the outcome of the past few minutes and in their wild desire to even up, Iberg and his men might not use that fine judgment. That was the gamble Rick had to take.

On either side the gray sage flowed past, as the broncos, heads level and outstretched, spurned distance backward. Hardy little devils, these broncos, with a lot of run in them if handled just right. Rick watched that strung-out bunch of riders over to his right.

They were drawing up more nearly level now, slowly but surely. Yet, to do so, Rick knew they were pushing their broncos full out. Which was what he wanted. The next couple of miles would tell the story.

His glance reached beyond those riders, to the rim itself, then moved on ahead to where, already in the distance, showed the thin, green line that was Chinquapin Creek. Up this he and Scat would have to turn, because the gorge at the head of the creek was the only means of access over the rim for several miles.

Evidently Matt Iberg had this figured, also, for he had his riders pulling slightly ahead now. Yet Rick waited, judging distance and speed with a shrewd eye. Even if he and Scat did succeed in cutting across ahead of the pursuit, it would mean they would pass within rifle range. One or the other of them, maybe both, might stop a slug. Which would have made the whole effort useless.

Rick glanced at Scat and was met with a wide and flashing grin. Good old Scat! The reckless devil was actually enjoying this thing. Scat was ready for any chance, any gamble. His spirit fired Rick anew, who took another gauging look at the prospect then yelled: "Let's go, cowboy!"

The gallant little broncos answered the urge of rein and spur. They began moving away from the pursuit, and, as they did so, Rick swung slowly but surely to the right.

The pursuit was quick to recognize the move. Quirts began to lift and fall, spurs to dig deeper. Now the full-out race was on, and the speeding riders converged. Rifles began to snarl, although speed and distance left the lead wide. But there would be closer shooting before this thing was done. Rick tried for another notch of speed and got it.

The ground and the sage were a blur underfoot now. The wind of progress whipped the brim of Rick's sombrero back and held it flat. Beneath it his lean profile jutted, grim and set. Foam gathered in rolls along the edges of saddle blankets. Flecks of it began whipping back against Rick's face. A couple more minutes would tell the story. And now that gamble of judgment on speed began to pay off. He and Scat were gaining. That extra edge that Iberg's crowd had spurred from their broncos, in the initial effort to draw even, was beginning to take its toll. The members of the pursuing party began stringing out more and more. But the converging angle brought them remorselessly closer.

Rifles rattled steadily and Rick heard the whine of lead overhead. Other slugs gouged gouts of dust from the earth, wailed away in ricochet. The range was still far too long for a six-gun, but Rick drew one and emptied it anyhow, hoping for some long-chance hit that might upset or delay the pursuit.

Now the sheltering thickets along Chinquapin Creek were just ahead. Once that vantage was gained, half of the battle would be won. Rick leaned lower in his saddle, muttered through set teeth.

"I hate to ask it, bronc'. You've done a grand job of running. But now . . . if you had just a little more . . . just a little more. . . ."

Somehow the gallant little animal found that last necessary ounce and Scat's mount matched the effort. They sped across that ever-narrowing crucial angle and gained the temporary shelter of the first thicket along the creek. But that rifle lead was cutting in all about them now, ripping through sour willow clumps, showering leaves and twigs. On the smooth, gray bole of an alder right in front of Rick a wicked white scar leaped into being, jagged with splintered wood.

Upcreek Rick and Scat sped, drawing down now a little from that killing pace. Rick grinned across at Scat, who let out a shrill, high yelp of defiance.

The pursuit had not given up, however. Still

that rifle lead searched and searched, and, when the brush thinned somewhat, Rick threw a hasty glance to the rear, to see riders still pounding after them.

There would be no chance to stop at the cabin for any supplies or equipment, or fresh broncos. It was still all or nothing and the gorge was the answer. And so, with savage regret, Rick saw his cabin flash into view and as quickly be put behind.

There was one spot on that gorge trail that would be bad, a cutback across the short face of sheer rock that would make them open targets to those rifles. But it had to be chanced and Rick took it first, bronco laboring and gasping. Lead smashed into the rock all about him with malignant fury, showering him with stinging particles, filling the air with the hot odor of brimstone. But he made the crossing, somehow unhit, and the turn beyond which meant safety. Then he held his breath for Scat.

Scat made it, a slight smear of blood along the angle of his jaw where a rock splinter had cut. But nothing worse. And they pulled their broncos to a stop for a well-needed rest.

"Dog-gone!" gulped Scat with a wide grin. "I never thought we'd make it with whole skins. I reckon the devil looks after his own, all right. Cowboy, I think them jiggers actually had mean intentions toward you and me."

"Plenty!" affirmed Rick grimly. "But they won't try and follow us any farther. They know we could hold this gorge trail until hell freezes with nothing more than a handful of rocks. We might as well keep moving. From here on out, for better or worse, our fortunes ride along with the High Plains folks."

"Suits me." Scat shrugged. "Too many polecats down in the valley, anyhow."

They went on up the gorge, their broncos climbing at a slow walk. When they finally topped out, Rick cut back to a point of the rim and looked down. What he saw jerked a bitter cry from him. Down there, far out and below, where his cabin had stood, was now just a pillar of towering flames. Matt Iberg had burned him out.

Scat looked and swore softly. "That guy is storing up a heap of hell for himself. Rick. Keep your chin up, old boy. We can always build another cabin."

"That's right," admitted Rick grimly. "But right now that fire leaves me with just about all I possess on my back and on the bronc'. My cattle should be waiting, maybe, if Iberg and the rest of the buzzards don't gobble 'em up. But if they try, I'll have plenty to say about it. This hand ain't played out yet, not by a jug full."

On the way home from his fruitless chase of Rick Dalton and Scat Kelly, Matt Iberg stopped in at the Rocking R, telling his men he would follow later. At the Rocking R he found George Rowan prowling moodily and savagely about, going through the motions of soaping down a saddle hung on the corral fence.

"Do any good?" growled George Rowan.

Iberg shook his head as he dismounted. "That *hombre* has the luck of hell riding with him." He cursed savagely. "Thought sure me and the boys had Dalton and Kelly trapped. But by an eyelash they squeezed by and got away from us up that Chinquapin Gorge. I burned his damned cabin for him, though."

"Small profit in that," grunted Rowan. "Them two jiggers running loose can throw plenty of monkey wrenches into our plans. They're liable to organize those High Plains ranchers, and, when we try and move in, we'll meet up with hell five miles wide."

"I was thinking of that myself," admitted Iberg. "So . . . just to be sure we don't waste any time, I'm going to round up the rest of the boys and we ride tonight."

George Rowan jerked his head up. "Tonight! Ain't that kinda sudden?"

"What of it? By your own admission Dalton may try to organize the High Plains country. Our best bet is to hit 'em before they get a chance to organize. We know what we want, what we figure on doing. I say, all things considered, the quicker we make our drive and get it over with, the better. Delay might stack the cards against us."

Rowan scowled in moody thought. Then he shrugged. "Maybe you're right, Matt. If we're going to move, there's no profit in hanging around."

"Good! Then I can count on you. How many men can you furnish?"

"None at all if that fool sister of mine gets hold of 'em first. She's on the rampage, and how!"

Iberg was startled. "What do you mean? Maybe I better go have a talk with her."

"Not if you're wise you won't. She's liable to scratch your eyes out."

"Not my eyes. I can handle her." And with that, Iberg dismounted and swaggered up to the Rocking R ranch house. At his knock, Kit Rowan opened the door, saw who was there, and started to slam the portal in Iberg's face. But Iberg got a boot in the opening, pushed the door wide with sudden roughness, and stepped inside, face dark with anger.

"What's the matter with you?" he rasped. "You can't treat me this way."

Kit's face was white, but it was the pallor of anger. Her eyes were blazing. "I've been a fool in several ways," she admitted. "But no longer. I see you as you really are now, Matt Iberg. A smooth, scheming, lying scoundrel. Thank heaven, I've come to my senses in time. Whatever your dirty schemes may be, no member of the Rocking R will be aiding you. Now get out of this house, and never come back!"

All of the deep-seated malignancy in Matt Iberg's make-up came to the surface and glittered in his murky eyes. His face twisted into a snarl and his hands opened and closed as though twitching to get at the soft throat of this slim girl who defied him. Kit read his thoughts accurately.

"You could never stop me from screaming," she lashed. "And that would bring a number of people, capable ones, who are rather faithful to my interests. What they would do to you would be rather messy and complete. Leave this house!"

Iberg fairly shook with the fury seething in him, but he made no move toward her, realizing all too well the truth of her words. And he realized he was playing this hand all wrong. He fought that malignant fury back, fought the snarl on his face back to a grimace of a smile.

"Sorry, Kit," he said thickly. "I didn't mean any of this. I'm a little upset, I reckon. Bat Tulane was a good friend of mine. And when that killer, Dalton, cut him down, I. . . ."

"You're wrong, Matt Iberg," cut in the girl coldly. "Rick Dalton is not a . . . a killer. He's one of the few honest, decent men in this valley. Bat Tulane was the killer, that lowest, most cowardly of all killers . . . a dry-gulcher. The mask is off, Matt Iberg . . . and you might as well realize it. Will you kindly leave?"

There was nothing else Iberg could do about it, not at the moment, anyhow. He turned without another word and stamped out. At the corral, George Rowan was still tinkering with his saddle. "Well?" he asked.

Iberg forced what was meant for a careless grin to his face. He shrugged. "You were right. She shore is on the warpath. Best thing to do is leave her alone until she gets over it. I'll be expecting you and your crew at the Box I right after dark, George."

"All right," said George. "We'll be there."

Iberg spurred away, and, as soon as he was beyond sight and hearing, he let all the banked-up, vindictive fury in him find voice and expression in a sinister burst of scalding cursing. Shaken, dripping with sweat from the outburst, he threw a glance back at the Rocking R.

"A scheming, lying scoundrel, am I?" he snarled. "Before I'm done with you, you'll weep tears of blood for those words, my fine young lady. After tonight there'll be just one boss in this valley and that'll be me . . . Matt Iberg. And from then on, when I snap the whip, you'll dance. And you needn't think that thick-skulled half-brother of yours will be around to help you. He won't. I'll see to it that George Rowan stops a slug tonight, if I have to throw it myself. Yeah . . . after tonight, we'll see."

X

Kit Rowan was a pretty forlorn, dispirited young lady. Even if Frank Orland had not given her the answer to a number of things that had been troubling her, she needed no further proof than the answer she had seen in Matt Iberg's face when, for a moment, he had let the dark, malignant devil in him show. It gave her some slight satisfaction to have told Iberg off, so that he knew, once and for all, just where he stood with her. But this was poor comfort indeed, in view of her complete estrangement in Rick Dalton's eyes. For where Rick had been right all along, she had been wrong. This knowledge gnawed at her ceaselessly, and, when blue dusk crept over the world and the black of night settled down, Kit was the most disconsolate she had ever been except at the time of her father's death.

Curled up in the depths of a big chair, she viewed her future. There was only one thing she could do now to square herself with her own conscience. And that, she vowed, she would do, first thing on the following morning. She would have an understanding with every rider in the outfit, an understanding that would guarantee that no Rocking R man would ever in any way aid the evil schemings of Matt Iberg. If the Rocking R took sides actively in this coming convulsion of the range, it would be on the side that Rick Dalton favored.

Kit had no illusions about her half-brother George. All too well she knew his sulky, sullen, stubborn disposition, knew that his intelligence was none too great, and that he was easily swayed by a man like Iberg. She was going to have a job keeping George in line, but she vowed to do it, no matter what the cost. It would be a pretty unpleasant session, she knew, and probably, before it was done with, she would have to threaten all manner of dire things.

The more she thought of this, the more the conviction grew that the sooner she had this understanding with George, the better all around. Tonight, for instance. She jumped to her feet, thought for a moment, and made her decision.

George would probably be down at the bunkhouse. He generally spent his evenings there, playing low-stake poker with the crew. Kit went out onto the verandah, glanced down through the darkness. At once something struck her as wrong. Mainly there was no sign of light about the bunkhouse. This was strange, yet tonight might be one of those nights when a discussion of some sort had started somewhere outside and the boys were still there, smoking and arguing. Kit went down to the bunkhouse.

It was empty, silent. She went down by the corrals, by the saddle shed, then, with growing fear, over to the cavvy corral. By the fitful light of the stars Kit made a swift count. And then she knew. George and the crew were out and riding—somewhere. But one of two answers was possible.

Either they had all gone to town—or they had
gone to join Matt Iberg. And if it were the latter, it
meant that Iberg intended leading a raid up on the
High Plains ranchers—tonight!

There was a lot of her father in Kit Rowan. In a
real emergency she grew cool and clear-headed.
There was only one answer to this. It was up to her.

She ran back to the ranch house, hurriedly discarded the gingham dress she was wearing, jumped
into her riding clothes. Then she sped back to the
cavvy corral, caught up one of her favorite ponies,
cinched her saddle in place, hit leather, and went
tearing through the night, straight for the Box I
headquarters. She was going to call her riders off
on this cruel madness being directed by Iberg.

The pony was fresh, spirited, full of run. Kit had
no idea how far she was behind George and the
crew. Maybe an hour, no more. She would be in
time. She settled low in the saddle and let the
bronco run full out. The night wind pulled and
tugged at her hair until it loosened and rippled
back over her shoulders in a dark cloud. Underfoot
the dim sage poured backward, and ahead the
black curtain of night opened and let her through.

When her straining eyes picked up the lights of
the Box I headquarters, Kit let out a little sob of relief. She was going to be in time. For if the assem-
bled ranchers had left on the raid, the Box I would
have been dark.

Past the ranch house and bunkhouse Kit raced,
to pull to a rearing halt by the corrals. "George!"
she cried. "George Rowan!"

Her reply was an exclamation of surprise and
a growling curse. "Hell, Matt . . . it's the Rowan
girl!"

Two dark, hulking shapes moved up, one on either side of Kit's pony. One of them was Matt Iberg, the other Cass Denio. "Where's George . . . where is he, and the rest of my crew?" demanded Kit.

Matt Iberg laughed mockingly. "Figured something was in the wind for tonight, and aimed to head them off, eh?" he growled. "Well, you're right on the first. Tonight we hit the High Plains. And you're too late to stop the Rocking R men. They and your brother left about fifteen minutes ago for the main gather below Bottle Rock Chute. Cass and me were just about to leave to catch up with 'em. And . . . ah, no you don't!"

As Iberg mentioned the place, Bottle Rock Chute, Kit leaned forward in the saddle, dug in the spurs. But even as the pony gathered itself to leap ahead, Matt Iberg grabbed the reins, held the horse back. "Grab her, Cass!" he yelled.

Kit fought like a fury to break free. But she had never a chance. The long, gorilla arms of Cass Denio reached far, pulled her from the saddle, then held her powerless despite all she could do. Denio was laughing thickly, tauntingly. Iberg swiftly tethered Kit's pony to the corral fence, then came to aid Denio.

"What you aim to do with her, Matt?" asked Denio. "We can't afford to have her running around loose now. She might even take it into her head to hightail up above the rim and warn them jiggers what to expect."

"I know," snarled Iberg. "She's a damned nuisance. Into the ranch house with her."

They carried her in, kicking, struggling, flaming and furious. And they thrust her into a small room that apparently was a storeroom of some kind, for it had no window, only a heavy door. They tossed her in a heap in one corner, and Iberg, standing in the door with a lamp held high, leered down at her.

"You'll have time to think a lot of things over, my dear," he mocked. "It won't do you a bit of good to yell, because nobody will hear you. You'll have a chance to get it through your head, once and for all, that from here on out, Matt Iberg is the boss on this range. I'll have a lot of other things to tell you when I get back, sweet lady. Rest easy."

He stepped back, the door was slammed, and Kit heard a lock snick into place. Footsteps echoed hollowly, faded, and were gone. A moment later came the *thud* of departing hoofs, and then was only complete silence and the blackness of a tomb.

When Rick Dalton and Scat Kelly rode away from the rim, after their escape from the Box I riders, and after watching Rick's cabin go up in flames, they headed straight back into the High Plains country to Charley Curtiss's ranch. It was just sundown when they got there and they saw Curtiss in the act of stripping a sweat-caked saddle blanket from the back of a very weary bronco.

Curtiss greeted them grimly. "Just got back from riding a big circle," he said. "I've contacted every rancher within ten miles of the rim, Rick. And they're all strong for that organization idea of yours. In fact, they're gathering tonight at Buck Millikan's place, which is about central for everybody, to talk the whole thing over and get all the details straightened out. I'm glad you're here. The boys will be glad to hear all you got to tell 'em."

"You're all damn' wise," said Rick somberly.

"You can't get set any too quick. Maybe this very night something may break."

Curtiss jerked a sharp look at him. "What makes you think that?"

Rick told him of Iberg's desperate try to get him and Scat, and of the burning of his cabin. "Iberg knows Scat and me got away up into this country," Rick ended. "He knows that I know what he has in mind. Therefore it's reasonable he'll figure me to warn you folks of what to expect and he may strike before that warning can carry full effect. That's why I say tonight may be a red night along the rim."

"Let's hope he does," growled Curtiss. "Long as this thing has got to come to a showdown sooner or later, the quicker the better, say I. And tonight is one night we'll be bunched for a fight. We'll grab a bite to eat and light out for Buck Millikan's right away. Sorry to hear about your cabin. But what set Iberg after you so hot and fast? Have a row with him?"

"Some," said Scat Kelly. "Rick evened up for Jim Prentiss, Charley." And then Scat told of the end of Bat Tulane, the dry-gulcher who had murdered Jim Prentiss.

Charley Curtiss grabbed Rick's hand, wrung it tightly. "Tulane rode for Iberg," he rumbled. "Which means Iberg put him up to that dirty trick. Yet why . . . why should Iberg have wanted Jim Prentiss moved out of the picture? Why Jim in particular?"

"I been thinking about that," admitted Rick. "My answer is this. Jim Prentiss was the most popular man on the High Plains range. He would have been the perfect leader to hold the High Plains ranchers together in a fight. So Iberg had him moved out. Iberg is a schemer, Charley . . . a deep one. He don't overlook any angles. So, that's about the way I figure it."

Curtiss nodded thoughtfully. "As good an answer as any, I reckon. Well, let's grub. We got things to do."

The stars were bright and high when Rick and Scat and Charley Curtiss rode in to Buck Millikan's spread. They found a number of riders already there, with more coming in every minute. On the ride over, Rick had been thinking and the more he thought the stronger there grew in him a strange hunch. He shook hands with Buck Millikan, pulled him aside, and explained that hunch.

"We should have guards out now, Buck," ended Rick. "This very night. At three places. The gorge trail behind my place, at Bottle Rock Chute, and at Bob Shelly's old place."

Buck Millikan nodded. "Think you're right, Rick. I'll send 'em out right away."

The gathering of the High Plains ranchers took place in Buck Millikan's bunkhouse, and, when they were all present, the long, low building was jammed to overflowing. At Charley Curtiss's suggestion, Rick took the floor. He sketched briefly the whole case as he saw it against Matt Iberg. Things Iberg had done and things he had said, over the past year or two. The trumped-up evidence on which he had lynched Bob Shelly and gotten control of the Six Springs water. The equally faked evidence on which he had ordered the bullwhipping of Slip Hankins. The dead proof that Bat Tulane, one of Iberg's riders, had dry-gulched Jim Prentiss.

Then there was the meeting of the valley ranchers that Rick had surprised at the Rocking R and his opinion of what they had met for.

"Iberg has organized those fellows," he ended. "And it can be for only one reason. The valley range itself is menaced by no outside threat. So that organization can have but one meaning. They intend to attack someone else. Who else is there to attack but you fellows? And why? Because they want your range for spring and summer range, that's why. To hang on to what's yours, you've got to fight back, meet organization with organization. If you're wise, you'll get together on this, one for all and all for one. Put the whole thing in the hands of a capable leader, take turns holding guard along the rim day and night, and be set at all times to fight. That, as I see it, is your only hope. If you try and stand alone, Iberg will pick you off, one by one. It's up to you."

Not one voice was raised in disagreement. Grimly and curtly these stern-faced men pledged themselves to fight together in a common cause. One for all, all for one. They made Buck Millikan, a grizzled, blunt-jawed man, their leader and agreed to follow out his orders without question.

When the meeting was over, men came to Rick and silently wrung his hand. Charley Curtiss had let the story out of Rick's shoot-out with Bat Tulane. The philosophy of these primitive men was fundamental. An eye for an eye. To them, justice had been served in the case of Jim Prentiss's murder.

At the corrals they hung around for some time, talking matters over, perfecting their plans. It was late when they started to break up. And then it was that, through the night, came a madly spurring rider. It was the guard Buck Millikan had ordered out for Bottle Rock Chute.

"They've moved in, boys!" yelled the guard. "They've moved in! Up Bottle Rock Chute. They've already set fire to Slip Hankins's layout!"

All eyes turned in one direction. Sure enough, piling up against the black dome of the night was a ruddy reflection. A hoarse, deep-toned roar rose from the crowd.

"They've asked for it!" yelled a rider. "And now we give it to 'em! Tonight's the night!"

XI

Along with the night wind a deep, savage exultation swept over Rick Dalton as he rode wildly through the darkness. Here it was at last. The chance to smash Matt Iberg's unholy scheme of empire, once and for all. No longer would he have to face lies and evasion, deceit and tricky scheming. No longer would he have to carry with him the gnawing, maddening consciousness of what Iberg was up to and be unable to do much about it. Here at last the chips were down. Now the cards were dealt and the game would go to the man who best played his hand.

Roaring along through the night with Rick was faithful Scat Kelly, Charley Curtiss, Buck Millikan, Slip Hankins, and all the rest of the High Plains riders. They rode silently now, but across saddles were poised rifles and six-guns hung heavily and deadly at saddle-leaned waists.

While they rode, they watched that crimson glow ahead of them climb to a peak, then begin to fade. Slip Hankins watched it, also, and his pinched face grew grim and bitter. "The whole layout's gone now," he snarled. "But what the hell! Be worth it if we can comb that pack of coyotes to tatters."

Those close enough to Slip to hear him said nothing. They merely tightened taut fingers around cold gun steel. They knew just how Slip felt.

Wisely enough, Buck Millikan halted the headlong rush. "With everything burnin' good, they won't waste too much time at Slip's place," Millikan told the impatient riders. "They'll be moving on to the next place. What's your guess, boys?"

The answer was almost unanimous: "Joe Ivory's spread!"

Millikan nodded. "Think so myself. We go that way."

They tore on again, hammering through the night, swinging back a little farther from the rim. From the rear a rider moved up even with the leaders, a tense, bent shadow in his saddle. It was Joe Ivory. At home he had left a wife and two children.

Rick did not question the choice. It was a logical one. The closest ranch to Slip Hankins's place was the Ivory home. It was a good gamble that Iberg would hit each place as he came to it. It was his safest bet to make his anticipated surprise attack a crushing one.

They breasted a low slope, topped a crest, where Buck Millikan called another halt. "Listen!" he growled. "Everybody!"

Rick strained his ears above the hoarse panting of the hard-run broncos. Then it came, thin and faraway. The sound of a shot! Then another and another.

A strangled cry broke from Joe Ivory. "I know that gun!" he shouted. "That's the light carbine I gave my wife for a present last Christmas. Boys, my Lucy is putting up a scrap for herself and the kids. I'm going in!"

There was no stopping him. Nor any of the others, for that matter. Out there in the grim night a devoted, valiant wife and mother was putting up a battle for her home and loved ones. The flame of utter ferocity that flared through these riders of the High Plains was like a roaring conflagration in high, sun-dried grass. All it touched caught fire. Instead of a charge, it became a race to see who would get there first.

The lack of opposition to the raid on Slip Hankins's layout at first made Matt Iberg a little wary. Then he concluded that Hankins was probably off visiting somewhere, and, when, at his orders, the torch was touched to the place and the red flames leaped high, Iberg sensed the lust for raid and destruction that swept over his followers. It suited him just right. They were set to make a night of it now, a night that would never be forgotten along the High Plains.

"Joe Ivory next!" had yelled a maddened rider. "Let's go get him!"

Iberg made no attempt to stop the rush. But here and there through the racing raiders he pulled in beside a man, to grip his thigh and shout a cautious word. And gradually, as the group lengthened out, Iberg began dropping back in the darkness, while the men he had accosted dropped back with him. Among these were Cass Denio and Howdy Orleans. They understood and were laughing ferociously to themselves.

"Smart thinkin', Matt," approved Cass Denio. "They tell me this Joe Ivory can shoot a wicked Winchester. Let some of those other damn' fools stop the first lead, if it comes. Right?"

"Right . . . right as rain. The more results we get without endangering our hides, the better it suits me. And if I let these other outfits weaken themselves with losses far enough, there won't be any argument as to who is boss when this night's work is over. There are some changes I want to make down in the valley as well as up here. So, watch yourselves, boys . . . keep your skins whole."

When the first group of attackers stormed up to the Ivory place, left their saddles, and tore to touch off barn and feed shed, bunkhouse and other buildings, the worried woman in the ranch house was not long in doubt of their intent. And it was then that her light carbine began to snarl.

A small pile of hay at one end of a corral was the first set to blaze, and in the growing light of the flames the rider who had started the thing was limned, sharp and clear. At the first *crack* of the carbine he whirled drunkenly, threw his hands high, and went down.

A speeding horse collapsed at the next shot, throwing its rider headlong. Then a third rider spun from his saddle in a limp tangle of arms and legs. Lucy Ivory was shooting for keeps.

This savage reception broke the first fury of the charge. Riders began to scatter a little wildly. "Get around . . . get around!" yelled Iberg. "Get around and don't forget you brought guns along to use." To punctuate this, he dragged a six-shooter and emptied it toward the dark bulk of the ranch house.

The raiders caught the order, swung out to each side, and completed a surround of the ranch house. A score of rifles and six-guns began to snarl and growl, while the ranch house fairly trembled under the terrific hail of lead crashing into it.

Lucy Ivory had grown up on the hard, dangerous frontier. She knew a little of how to play this game. She made her scared and whimpering children lie flat on the floor and stretched herself beside them until that first terrific volley should cease. And so it was that, although savage lead *whizzed* and *crashed* through every room, filling the air with dust and splinters, neither she nor her two little ones were scratched. The deadly danger would come with the rush that would follow the first smash of gunfire. She knew how small was her chance when she rose to stop that rush. Yet she was determined to try, and, while she lay there, waiting for the terrible moment, she whispered a little prayer. If only Joe—her Joe—could be there to help!

Faintly above the rumble of gunfire rose Matt Iberg's yell: "Close in! Close in!"

Lucy Ivory choked back a sob. Here it was!

Then the vengeance-chilled men of the High Plains struck. They came in at a reckless, savage speed, the rumble of their approach hidden from the raiders by the snarl and crash of the raiders' own guns.

In the lead, Joe Ivory, Rick Dalton, and Scat Kelly rode neck and neck, and they hit into the startled ranks of the raiders like the clap of doom. Joe Ivory was a regular madman and would have surely ridden to his death had not his pony stopped a slug and gone down like a shot rabbit, sending Joe rolling end over end, dazed and half stunned.

Neither Rick nor Scat wasted any lead. Each picked out shadowy riders ahead of them and drove home deadly lead. And now Matt Iberg's scheming came back at him. He and his men, who had held back, were the first to feel the impact of the High Plains men.

Howdy Orleans, about to give a yell of warning, died with the words in his throat. Others of the Box I outfit died with him, with Rick searching the night frantically, but without success, to try to identify Matt Iberg as a clout for his lead.

The attack charge of the High Plains men carried them straight up to the ranch house door. Joe Ivory, who had recovered his senses, raced in afoot, calling brokenly to his wife. And she heard him and ran out to meet him and take refuge in his thankful arms.

The other High Plains men did not halt. With Rick leading one bunch and Scat the other, they circled the ranch house and fanned out to smash into the circle of raiders. It was close, savage work, but there was no stopping or resisting these maddened High Plains riders.

They shot and beat and clawed and cursed. Then shot again. Raiders, upset by surprise, overcome by the sheer fury of the defenders, began going down on every side. Others tried to break and run, only to be shot from their saddles as they fled. What had started as a murderous surprise raid on the Ivory Ranch, now became a mad, broken rout of the raiders themselves. They had expected nothing remotely like this. At the worst, they figured only a little scattered resistance here and there along the infamous route they had planned for the night. But nothing like this, no massed, organized numbers that fought with the utter ferocity and abandon of maddened tigers.

Rick found it was impossible to make anything a definite objective in this wild, red chaos of lead and flame and death. He knew that his comrades were within the circle, so any man who made up the outer limits of that circle was legitimate prey to his leaping, reeking guns.

At first lead came back at him from guns that were at times so close to him the flame of them seemed to scorch his very eyes. Invisible fingers tore his hat from his head. Something else unseen tugged at the collar of his shirt. A thin line of white-hot fire ran along his ribs to be followed by a moist warm clamminess. But Rick noted these things with a consciousness that seemed far removed, incredibly remote. Automatically he rode on and on, seeking targets, living targets, and throwing lead at them until empty guns *clicked* uselessly in his hands.

Matt Iberg lost his horse early in the fight. He crouched low, trying to work toward the outer darkness where he might find safety. For he knew that his mad scheme of domination over the High Plains had blown up in his face. He knew that the men following him would soon lose all stomach for the whole affair under punishment of this sort. Now it was every man for himself, and Matt Iberg was trying to find a horse to make a getaway.

A hulking rider bore down on him, and, glimpsing the fellow against the stars, Iberg instinctively recognized him. "Cass!" he called hoarsely. "Cass Denio! Over here. This is Matt. I lost my bronco.

Give me a leg up to get clear of this hell. Cass! Over here!"

Cass Denio heard and whirled his bronco that way. "We're whipped, boss . . . we're whipped!" raged Denio. "They've cut us to pieces. And Dalton's out there somewhere, damn him. I heard somebody yell to him."

"I know," snarled Iberg. "I'll tend to him . . . later. Right now . . . we got to get away. I'm coming up behind you."

Yet, before he could do it, another rider bore down on them through the blackness. It was George Rowan and he was calling to Iberg. "That you, Matt? Thought I heard your voice. That you?"

"Yeah," spat Iberg. "It's me. You got here just in time. I need your bronco . . . but I don't need you . . . no more."

And then Matt Iberg shoved a gun out and shot George Rowan through the body. Rowan gasped, doubled up, and slithered from his saddle. Before the startled bronco could whirl away, Iberg had it by the rein and was in the saddle. And then he and Denio spurred savagely away into the sheltering blackness of the far, wondering night.

XII

As soon as Joe Ivory found that his wife and children were unhurt, he rustled up several lanterns, and by the light of these the victorious High Plains ranchers began combing the battle ground for casualties. One of the first they found was Scat Kelly. Scat was sitting on the ground, swearing steadily and clutching at a leg cleanly broken by a slug. While some carried him into the house, others searched farther. They found several more of their friends wounded and one dead, a young bachelor rancher named Bert Rothrock.

But for every one of the High Plains casualties, they found three of the raiders. They found Bosco Scarlett out by that still smoking little pile of hay. He was the one who had started it and who had been cut down by Lucy Ivory's first shot. Bosco Scarlett was quite dead. They found Stooly Maxwell, humped on the ground, bleary-eyed and stupid with a smashed shoulder. They found old man Guest, spread-eagled, dead face to the sky, a bullet hole between his eyes. And, finally, they found George Rowan, still alive, faintly conscious, but very, very seriously wounded.

George Rowan blinked dazedly at the lantern light in his eyes. "Dalton . . . Rick Dalton," he mumbled. "I got . . . to tell . . . him something. Where is he? Rick Dalton . . . ?"

They called Rick over, and Rick knelt beside Kit Rowan's half-brother. George Rowan caught at him.

"Rick . . . Rick . . . you got to . . . stop him," Rowan gasped. "Iberg . . . he shot me. Did it deliberate . . . took my bronco. Said he had . . . no more use . . . for me. Iberg and Denio . . . they were together. I'm afraid . . . for Kit . . . for Kit. Rick . . . you got . . . stop him. . . ."

Then George Rowan fainted.

They carried him into the house, where Lucy Ivory, calm and cool again, was caring for the wounded. She looked at George Rowan's wound, studied the angle of it a moment, then nodded. "I think he'll make it all right," she said quietly. "The bullet went clear through. I think he'll make it."

Rick waited to hear no more. He was out, into his saddle, and gone, racing through the night toward the rim. His thoughts were as cold and brittle as the gleam in his eyes. Strange how the pattern formed, how the cards fell. Here, at last, the issue lay clear-cut. Here was the final showdown. Between him and Matt Iberg. Just as though it had always been written that way by the Fates. And the final issue—Kit Rowan—the most important issue of all, at least to Rick Dalton.

Rick reloaded his guns as he rode, his senses straining and leaping out ahead of him. Which route would Iberg and Denio take in leaving the High Plains? The closest one, no doubt, which would be Bottle Rock Chute, the way they had come up. And that was the route he had to take himself, because to cut far north to the gorge of Chinquapin Creek would be the long way around to the Rocking R, and Iberg would get there before he could. The only thing to do was to make this a stern chase, albeit a long, hard one.

At best, Iberg and Denio did not have much of a start on him. Not over half an hour. And smart riding could cut that down. Perhaps the two renegades would feel that they were in no immediate danger of pursuit. Obviously Iberg had left George Rowan for dead. He would not know that Rowan had been able to speak, or guess the urgent message he had given.

Rick rode into a miasma of low-hanging wood smoke. It was the smoke from the still smoldering ashes of what had been Slip Hankins's layout. Already he had come that far. Bottle Rock Chute lay just ahead.

In mechanical caution Rick pulled to a stop at

the crest of the night-blackened chute. There was no sound down there, but, as he listened, far below and off to his right sounded the last fading echoes of hoofs. The gleam in his eyes grew colder. Already he had cut down much of the lead the renegades held.

Rick put his bronco to the descent, dropping down the steep, twisting road that followed the chute from the rim to the sage-cloaked slope of the valley below. Once into that sage, Rick turned north, in the same direction those fading hoofs had sounded.

At a fast walk, Rick pushed his bronco along through the sage, eyes searching the blackness ahead. He caught his breath in a long drawn hiss of satisfaction as he saw a pinpoint of light glow into being out ahead. His guess was right. Iberg and Denio had stopped at the Box I.

Rick rode a cautious way to within a couple of hundred yards of the ranch headquarters before dismounting, tying his bronco to a sage clump, taking off his spurs, then prowling noiselessly in on foot.

He reached the first corral, slid shadow-like along beside the fence. That pinpoint of light had disappeared. Rick paused, every sense testing the night about him. Maybe they had heard his running before he had pulled to a walk. Maybe they were laying for him with bared and ready guns. Maybe they were within only a few yards of him this moment. At any time one or both of them might cut down on him with savage lead.

Noiselessly Rick slid both his guns free. Then step by step he closed in. The dark bulk of horses loomed before him. Two of them, still panting heavily from the run they had made. The sweat that foamed on them laid a rancid odor on the air. They were too weary to pay Rick a bit of notice as he sidled past them and kept up his stealthy approach to the house.

A slight angle of change in his approach brought a relieving discovery. He saw light once more, glinting palely through a window. At least one, probably both, of the renegades were in the house. Rick went ahead faster, until the porch was before him, with steps to climb.

Up he went, on tiptoe, his nerves singing, taut and bitter. The front door, he discovered, was ajar, and he pushed it carefully open. Across the width of the room ahead stood another door, open, showing as a pale yellow rectangle from the light glowing beyond.

Now Rick heard a voice, the voice of Matt Iberg. "Hold on to this light, Cass. I'll bring her out. She'll probably put up a scrap."

Rick didn't wait to hear any more. Kit Rowan was in this very ranch house! How she had got here, Rick did not know. That explanation would come later. The thing he had to do was get at Iberg and Denio before Kit was brought into the scene and maybe got hurt in the showdown coming up. And so, with this in mind, Rick slithered quickly across the room and threw a glance beyond.

There was Cass Denio, holding a small kerosene lamp guttering and smoking in a grimed chimney. The light of it threw his shadow, huge and distorted, against the wall behind him. And there was Matt Iberg, half bent as he fumbled at the lock of the door before him. Rick drew a deep breath.

"Iberg! Denio!" he rasped. "This, I reckon, is it!"

Cass Denio grunted as though someone had hit him. He spun around, staring with sagging jaw at the lean, cold-faced, blood-stained apparition in the doorway. Matt Iberg jerked erect, spun around. "You!"

"Yeah," droned Rick tonelessly, "me!"

Rick saw Cass Denio's fingers open, saw the lamp start to fall, saw Denio's clawing hand snake toward his gun. And Rick shot once, twice—just as the lamp crashed on the floor.

The groan of a mortally wounded animal belched from Denio. But there was no crash of his fall, so Rick drove two more smashing shots, before turning his guns on where Iberg had been.

For a moment the room was black. Then, where the lamp had smashed, spattering a flood of kerosene in all directions, a tiny red flame glowed and almost instantaneously rippled half across the room in a curtain of roaring flame.

Acrid, stinking smoke billowed out, fogging Rick's eyes, choking his lungs. But through it and the sheet of flame beyond he made out a wavering figure and he pounded lead at that figure in a re-morseless roll. He saw a gun flash, but no lead came his way, for Matt Iberg was blind, dying and shooting the same way.

As the gun thunder died, Rick shielded his face with an arm and raced to that locked door. "Kit!" he shouted. "Kit! You in there?"

Her answer was his name in a sobbing cry. "Rick! Oh . . . Rick darling!"

The door was stout and soundly locked. The key must still be with Matt Iberg, dead in the center of the flames.

"Get to one side, Kit!" yelled Rick. "I've got to shoot the lock out. This place is on fire. Get to one side!"

Then Rick turned his guns on the lock, firing them until empty. The door shivered and clouds of splinters flew. And Rick, drawing back a stride, smashed a foot into the door with all his weight and power. The lock squealed and crumpled and the door crashed open. Rick staggered in, gulping at the smoke-free air.

A lithe figure launched itself at him, clinging to him, sobbing wildly. "Rick! Rick!"

Rick swept her up like a child. "Take a deep breath, put your face against my shoulder, and hold tight," he ordered. "Here we go!"

The flames had spread clear across the room now. To get clear, Rick had to go through them. He held his breath and made the dash. For one split second of hell he was in the midst of a searing inferno. Then he was through, into the room beyond, across that and out on to the porch beyond.

Strength ran out of him strangely, and abruptly he was down on the ground, half sitting, half lying.

Rick must have gone out for a time himself. That wound across the ribs had bled more than he thought. He came to with the realization that someone had him by the shoulders, dragging him farther and farther away from a terrible, beating heat. A vast roar filled the world, the roar of mounting flames.

Rick got enough strength to sit up again, and Kit Rowan dropped down beside him, holding him in her arms. And they sat that way while the flames towered and towered, while roof and walls caved and flattened, and until the flames began to die, their fury done.

Rick stirred, got stiffly to his feet, lifting her up beside him. "I . . . I got things to tell you, Kit," he said hoarsely. "About. . . ."

"There is only one thing I want to hear," she cut in, giving him a quick, fierce little tug. "Not so long ago, though it seems years now, you told me you loved me, Rick . . . that you would always love me. That is what I want to hear you say again. That you love me . . . that you'll always love me. That's all that counts now, Rick darling . . . just that."

So Rick told her. And she crept into his weary arms and kissed him and whispered the same words back to him. And when Rick finally lifted his head and looked toward the black rim towering to the east, he was a little startled to see the cool, quiet silver of a new dawn climbing into the patient sky.

Horse Thief Trail

"Horse Thief Trail" was L. P. Holmes's story #221. He sent it to his agent, August Lenniger, on November 18, 1938. When Lenniger returned it unsold, Holmes undertook to revise it extensively, changing the title to "Justice Counts" and assigning this draft a new number as a new story, now #233. This version he sent to Lenniger on September 9, 1941, and Lenniger sold it quickly on October 19, 1941 to A. A. Wyn at Periodical House. It appeared under the title "Make Way for a Maverick" in *Western Trails* (7/42). For its first reappearance since magazine publication, L. P. Holmes's original title has been restored.

I

After the others had gone, Jeff Hawn still stood beside the freshly filled grave, his feelings locked deeply within him. His eyes, however, were bleak, his thin young jaw set.

He was thinking that in this grave lay the only human being who had ever shown him kindness. He was thinking how, despite the emptiness and loneliness, the bleakness and desolation that had been her empty cup of life, Sarah Hagee had found time to be kind and patient and understanding with a homeless boy who had lost all grip on life and had needed, desperately, some kind of anchor. And he was remembering what she had told him, the last time he had seen her alive, this tired, cheated woman with her faded, haunted eyes. She had said: "You mustn't mourn for me, Jeff. Now I shall be able to rest . . . rest. But you, don't you string along with Alec Hagee and his crowd. Alec will ruin you, Jeff, like he has ruined everything and everyone he ever touched in this world. You must leave, Jeff. You saddle and ride . . . far. Never lie, never cheat, never steal, Jeff. And somewhere you'll find happiness."

These things she had said to him and Jeff had listened, voiceless with the choked emotion within him. This had been—farewell.

Remembering it all, Jeff swallowed thickly. And then, not knowing why, he reached for one of the low-hung branches of the live oak which shaded the grave, twisted off a sprig of green, glistening leaves, and laid them gently on the grave. Then, squaring his loose-hung young shoulders and lifting his sun-browned chin, he went over to the ramshackle corral near the equally ramshackle barn.

Jeff knew the horse he wanted, a big sorrel with white points. He roped the animal, brought it up to the snubbing post, then went into the barn. Alec Hagee's saddle was there, and it was a good one. But Jeff lifted down the old, battered one Hagee had let him use, and this he carried out and cinched in place on the sorrel.

The bridle was one Jeff had made himself. He had found the bit, lying ancient and rusted, back up the old Mescalero trail. With patient, painstaking care he had scrubbed and polished it, then fashioned the headstall from scraps of leather he had picked up here and there. When he finished with the horse, Jeff went up to the ranch house.

They were at it again, Jeff thought bitterly, at their drinking and carousing. From bitter experience Jeff knew it would go on until the last drop of liquor that Shell Darrough had brought in with him was gone. But Jeff wasn't caring about that any more. He would soon be on his way, and he'd never come back.

Jeff's first thought was to go around and slide in the back way. But Sarah Hagee had told him never to lie or cheat, and Jeff figured that to sneak around was just as bad. So he went in the front way, right through the room where they were gathered.

Alec Hagee was maudlin drunk. Shell Darrough had the same look about him, his huge, bony face sagging and brutal. Lobo Skurr was as always, after the liquor had taken real hold of him. He was backed up in a corner, his yellow, restless eyes sort of glazed and deadly-looking. In this condition, Lobo Skurr was as dangerous as a coiled rattlesnake, ready to lash out at anyone on the slightest provocation. Hoke Burdick and Tobe Nero were just hunkered down against the wall, stupid as animals.

They paid Jeff no attention, for he had been around the place ever since they had started coming here. So Jeff went on to the little cubbyhole of a room off the kitchen where he had slept on a husk mattress and where the few odds and ends that he could call his own were hoarded.

There was a battered old pair of saddlebags that a stray wild-horse hunter had discarded and that Jeff had reclaimed with patient mending and patching. Into these he wadded his only spare shirt and socks and a pair of faded, patched jeans. There were a few other items, one of which was a yellowed, faded picture. Sarah Hagee had given that to Jeff with the words: "Once I was that girl."

The picture showed a slim, laughing, pretty girl with a wealth of fair hair framing her face. She stood arm in arm with a big leonine man with heroic features and a thick, square beard. She had never said who the man was. Jeff put the picture away carefully.

That was about all, except the old carbine rifle with the scarred and wire-mended stock. From the top of a dusty rafter Jeff recovered half a dozen cartridges for that rifle. Carefully he wiped each one off and slid them into the loading gate of the weapon. Then, rifle over one arm and saddlebags over the other, Jeff went out the way he had come.

He had reached the door before Alec Hagee took notice.

Hagee snarled thickly: "You, Jeff . . . where you goin'?"

Jeff did not answer. He just kept right on, down to the corral. He led the sorrel out of the corral, hung the saddlebags across the cantle, and tied them there. Then, laying the carbine across the saddle in front of him, he mounted.

Alec Hagee had come out of the house and down off the ramshackle porch. Shell Darrough stood in the doorway, big, bony, and full of drunken slouchiness. Jeff reined the sorrel toward Alec Hagee and sat his saddle quietly, looking down at the man.

Hagee said again: "Where you goin'?"

"I'm a-going," said Jeff slowly. "Like Miz Hagee told me I should. I'm a-going, and never coming back. I'm taking this bronc'. I've earned it. I've worked like a dog for you and never a single cent did you ever pay me. All I got from you was cuss words and kicks and abuse. You owe me this bronc', so I'm taking it."

It took a moment or two for Alec Hagee's befuddled mind to grasp the import of Jeff's words. When he did, he went into a savage fit of rage. He cursed viciously.

"You git down. You ain't leavin'. You ain't takin' no bronc' of mine, you dirty little thief. Git down, I say . . . or I'll pull you down and manhandle you within a inch of your life. You heard me . . . git down!"

Jeff shook his tawny head. "I'm a-going," he said again.

Jeff thought that Alec Hagee was too deep in the liquor to move as swiftly as he did. And so, with a quick lunge, Hagee got one hand on the sorrel's rein and the other on Jeff. Jeff tried to fight him off. The sorrel, high-strung, began to snort and whirl. They went around and around in a scurry of dust. Up in the doorway Shell Darrough seemed to think the whole thing funny, for he roared with rough laughter.

But there was no laughter or mirth in Alec Hagee. Jeff had seen Hagee's black, poisonous fury on the rampage before and he recognized it now. Hagee's eyes were congested and crimson and his lips peeled back from his yellow teeth. It was all Jeff could do to keep from being hauled from the saddle. Only by locking his young and sinewy legs about his horse with all his power did he manage to keep his place.

Then into Hagee's cursing came a thin and deadly note. Still hanging onto Jeff with one hand, he let go of the sorrel's rein with the other and grabbed at the holstered gun at his hip. And Jeff, knowing that the man meant to kill him, did the only thing he could do. He drove the steel-shod butt of his carbine into the very center of Alec Hagee's convulsed face—drove it hard!

There sounded the *crunch* of shattered bone, followed by the swift, leaping crimson of blood, and Alec Hagee's grip on Jeff loosened and fell away. Jeff, sick and numbed and desperate, let the jittery sorrel run.

No shots followed him. Only the wild, brutal laughter of Shell Darrough.

Jeff headed south and west. Out there lay the Moencopee Desert. Somehow he knew that there lay sanctuary and escape. For he knew that he was not done with Alec Hagee, who would, as soon as he was able, follow him, vengeful as a wolf.

The younker had never been on the Moencopee Desert. All he knew was that, on certain days when the sun haze was not too blinding, a person could, from the higher slopes up along the Mescalero trail, look southwest and see, away out there, a vast sea of coppery crimson. That was Moencopee.

Jeff slowed the sorrel from its first wild run, holding it down to a strength-conserving pace. From time to time he twisted in the saddle and looked back. But he was a full two hours gone before he saw it, a thin and distant funnel of dust lifting. They were after him!

That blow in the face with the carbine butt might have knocked the senses out of Alec Hagee for a time, but it would also knock the liquor out of him. And he would have roused the rest from their drunkenness and made them join him in the chase.

Jeff fought back the impulse to spur the sorrel into a wild run. That would never do, for Jeff's life now lay in the strength and staying power of the horse under him, and it would be criminal folly to waste the animal's reserve.

The low slopes ran out flatter and flatter and almost imperceptibly merged with the burning immensity of the desert. Brush grew scantier, scrubbier. The earth began to scab with leprous patches of alkali, and, even though the sun was dropping low to the west, heat laid an invisible but smothering weight on him. The sorrel began to lather and Jeff held it to an even slower pace.

Looking back, Jeff saw them come off the slope and on to the desert. Just moving dots, and he counted five of them. Which meant that all had joined in the chase.

The first swift terror of the thing had left Jeff. He was able to calculate distance with calm judgment. His lead was a good three miles, maybe more. They would have to push their horses heavily to close the gap, and, even though the sorrel was lathering, there was plenty of run left in the horse. Sundown and darkness were not too far off. If he kept his head, his chances were good.

By sundown they had cut the three miles down to less than one, but were still out of rifle shot. Jeff picked up the sorrel's pace a bit and held the interval, and figured ahead. Smoky blue dusk came down and washed out the feral crimson of the desert under a cooling tide of shadow.

When darkness followed and Jeff knew they could no longer see him because he could not see them, he turned abruptly east and let the sorrel run for a couple of miles. Here a gaunt backbone of rock lifted and Jeff pulled to a halt closely beside it. He unsaddled and, holding the sorrel by a long lead rope, let the animal roll, then rest.

The massed glow of the new stars pushed the first blackness back and Jeff found he could see for quite a distance. Alert as a hawk, he watched and waited, letting Hagee and the others get well away. Then he saddled up again and was just about to swing into the saddle when he heard the sneeze of a weary horse. Taut with strain, Jeff swung the sorrel close to the protective shadow of the rock backbone and laid a hand on the sorrel's nostrils, to cut off any whistle of recognition on the part of the animal.

They passed by little more than fifty yards distant. They were heading back home. In single file they passed, five of them, so close that Jeff could see the starlight gleaming on the silver mounting of Lobo Skurr's saddle.

Death was passing out there, and Jeff knew it. His mouth was dry and the chill of it lay in his veins. He held his breath, cold sweat rolling down his thin, angular face. If the sorrel stamped—or even moved. . . .

The five melted into the night and were gone. Jeff leaned against the sorrel, dizzy with relief. They must have realized they had overrun the trail and had ridden a circle, on the thin chance they might stumble into him. And it had been that close—that close.

Jeff made himself wait an hour, two of them. Then, heading the rested sorrel out at a jog, he marked the stars and rode west into the desert. All night he rode and all the next day. And with another dusk settling about him he stared with sunken, feverish eyes at the black bulk of a mountain rising dead ahead. The past day had been one of hell, no less. Jeff's tongue was thick and swollen and thirst lay in him like some demoniac, consuming fire. Throughout the latter part of the afternoon Jeff had begun to see things— things that he knew were not there.

The sorrel's pace was just a crawl now. That terrible day had melted the flesh off the horse. It was a bony, shambling nag. But there was that mountain out there and it would mark the end of the desert.

Jeff knew he couldn't stop. Another day, or even a portion of one like the last, and the desert would win. He knew that, in a numbed, fatalistic sort of way. He had to keep going. He had to! And so he kept the sorrel moving at a slow walk. It was all the sorrel had left.

Midnight came and passed, and the mountain loomed higher, blacker against the stars. Of its own volition the sorrel broke into a shuffling trot. It flung its head, questing the air with parched, dusty nostrils.

Dimly it seemed to Jeff that things were changing. The stunted, starved brush had thickened, was high enough to pull and drag at his stirrups. The sorrel's pace picked up still more. And then, abruptly, there were cottonwoods and alders and willows all about and the smell and sound of running water. The sorrel slid down a cutbank, clattered across a gravel bar, and splashed into a shallows.

Jeff slid from the saddle, instinctively fighting the sorrel back. Not too much water all at once—not enough to founder it. A little now—a little more later—and then all the frantic animal wanted. And after that, the same method for himself.

Jeff had just enough left to drag saddle and bridle from the animal. Then he sprawled at full length on the gravel bar and sleep hit him like a club.

II

The sun was in his face when he awakened, stiff and sore and famished and bleak with thirst again. But there was the water close by, and Jeff doused his head and drank his fill and knew that one wicked portion of trail was behind him.

He found the sorrel downstream a bit where a

patch of bitter clover grew, rank and green, against the creekbank. The horse whickered gladly at Jeff's approach and Jeff led it back to where his saddle lay. Astride once more, Jeff crossed the creek and moved out into a meadow land beyond, where a scattering of white-faced cattle grazed.

Through the meadows a fair trail ran, which presently swung away and climbed to a rolling rangeland beyond, giving off in a long slope to a wide valley below. The trail forked and Jeff took the fork leading into the valley.

He was gaunt, almost weak with hunger, but he forgot this as his eyes searched eagerly ahead. In the near distance he saw a town. Here was the real beginning of that other world that Sarah Hagee, with dying breath, had told him to go in search of.

Jeff had never been in a town before in his life. At least, not that he could remember. The thought of entering this one thrilled and scared him, at the same time.

Round Mountain was an ordinary cow country town, a trifle larger and of more importance than some because of being the county seat. In Jeff's eyes it was tremendous.

He came in at the east end of the street and rode slowly along. There were hitch rails on either side with a scattering of cow ponies tied here and there. Farther downstreet a couple of buckboards were tied. The gusty breath of a hash house touched Jeff's nostrils, a sharp reminder of the wolfish hunger that gnawed at him. He pulled to a hitch rail, slid out of the saddle, and tied the sorrel.

As he stepped up onto the board sidewalk, three riders emerged from a nearby saloon, boot heels *clicking*, spur chains *clanking*. Jeff, watching them,

GET
4 FREE BOOKS!

You can have the best Westerns delivered to your door for less than what you'd pay in a bookstore or online. Sign up for one of our book clubs today, and we'll send you 4 FREE* BOOKS, worth $23.96, just for trying it out...with no obligation to buy, ever!

Authors include classic writers such as
LOUIS L'AMOUR, MAX BRAND, ZANE GREY
and more; PLUS new authors such as
COTTON SMITH, TIM CHAMPLIN, JOHNNY D. BOGGS
and others.

As a book club member you also receive the following special benefits:
- 30% OFF all orders through our website & telecenter!
- Exclusive access to special discounts!
- Convenient home delivery and 10 days to return any books you don't want to keep.

There is no minimum number of books to buy,
and you may cancel membership at any time.
See back to sign up!

*Please include $2.00 for shipping and handling.

YES! ☐

Sign me up for the Leisure Western Book Club
and send my FOUR FREE BOOKS! If I choose to stay
in the club, I will pay only $14.00* each month,
a savings of $9.96!

NAME: _____

ADDRESS: _____

_____

TELEPHONE: _____

E-MAIL: _____

☐ **I WANT TO PAY BY CREDIT CARD.**

☐ VISA ☐ MasterCard ☐ DISCOVER

ACCOUNT #: _____

EXPIRATION DATE: _____

SIGNATURE: _____

Send this card along with $2.00 shipping & handling to:

Leisure Western Book Club
1 Mechanic Street
Norwalk, CT 06850-3431

Or fax (must include credit card information!) to: 610.995.9274.
You can also sign up online at www.dorchesterpub.com.

*Plus $2.00 for shipping. Offer open to residents of the U.S. and Canada only.
Canadian residents please call 1.800.481.9191 for pricing information.
If under 18, a parent or guardian must sign. Terms, prices and conditions subject to change. Subscription subject
to acceptance. Dorchester Publishing reserves the right to reject any order or cancel any subscription.

JOIN NOW!

did not see the slim, bright-haired girl who emerged from the store next door but a split second later. Jeff took his courage by the scruff of the neck and accosted the three riders.

"Do you know of a mite of work a fellow might do to earn a square meal?"

They halted the casual conversation among themselves and looked him over. Jeff realized of a sudden that they were three pretty tough-looking customers. One in particular, a big, thickset, black-browed sort who, after looking Jeff up and down in a sort of mild contempt, asked: "Where in hell did you drop from? You look like something a pack rat dragged in. Beggars ain't popular in this town. If you're smart, you'll shag along somewhere else."

Hot blood burned in Jeff's gaunt, thin face. His sunken eyes were level and steady.

"I'm not begging. I'll work for a meal. Sorry I bothered you."

He would have moved on, but one of the others caught him by the arm.

"Just a minute, you," he growled. "Blackie, take a look at that sorrel bronco yonder. I think it is . . . yes, I know it is!"

The black-browed one turned and looked, stiffened and walked over to Jeff's bronco. He ran a hand up under the gaunt, sweat-stained animal's mane, pushed the mane aside, and looked intently at a spot high on the animal's neck, almost between the ears. He swung around and came striding back, a hot light in his black eyes.

"That's the bronco," he said curtly to the others. He shot out a thick arm and caught Jeff by the slack of his faded old shirt. "So!" he snarled. "You're not only a cheap grub-moocher, but a horse thief, too.

You got a hell of a nerve, riding that bronco right back into the town you stole it from."

Jeff was stunned. He blinked, his jaw dropped.

"You . . . you're wrong, Mister. I never stole no bronc'. I . . . I worked for that horse. I. . . ."

"Don't lie to me, you miserable, brush-popping thief," spat Blackie. "So you wanted a meal, did you? Well, you'll get a noosed rope around your neck instead."

Jeff was too dazed and startled to get the significance of these words immediately. But when he did, he started to struggle, trying to get free of the grip on his shirt. He struck out awkwardly and in return got a heavy fist in his face that knocked him flat.

For a moment Jeff lay there, dazed and half blinded by the blow. Everything seemed a jumble and through that jumble it seemed he could hear a feminine voice crying out indignantly. Then everything was swept away in a gust of hot, bitter fury.

He lurched to his feet and saw that black-browed face leering at him. Jeff hit that face, hit it with a clenched fist as hard as he could swing. It was an awkward blow and not nearly hard enough. Blackie's head jerked back and a thread of crimson seeped from his lips. He spat a flurry of savage cursing and put all his weight into another crunching blow.

It seemed to Jeff that a post maul had crashed into his face. In a numbed sort of way he felt his shoulders strike heavily on the board sidewalk. Then blackness completely engulfed him.

Cold wetness spread over Jeff Hawn's face and something hot and pungent scalded his throat and made him choke and cough. The dazed shadow left his brain and he remembered and he began to thrash and struggle. Strong but not unkind hands held him down and a deep voice rumbled:

"Easy, son, easy. Nobody is going to hurt you."

Jeff choked some more, then got his voice going. "That black guy," he mumbled. "I'll kill him! He called me a bronc' thief and knocked me down. I'll smash his lying teeth out!"

But Jeff wasn't smashing anything just now. The big hand on his chest held him effortlessly, while that deep, kindly voice took on a biting power.

"If he wasn't a half-starved, scrawny kid, I'd let him up and let him have at you, Blackie. I'd even give him a pick handle and wish him luck. I hope I never have to tell you again, Crowe. You go throwing your fists so free and easy again and, old as I am, I'll strip off this star of mine and then, man to man, give you a licking you'll date time from. That's a promise. Somehow, it's an idea of mine, that should you go up against somebody your own size and weight, that black streak in you might begin to show a little saffron."

Came the harsh growl of Blackie Crowe's voice: "Ah . . . why all the soft stuff? He's just a damned, cheap horse thief. That sorrel he rode into town is the same horse Bert Laven had stolen right off the street of this town. You know that, Bill Jacklyn, just as well as I do."

"It is the same horse, no doubt," said that deep voice. "But that's no proof this kid stole it. And no excuse for you to bullyrag him. You can get along now. Just to teach you a lesson, I think I'll have Judge Alcott put through a warrant for you for disturbing the peace. That will get you maybe thirty days in the cooler."

Blackie Crowe's sneer deepened. "Who's going to swear to the warrant, Jacklyn? You never saw me hit him."

"But I did," said a clear female voice. "I saw you, Blackie Crowe. I'll swear to it . . . and be glad of the chance."

"You see, Crowe," came the deep voice. "You better get out of town for a couple of weeks. My temper is getting thin. Git!"

The fading *clank* of spur rowels sounded. Then some more wet coolness was spread on Jeff's face. "You'll be as good as ever in a little while, son," said the deep voice kindly.

Jeff came out of it fast, after that. There was a lean toughness in his lanky frame that even the hardships of the past few days could not down. He found himself lying on a blanketed bunk. Now he sat up on it, staring at the big man with the square, grizzled beard who stood above him, and at the slender, bright-haired girl beyond. The big man wore a sheriff's star on his shirt.

"When did you eat last, son?" asked the man.

"Two, three days ago," mumbled Jeff.

The big man made a sound of concern. He turned to the young woman. "Go over to Sam's and get a tray of food, Janie."

The girl hurried out. She was soon back, bearing a tray covered with a clean cloth.

The big man said: "Pull a chair up to the table and eat, son. After that we can talk."

Jeff felt abashed, with the girl watching him eat. Remembering some of the things Sarah Hagee had told him about table manners, he followed them painfully, eating slowly when he wanted to wolf the food.

The food took hold right away and by the time he had finished, aside from his bruised and aching face, he felt almost normal. He got to his feet.

"I'm thanking both of you," he said simply. "And I'd like to do a mite of work for you to pay for that food. I aim to pay my way as best I can. I'm no grub-moocher, like that black guy said I was," he ended fiercely.

"The treat is on me, son," said the man with the star. "Now for a little talk. Who are you? What's your name?"

"Jeff Hawn."

"How old are you?"

"Nineteen, I reckon."

"Where did you come from?"

"From over in the San Vargas Hills country, past the Moencopee Desert, out along the Mescalero trail."

"Got any kin?"

"Not that I know of. The Mescalero Apaches killed my father and mother. I was pretty small then. I just remember it kind of faint. I hid in a dark corner and the Apaches never found me. I can't remember what happened after that. But Miz Hagee, she told me a wild-horse hunter found me laying out in the brush more dead than alive. He took me to Miz Hagee, who was the nearest lady, and she took care of me after."

A strange quiet fell over the room. Jeff wondered if this big man with the star was believing him. He stole a glance and was startled at the look on the sheriff's face. A sort of frozen look, full of an old agony.

The sheriff said slowly: "You run along, Janie. Jeff and me . . . we're going to have a long talk."

After the girl slipped out, the sheriff asked slowly: "I want you to tell me everything, son . . . from as far back as you can remember."

It was pretty awkward at first, but after he got going, the words came faster and faster to Jeff. He told everything he could remember.

"I couldn't ever have stuck it out if it hadn't been for Miz Hagee," he ended. "Alec Hagee was mighty mean, 'specially when he was drinking, which was about all the time toward the end. But I stayed on for Miz Hagee's sake because she'd took . . . taken such good care of me. But just before she died, she told me to leave . . . to get away from Alec Hagee. So I did. Alec Hagee, he'd never give me nothing but kicks and cussing and hard work, and I figured I had a right to a horse. So I picked that sorrel I rode into town. It was one that Alec Hagee had showed up with one time. He never said where he got it, and I never bothered to ask. Well, when I was ready to leave, Alec Hagee tried to stop me. He tried to pull me out of the saddle. When he couldn't, he went crazy and started to pull a gun on me. I hit him in the face with the butt of my carbine, and then broke for it. Him and Shell Darrough and Lobo Skurr and the others tried to run me down, but I got away from them in the desert. Then I lit out. It was pretty tough before I got clear of the desert. But I did it and hit this town. And then that black guy jumped me about that bronc'. That's all."

The sheriff had slouched deeply in a chair, his face seamed and suddenly very old-looking. "Missus Hagee . . . her name was Sarah, wasn't it, son?" he asked.

"Why . . . yes, it was. How did you know?"

"I knew. Tell me, did Alec Hagee mistreat her?"

"If you mean hit her, or anything like that . . . no. He made out as to . . . a couple of times. But she would just straighten up like a queen and just look at him, and he'd back away. Once, when he was drunk, he was going to, anyhow. But I . . . I drove him off with a gun. I'd've killed him that day, I think, only Miz Hagee stopped me. I wish now I had," he ended fiercely.

The sheriff seemed to hesitate. "I'm wondering, Jeff . . . if you have any little thing to remember Sarah Hagee . . . some trinket maybe?"

"I got a picture. It's in my saddlebags. I'll get it, if you want."

"I wish you would, son."

Jeff hurried out to where the sorrel still stood at the hitch rail. He got the picture, glanced at it. And suddenly knew something. The big man with the square beard who stood beside the girlish Sarah Hagee was the sheriff! That kind of floored Jeff, but he didn't say a word about it when he handed the picture over.

The sheriff looked at it a long time, then said: "Thanks, Jeff . . . thanks. This means a heap to me. I'm wondering, could I keep it?"

"Sure you can . . . sure." Jeff nodded.

"You're a good kid, Jeff. I want you to stay around Round Mountain for a time. You take that sorrel bronco over to the livery barn. Tell Pete Manners that Bill Jacklyn said he was to take care of the animal, and to let you use his spare bunk and do odd chores for him. I'll have a better job for you, later on."

"Then . . . then I ain't going to be arrested for stealing a horse? 'Cause I didn't steal it, 'less you could say it was stealing for taking it from Alec Hagee and telling him to his face that he owed me a bronc'."

"You never stole anything, Jeff. That sorrel is your horse. You, keep it. Maybe so you'll ride it back across the Moencopee Desert again, one of these days."

III

For the next two weeks, as soon as the newness of things wore off, Jeff Hawn was happier than he had ever been in his life before. Pete Manners was a fat, kindly, incredibly lazy individual. He had let the stable and corral run down considerably, so there was plenty to do. Jeff worked from dawn to dark, caring for horses, soaping harness, greasing buckboards and livery rigs, fixing the corral, re-swinging doors on the stable, and numerous other things that needed doing.

Jeff had said from the first that he aimed to earn his keep and he meant it. He had a good bunk and all he could eat, and he began to take on weight. The swelling and bruises left his face and his old life began to fade into the limbo of forgotten things. All except Sarah Hagee. He knew he'd never forget her.

Twice that slim, bright-haired girl, Janie, came down to the stable in riding clothes, and Jeff it was who saddled up a trim little pinto mare for her. Her clear, bright smile of thanks abashed Jeff, but from then on that pinto mare received double attention, being brushed and curried until its sleek hide shone like silk. And her saddle and other riding gear were kept in meticulous order.

Several times Jeff saw Sheriff Bill Jacklyn and grew to have a tremendous admiration for the deep-voiced officer of the law. One day, after Jacklyn had had a talk with Pete Manners, Pete sought out Jeff and handed him a couple of gold double eagles.

"You're plumb particular, Jeff, how you keep the stable broncos brushed and curried, especially"—and here Pete's eyes twinkled—"that pinto mare of Miss Janie's. Now you could stand a currying yourself. You go down to Frenchy's barbershop and get your own mane curried. Then you go to Ed Porter's store and get yourself a new outfit of clothes, from toe to topknot. 'Cause you're done with stable work. Bill Jacklyn's got a new job for you. When you get all prettied up, you go over to Bill's office."

Jeff had his first haircut in a real barbershop. Always before, Sarah Hagee had kept his thick, tawny mane under control with her old scissors. When he had an armful of new clothes, including a new, genuine Stetson sombrero and a pair of new cowboy boots, Jeff remembered something else Sarah Hagee had told him: "There's self-respect in honest soap and water, Jeff."

So Jeff carried his new purchases, along with a towel and soap, out to a sheltered pool in the little creek that ran east of town and gave himself a rare scrubbing. Dressed in his new clothes, he realized the shabbiness of the old and threw them away. Then he headed for Bill Jacklyn's office.

As Jeff was about to pass the Oberon Saloon,

Blackie Crowe came out. He looked Jeff up and down and a sneer twisted his swarthy face.

"Well, if it ain't the horse thief himself . . . all prettied up. Them new clothes ought to be christened by a roll in the dust."

Jeff faced him, trembling a little but not with fear. "I want no truck with you, Crowe," he said. "But I'm telling you something. You lay off that horse thief stuff or . . . or I'll kill you!"

Blackie Crowe might have scoffed at the words, but he was startled by the cold, blazing fire in Jeff's gray eyes. Blackie Crowe took a good look, said no more, and walked away. Jeff did not realize that some of that fire was still there when he went in and confronted Bill Jacklyn.

Jacklyn said: "You're stirred up, son. Why?" Jeff told him, and Jacklyn said slowly: "Blackie Crowe is one of them peculiar knot heads who cannot learn anything until they've been hit with a club. But we got more important things to talk about than that. Lift your right hand."

Jeff did, startled.

Jacklyn said: "Repeat this oath after me."

Jeff did that, too—more amazed.

Then Jacklyn handed him a deputy's star. "Pin this on your shirt, son. You're a deputy sheriff, now. Can you shoot?"

"I . . . I'm pretty good with a rifle," Jeff stuttered.

"You got to be twice as good with a short gun," said Jacklyn. "Those guns hanging on yonder pegs are yours, so strap 'em on. There's plenty of cartridges in the closet yonder. You get busy practicing. Don't worry about long shots. The rifle is the gun for that sort of stuff. Work on drawing smooth and fast and hitting something the size of a man at close range. In a few days I'll see how you're coming along."

Jeff started practicing that very afternoon. He saddled up the sorrel and rode a couple of miles from town, well away from anyone. He found the old, burned stump of a lightning-struck tree and he went to work on that.

At first he was pretty clumsy and did a lot of missing, but concentration and determination began to get results. He found he was hurrying the draw too much and was too tied up. He made himself relax and kept saying to himself: "Smooth . . . smooth."

In the next five tries Jeff saw charred chips fly from the trunk three times. He decided that was enough, for the heavy recoil of the big .45 Colt guns was tiring his arms. When he turned back to his horse, he got a surprise. There, sitting easily on the pinto mare, was the slim, bright-haired girl.

She laughed softly at his confusion.

"I heard the shooting, so came over to see what was going on," she explained. "Uncle Bill told me he'd made you a deputy. You were doing pretty good at the last."

They rode back to town together. Jeff was tongue-tied at first, but he loosened up pretty soon. By the time they reached Round Mountain, he was doing a lot better and thinking that the way that bright, silken hair curled softly about her face was the prettiest thing he'd ever seen.

More than one pair of eyes marked Jeff's and the girl's approach and one of them, Blackie Crowe's, burned sullenly.

"Look at that punk horse thief," Crowe growled to Slim Ankers. "All duded up with a star and guns. Jacklyn must be loco, making an *hombre* like that his deputy."

Slim Ankers laughed. "It ain't the star and it ain't the guns you're griped at, Blackie. It's the fact that Janie Jacklyn is riding with him and smiling at him that's got you hot under the collar. Well, take a tip from me, Blackie. That girl will never fall for your brand of manly beauty."

Blackie Crowe cursed harshly.

The days went by, moving into weeks. Every afternoon Jeff rode out and had a session with that lightning-struck tree stump. Soon the stump began to be too easy. He picked smaller, more difficult targets. He tried all kinds of ideas, all kinds of tricks. He would put his back to the target and walk away, then suddenly whirl, draw, and shoot. He would whirl to the right, then the left.

He tried straight ahead work, then the cross-body draw, and shooting with either hand. Standing, he would suddenly throw himself headlong, cushioning his fall with one hand and arm, while drawing and shooting with the other.

Young, naturally swift in reaction, he became better than he knew. Plenty of good food was having its effect, too. He began to fill out, his back and shoulders packing with smooth, sinewy muscles. He lost that scrawny, sunken-eyed look.

Other changes were taking place, changes Jeff hardly realized. A boyish shyness was still on him, but there was an assertive manliness about him, also a confidence and dignity that were lacking before.

Several times, when Jeff finished his gun practice, he would find Janie Jacklyn waiting to ride back to town with him. He was still boggled with wonder at the bright and stirring beauty of her, but he was much more at ease in her presence and their acquaintanceship progressed famously.

Every day Jeff saw Sheriff Bill Jacklyn. Jacklyn was always busy writing letters, so it seemed to Jeff. The sheriff was sober and grim and grave. Jeff couldn't help wondering if all there was to being a deputy sheriff was to eat and sleep and practice with a six-gun.

Then one day Jacklyn said: "We're ready for business, Jeff. I'm going out with you to see how you've come along with those short guns."

When they got out to Jeff's favorite practicing ground, Jacklyn said: "Go ahead. Show me, son."

At first Jeff was a little self-conscious. But he soon forgot this and warmed up to the show. He put on all the tricks he had worked out. He finished off by throwing himself on the ground, drawing both guns as he went, and then rolling over and over. And each time a shoulder came up free, a gun would bellow and charred splinters of wood would leap from the stump. He got up, brushed himself off, and looked at Bill Jacklyn hesitantly.

"That's as far as I've got, Mister Jacklyn," he said.

"As far as you've got, eh, lad?" rumbled Jacklyn. "Well, I rise to tell a man it's far enough. One more gun lesson, Jeff. Never throw a gun on a man unless there just ain't any other way out. And never go for a gun unless you mean business."

When they got back to town, Jeff took both horses down to the livery barn. Pete Manners did not seem to be around, so Jeff made out to put the broncos up himself. He unsaddled Bill Jacklyn's animal first and carried the saddle into the stable. As he did so, he heard Janie Jacklyn's voice out at the rear of the place. Her voice was indignant and a trifle shrill with fear.

Jeff dropped the saddle. He went back and around and down the line of stalls. Janie's little pinto mare was kept in a box stall at the far end, and Janie was down at the entrance of the stall, bridle in hand. Looming beside her was the thick figure of Blackie Crowe.

"I don't need any help, Blackie," Janie was saying. "I can saddle my own pony. And I don't like the way you've come prowling in here after me. I don't like you and I never did. You better leave right now, or I'll tell Uncle Bill."

Blackie Crowe merely laughed, and Jeff knew from the sound of that laugh that Blackie was half drunk. "You can't act so uppity to me, my pretty one," leered Blackie. "I'm tired of seeing you give all your smiles to that slick horse thief deputy of your uncle's. You used to be right friendly with old Blackie. And you can't give him the go-by like this."

"That's a lie!" rapped Janie hotly. "I never was friendly with you and I never want to be. You're drunk . . . and you get out of here!"

Blackie's answer was another gloating laugh as he made a grab for her. Janie dodged and hit him across the head and shoulders with her bridle. Blackie cursed, lunged for her once more. And then Jeff Hawn went a little bit crazy.

He went down behind the stalls at a run and his voice lashed ahead of him: "You! Crowe! Don't you touch her!"

Jerked up short by this interruption, Blackie

ried two gallon canteens of water slung to their saddle horns. Across the cantles of their saddles were strapped a few supplies. Under their saddle fenders they slung rifles—Jeff his old carbine, for which he had got a new supply of ammunition, while Bill Jacklyn carried a longer rifle of heavier caliber.

They were ready to swing into their saddles when a slim figure stole up through the gloom.

"Uncle Bill," Janie said softly, "you be mighty careful."

Bill Jacklyn brushed bearded lips against her cheek, gave her a fond hug. "I'll be all right, honey. Don't you worry."

Jeff's heart leaped as she came over to him and laid a light hand on his arm. "You too, Jeff," she murmured. "Be careful."

"I aim to be, Miss Janie," he answered.

She stood there a moment before adding: "What happened today . . . you must know how I feel. . . ."

"It was a heap of satisfaction," said Jeff sturdily.

She patted his arm softly as he reached for his stirrup.

By sunup next morning, Jeff and Bill Jacklyn were well out into the Moencopee Desert. Their horses showed the effects of grain feeding. They spurned the miles behind them easily, and even when the sun built up its blinding, savage blast and the foam began to roll, the broncos still kept steadily at it.

It was a lot different from when he had come across this same bleak and hostile country alone. Now his horse was stronger; he was stronger; he had company, and there was water in the canteens to take a sip of now and then.

At sundown they made a short stop, unsaddling to let the horses stretch and roll and rest a bit. They ate a frugal supper and poured a couple of quarts of water into the dished crowns of their hats, which the horses sucked up greedily. With the first stars they were on their way again. In the first gray light of a new dawn, they breasted the first long slope of the San Vargas Hills. The desert was behind them.

Now Jeff took the lead, for this was country he knew. And when the sun came up, Jeff and Sheriff Bill Jacklyn hunkered down in a copse of scrub oak. They were looking down at the ramshackle group of buildings that for so many years of his life Jeff had called home.

IV

Nowhere was there a sign of life. The corral was empty and no smoke showed from the chimney of the cabin, even though they waited until the sun was a couple of hours high.

"Looks like they might have skipped out," said Bill Jacklyn. "Not a soul around."

"They might be off pulling a chunk of dirty works somewhere," said Jeff. "Like as not they'll be back, sooner or later. We might as well go on down, Mister Jacklyn."

They circled and came in cautiously, using the old barn to hide them from view of the house. Jeff took one trip across the corral, head bent, eyes searching.

"Not a track in here under ten days old," he

reported. So they went up to the house without further pause.

Things were pretty frowsy inside. Empty whiskey bottles littered the floor and a mess of empty dishes stood on the kitchen table, needing a washing badly. But there were blankets on the bunks and a spare saddle in one corner. And a store of food on the kitchen shelf.

"They'll be back," declared Jeff. "All we got to do is wait."

When they went outside, Bill Jacklyn said slowly: "Where is . . . is she buried, Jeff?"

Jeff led the way out past the barn and up the slope to the gnarled live oak tree. There lay the long, narrow mound of fresh-turned earth, with the wilted sprig of foliage Jeff had placed on it still there. Jeff took off his hat. Bill Jacklyn did likewise.

Jacklyn's face was again seamed and tired and old. His lips moved, but what he said was only for himself. He sat down beside the grave.

"Jeff," he said slowly, "you got a right to know. Sarah Hagee was my daughter. And I was a fool. Sarah was a proud, headstrong girl. She made a mistake, only because I made a bigger one. I interfered with a love affair of hers. I upset things. In her anger and pride and grief over it, Sarah made her mistake. She ran off with a no-good young buck named Alec Hagee. Had I used my head and kept my mouth shut, Sarah would have seen through the fellow in her own good time and never in the world married him. But I forced her hand, and now I got a cross to carry the rest of my days. Even after she made her mistake, had I gone after her and shown her understanding and kindness, she would have come home with me and still found a decent share of happiness in life. But no. I was full of fool pride, too. And now . . . she's at rest . . . here."

Bill Jacklyn's head hung, heavy and sad. And Jeff stole away, going back to the horses.

After a time Jacklyn followed him. The sheriff was still grave and weary-looking, but he seemed to have struck some kind of peace with himself.

Jeff said: "There's a better place to lay in wait . . . higher up. There's a little spring there and some grass for the bronc's. And we're not so liable to be discovered."

So they rode up to the spot, which was at the head of a little gulch, screened with live oaks. Here they set up a frugal camp, picketing the horses to graze.

"No telling whether we'll have to wait a day or a week," said Jeff. "Our grub is pretty low. There's a scattering of little desert deer hang out in the roughs a couple of miles west. Maybe I better go get one."

Jeff was back by mid-afternoon, a plump little desert whitetail slung across his shoulders. They hung the deer, skinned it, and let it cool in the shade.

"Should be some old wool sacks down at the place," Jeff said. "I'll go get one to put around that venison to keep the blue bottles off it."

With the meat safely covered against the flies, they settled down for the wait. It was monotonous duty, but both knew it was the soundest course. For the San Vargas Hills country was vast. A man might ride it for months without cutting the trail of any of the renegades he sought. But in time, the renegades would show here. Sooner or later they would come.

Days and nights went by and ran into a week. They took turns watching. They slept a great deal. And they ran out of all food except venison, which grew tiresome as a straight diet. But still they waited.

Nights the stars glittered and the coyotes sang and mourned at a moon that reached its fullness and began to fade and grow later and later each night. Bill Jacklyn encouraged Jeff to talk about Sarah Hagee. And Jeff told him how, when Alec Hagee and the rest would be away on one of their many absences, Sarah Hagee would spend evening after evening teaching Jeff to read and write and study out of a few old dog-eared books she had produced from somewhere.

"My own mother couldn't have been better to me," he ended. "She kept me from going wild as any wolf cub. If I ever amount to anything in this world at all, it will be because of Miz Hagee."

Came an afternoon, well along, when Jeff was keeping watch. His exploring eyes caught a faint haze of dust, far up along the Mescalero trail. He watched that dust haze grow closer and finally there burst into view a bunch of some twenty horses. Driving them were five riders.

One of the riders spurred ahead, down to the headquarters, to swing wide the corral gate. The horse herd, kept well bunched, was put into the corral, and the gate closed. The five riders unsaddled and added their own animals to the group in the corral. Then they headed for the cabin.

Jeff marked each of the riders with narrowed

eyes, nodding. The same old bunch. Alec Hagee, Shell Darrough, Lobo Skurr, Hoke Burdick, and Tobe Nero. Just back from another rustling raid.

Jeff slipped back to camp, where Bill Jacklyn was dozing. "They just came in," reported Jeff excitedly. "Hazed in a bunch of bronc's, near two dozen of them. Been on a bronc'-stealing raid probably. They've unsaddled and gathered in the cabin. Shall we go get 'em?"

Bill Jacklyn was up on his feet and alert. He glanced at the sun. It would set within the hour.

"We'll hit 'em at dusk." He nodded.

Jeff had never seen time move so slowly. He was restless as a cat. Bill Jacklyn looked at him several times with troubled glance. Finally he said: "Maybe I've been a fool again, Jeff. I can't ask you to go down there with me. There's bound to be gun play. And you're still a lad . . . not yet twenty. I think you'd better hang back."

Jeff looked him straight in the eye. "I'm your deputy, Mister Jacklyn. I'll follow your orders in most things. But I won't let you go down there alone and take that crowd on, five to one. Hagee, Darrough, and Skurr in particular are plenty mean. Hoke Burdick and Tobe Nero ain't so much. I always figured them as better at dry-gulching than smoking it out face to face. They'd be the kind to get you when you wasn't looking. But even so, they hike the odds. When you go down, Mister Jacklyn, I go down."

A grim, prideful smile tugged at Bill Jacklyn's lips. He dropped a fond hand on Jeff's shoulder.

"Sarah did a real job of making a man of you, lad. And Janie, was she here, would give me fits.

Yet she'd want you to go along with me. So we'll go down together, Jeff."

They moved their horses down as far as the scrub oaks would offer shelter. Then they went the rest of the way on foot. They had their rifles with them but Jeff knew, if close-up work started, where he would place his reliance. On those two big belt guns, sagging at his hips.

They came in from behind the corral. The horses inside the enclosure were gaunt and weary with hard driving, and paid them no attention. There was still light enough for them to read some of the brands on the horses. Out of the first ten broncos he looked at, Jeff read four different brands. These were definitely stolen broncos, picked up here and there along the trail. If those men in the cabin had not been damned before, they were most definitely damned now.

The sheriff and Jeff stole around the barn. There was a light in the cabin. Jeff could smell wood smoke from the chimney and the odor of frying bacon.

"There's a back door, of course?" murmured Bill Jacklyn.

"Yeah, a back door," answered Jeff.

"You go around there," said Jacklyn. "I'll go in the front. You wait until you hear me call them. Then you come in. Caught front and rear, there's a good chance they'll quit cold."

"All right." Jeff nodded. "But while four of 'em might quit, Lobo Skurr never will. He's bad . . . plenty."

"There's always a cure for the real bad ones," said Bill Jacklyn grimly. "Good luck, lad."

"And you, sir," said Jeff. "Remember . . . Skurr is all wolf, like his name."

They split and circled. Coming up to the back door, Jeff moved very softly, eyes and ears straining. There was a repressed tumult building up inside him. Not fear, but a tingling, driving excitement, which set all his nerves to singing. He put his carbine up against the wall. This would be close work. He rubbed moist palms up and down against the front of his shirt, drying them.

The back door was open, for the night was warm. Standing back from the light, Jeff looked in. Hoke Burdick was at the rusty old stove, putting grub together. And through an inner door in the far room, Jeff could see the big, uncouth bulk of Shell Darrough, sprawled, loose and heavy, in a chair, a whiskey bottle in one his dirty paws. He had just taken a drag from it and was licking his lips.

Then Jeff saw Shell Darrough freeze, a man turned to stone, a vast and wicked surprise bugging his eyes. The voice of Bill Jacklyn rang, deep and harsh with authority.

"Don't anybody move! This is the law! You're under arrest, all of you! Don't move, I say!"

Jeff closed in swiftly. Hoke Burdick had jerked around from the stove, frying pan in hand. Now he set the pan back on the stove with exaggerated caution. He drew a gun and on tiptoe began moving toward that inner door.

Jeff, on tiptoe himself, slid in behind him, drawing both guns. Burdick flattened against the wall, tensing himself for a surprise shot. And Jeff, reaching out, slammed him solidly across the head with a heavy gun barrel. Burdick's knees buckled and he fell, half through the door. That seemed to set things off.

Bill Jacklyn's deep voice roared with warning. And then guns were shaking the confines of the place with trapped thunder. Jeff leaped across the sprawled figure of Hoke Burdick.

Strange how the whole picture limned instantaneously on his brain. Bill Jacklyn, big and towering, just inside the front door. Alec Hagee on one side of the door, Shell Darrough on the other, both whirling on Jacklyn and pumping lead as they went. Lobo Skurr, on Jeff's left, standing flat against the inner wall, with Tobe Nero, hunkered down as usual, beside Skurr.

Bill Jacklyn had both guns laid level, feet spread. He lurched slightly as Lobo Skurr got into action. Yet Jacklyn cut loose with both guns and Alec Hagee, a stream of poisonous curses on his lips, whirled, walked straight into a wall, and collapsed.

Skurr had the eyes and reactions of a cat. He saw Jeff burst in and swung his guns. Jeff didn't forget the weeks of practice he'd put in. He threw himself to the floor, both guns out. He rolled over and over, throwing first one gun, then the other.

Skurr's lead chopped and splintered the floor, always where Jeff's body had been a split second before. And Jeff saw the dust spurt, once, twice, three times from Skurr's shirt as his lead took him. Skurr crashed on his face.

Shell Darrough was roaring like a maddened and mortally wounded bull. Bill Jacklyn had pumped lead into Darrough and the big renegade had gone blind and berserk in his dying. He seemed to be shooting in every direction, wild but dangerous. One of his slugs ripped splinters not a foot from

Jeff's face. And Jeff hammered him with four crashing slugs. He cut Darrough down, like some great tree falling. Abruptly there was silence, dazed and horrified.

Jeff had been counting. Hagee, Skurr, Darrough—all down in this room. And Hoke Burdick gun-whipped in the kitchen. One more—Tobe Nero. Jeff came upright, looking for him, guns searching.

They were not needed. Tobe Nero lay against the wall, a still bundle where he had toppled sideways, with his knees drawn up in that hunkered position. There was a round blue hole in Tobe Nero's low forehead. Somebody's lead, maybe Shell Darrough's, had found him.

Bill Jacklyn was still in the doorway, but swaying from side to side. He held both guns, but they were pointing at the floor, his arms hanging limply. As Jeff watched, Bill Jacklyn slid down, like a man very, very tired.

Janie Jacklyn was wild with worry. A full month had gone by since her uncle and Jeff Hawn had headed out after a list of wanted men. And not a word from them. Janie carried her trouble to Pete Manners.

Pete didn't mince words. He'd been doing some worrying on his own.

"It looks bad, honey," he told the distraught girl. "No use kidding ourselves. I'm going to scare up a posse and go look. I don't know just where to look, but it's somewhere across the Moencopee Desert. Yeah. I'll go look. I can round me up a few boys who'll be glad to go."

There came the sound of weary horses *clip-clopping* to a halt in front of the stable. They went out and Janie gave a glad and tearful cry. Three riders were out there, on weary, dust-caked mounts. One of them was Bill Jacklyn, thin and gaunt and with one arm in a sling. There was Hoke Burdick, wrists bound to his saddle horn, ankles to cinch rings. And there was Jeff Hawn, lean and brown, but no longer a boy. Manhood was in his bronzed face. A youth who had gone through the crucible of life and who had been forged into a man, lean and tough and masterful.

"Uncle Bill . . . Uncle Bill!" sobbed Janie. "Oh, I've worried so! Uncle Bill. . . ."

Bill Jacklyn swung carefully down. He slid his sound arm about his weeping niece, hugging her. A grim smile was on his lips.

"There, there, honey," he comforted. "I'm back . . . thanks to Jeff Hawn. And thanks again to Jeff, the job is done. Jeff saved one prisoner to prove it. I'll tell the world I picked the real thing for a deputy. You might save one of these kisses for Jeff, honey. He's earned it."

Jeff had stepped down quietly. Now a small tornado hit him, a tornado of tears and encircling arms and warm lips. And the grim maturity in Jeff's face faded slightly to let the boy back again.

While Jeff looked after the prisoner, Bill Jacklyn sat in his favorite chair in his office and told Janie and Pete Manners the story.

"I wouldn't have had a chance alone . . . or with an ordinary deputy," he said flatly. "But that Jeff . . . he's a tiger. So we cleaned them out, all but Burdick. I figured I was done, with Skurr's slug in my shoulder. But Jeff wouldn't hear of it. He doctored me . . . he stayed with me. I swear that boy never slept for a week. He brought me through and kept Burdick prisoner all the time, besides. Finally Jeff had me ready to ride again. He got me back across the desert, and Burdick, too. Before we left, we turned them stolen broncos loose. Most of them will find their way back to their home range. And Jeff . . . well, along the trail of life, Sarah Hagee trained a man. When I'm ready to turn in my star, there's a better man ready to wear it."

It was night again and Jeff sat alone in the office. Bill Jacklyn was in bed, just for a safety measure. Hoke Burdick was safely behind bars and a stout lock. The Reward notices on the desk Jeff tore up and threw into the cracker box that served as an office catch-all. That job was done.

Jeff had no regrets. Life shoved things of that sort at a man. Duty was duty. It had changed him, of course. Bound to. But a fellow had to grow up complete, sometime.

A step sounded in the door. It was Janie. There was a shyness upon her now.

"Uncle Bill is asleep," she said. "I've come to thank you again, Jeff. You saved his life, twice over. You . . . you've been mighty fine."

Jeff's boyish smile flashed.

"The sample of reward I got sure made it all worthwhile. The next installment can come along any old time, far as I'm concerned."

Janie colored hotly.

"I was so relieved to see you both safely home, I guess I went a little out of my mind."

Jeff got up and walked over to her.

"I've been out of my mind that way about you for a long, long time, Janie. Ever since I first put eyes on you, matter of fact. I ain't going to cure easy."

Her head was bent, her cheeks scarlet. Then she looked up and met his eyes in a long, slow glance. She nodded slightly, and an elfin smile glowed.

"I expect we're both crazy then, Jeff."

River Range

The author completed "River Range" in early December 1945. He sent it to his agent who sent it on to editor Fanny Ellsworth at *Ranch Romances* who bought the short novel on February 15, 1946. It appeared under this title in *Ranch Romances* (2nd May 1946). Subsequently, when this magazine was sold by Warner Publications to N. L. Pines's Standard Magazines, the story was reprinted under this title in Standard Magazine's *Triple Western* (2/52). This is its first appearance in book form.

I

It was Buzz McClure, who Logan had sent out ahead to Castella Landing to see that all was in readiness, who brought the word. Buzz's report was brief and to the point. The loading corral at the landing was full of Broken Arrow cattle.

Boone Logan was silent while he built a smoke. Then he asked curtly: "What was Hoddy doing?"

Buzz hesitated, reluctant to answer. Logan bent a pair of gray eyes, now gone a little smoky, on Buzz. "Well?"

Buzz shrugged a trifle helplessly. "He was in the Oro Fino."

"Drunk?"

"Pretty drunk."

Logan swung his head and looked out across some three miles of brushy Colorado River bottoms toward the town of Castella. The muscles at the corner of his jaw crawled and bunched and a dark bitterness pulled at his lips. Buzz McClure, recognizing the signs, said: "All men haven't got your strength, or the same fidelity to the job. Not even your brother. And they can't always help it."

Logan said, a trifle thickly: "I haven't asked a

great deal from him, except trust. Now he falls down on that. We'll hold the cattle here for the present."

There were around 200 head of C Cross white-faced cattle in the herd Logan and his men had been bringing in to Castella Landing from the high grass meadows of the Indio Mountains, sixty miles back across the desert. Now, with Logan spurring back to pass the order to the riders in the drag and Buzz McClure taking the same word to swing and point riders, the drive pressure was taken off the herd and the weary, desert-dusty cattle began to spread and graze across the flats.

"You will hold them here until I send word to bring them on, Shane," Logan told Shane O'Leary.

With that, Logan swung his horse and set out at a lope for Castella.

Shane O'Leary said: "He's got the old, tough rawhide look to him, Buzz. Why?"

"It's Hoddy," explained Buzz. "Hoddy was supposed to hold the loading corral at the landing for this jag of cattle. Now the loading corral is full of Broken Arrow stuff and Hoddy is in the Oro Fino, lapping up booze. I'm going to stick my neck way out, Shane. I'm going after him and stand between him and Hoddy, if I have to. Should the old black hell get completely loose in him, he might do something that would haunt him the rest of his days."

"That kind of friendship for a man is rare, Buzz. I wish you luck."

Boone Logan heard Buzz McClure coming up behind him, pulled to a stop, and growled: "Where are you going?"

"With you," said Buzz quietly.

"You're not. Go back to the herd!"

"No!"

Boone Logan was a big man, without the slightest hint of bulk anywhere about him. He was lean, iron-hard. His jaw was flint, his will absolute. As foreman of the huge C Cross outfit, with holdings scattered up and down the river for a good 100 miles, and reaching back from the river as far as the Indio and the Tejon Mountains, Logan's reputation was that of a man who ran Buck Channing's outfit with a firm hand and whose fidelity to Buck Channing's interests was almost fanatical. He was a man who inspired in others either a deathless loyalty or a smoldering antagonism, a man who could be gentle, or ruthless, as the need or the mood swayed him. Now his mood was dark.

His gray eyes seemed almost black, what with that smokiness moiling in them. "You'll go back to the herd, Buzz," he grated.

"No," said Buzz again. "I'm going with you."

"You'll go back to the herd," warned Logan, "or you're done as a C Cross man, right here and now."

Buzz was stocky with broad, blunt features, usually cheery and with blue eyes full of laughter. Now Buzz's face was grim, his eyes very steady. "I don't believe that, Boone."

"You'd better. When I give an order to a C Cross man, he obeys it . . . or he's through. I'm ordering you to get back to the herd!"

Buzz ran the tip of his tongue across his lips, then said for a third time: "No."

Logan said, dangerously quiet: "You're through. Get your gear out of the chuck wagon. I'll have your time waiting for you at the River View Hotel, later today."

Then Logan touched his horse with the spur and rode on.

Buzz sat his saddle very quietly a long moment. A flush of anger ran across his face, but he subdued it quickly and murmured: "Easy, McClure, easy. Keep your shirt on. You can see what a damn' fool black anger can make of a man. It's up to you to control yours. You knew you were sticking your neck out, and, if the ride is going to be a rough one, you got to do your best."

Buzz set his horse to a full run, pulled up to Logan, went past him, and drove on to Castella. The town ran along a low benchland above the river. It was rough and ready, but pretty substantial for, as river towns went through those wild stretches of the Colorado River, Castella knew a certain steady prosperity. It not only had considerable cattle country trade, but was the central supply point for Kent Masterson's pack train business of taking supplies into the far, rugged back country, to isolated little ranches, to mining camps and little, interior towns that had sprung into being at some lonely trail crossing. It was a regular port of call for Captain Matt Corbee and his little sternwheeler riverboat, the *Mohave*, and would be for the big, new boat, the *Pathfinder*, that a new company in Yuma was about to put in the river trade.

Buzz McClure sent his bronco clattering along the single street to the hitch rail in front of the Oro Fino, where he dismounted and tied and *clanked* in. Hoddy Logan was still where he'd been when Buzz had found him on his first trip into Castella, before going back to report to Boone Logan. Still with a bottle and glass in front of him, and from the glaze of his eyes considerably further along the road to complete intoxication.

Buzz thought: *If I can only get him into the back room and on a bunk, he might be asleep when Boone gets here.*

Buzz leaned against the bar at Hoddy's elbow. "How does the idea of a good sleep strike you, kid?"

Hoddy looked at him blearily. "Not interested," he mumbled thickly. "Lemme alone."

There wasn't too much family resemblance between Hoddy Logan and his older brother Boone. Hoddy wasn't as big a man, and was fairer. His eyes were gray, as were Boone's, but lacked the fire and spirit. His mouth was sullen.

Buzz took him by the elbow and urged: "Come on into the back room, kid. You can take the bottle along."

Hoddy jerked away. "Damn you!" he snarled drunkenly. "I said . . . lemme alone!"

Over at one of the card tables Kent Masterson and Harvey Overgaard were playing cribbage. "No use, Buzz," said Kent Masterson. "Harvey and me both had a try at the same thing and with no better luck than you're having. Arch DeLong tried to get the bottle away from him and didn't have a chance. We'll just have to wait until it floors him."

Buzz bent his head slightly, for he could hear the pound of hoofs along the street. He sighed deeply, built a smoke, and waited.

The hoofs stopped outside, and a moment later Boone Logan came in. Kent Masterson and Harvey Overgaard put their cards down and sat, silent and watchful. Boone went straight to Hoddy, who was unsteadily pouring a refill into his glass. With a single sweep of his hand, Boone sent both bottle and glass flying. Hoddy turned to face his elder brother, clinging to the bar to steady himself. Angry curses were on his lips, but died unuttered at the look on Boone's face.

"You drunken, useless fool!" rapped Boone harshly. "You've had all the rope you're going to get. I've given you every chance, made every excuse for you, tried every other means I could think of. Now I'm going to try the last thing. If you can't get sense and backbone into you any other way, then, so help me, I'll whip some into you."

He reached for Hoddy, but his arm was pushed aside. It was Buzz McClure, and now Buzz stepped in between the two brothers. "No, Boone," said Buzz quietly, "that wouldn't do at all. You'd be sorry for it all your life."

Boone Logan's eyes went absolutely black. He said, and his tone was as thin and toneless as a shift of cold wind: "Get aside, McClure. I won't warn you again."

Buzz, going a trifle white about the lips, for he knew what was coming, said: "No."

Quick as a pouncing wolf, Boone Logan rolled his shoulder and hit him. The blow was solid, savage. It landed with a *crunch* and snapped Buzz's head back and would have knocked him down, had not the bar caught Buzz across the shoulders and held him up. Buzz weaved a little, but spread his feet and stayed erect. His lips were mashed and bleeding and a queer hurt shone deeply in his blue eyes. But he kept his place between Boone and Hoddy.

He said thickly, for his lips were already swelling

from the blow: "Hitting your best friend is bad enough, Boone. But hitting your brother would be worse. If you want to get me out of here, you'll have to lay me cold. Right now Hoddy is a better man than you are. He's taking his mad out by only hurting himself. You're hurting others."

It was a deadly tense moment. Buzz was set to take another blow, and he was sure one was coming. Yet he held his place and his blue eyes maintained the bleak ferocity of Boone Logan's glance without wavering. Then Boone's eyes fell and he brushed a hand across them as though wiping away some dreadful shadow. Buzz knew then that his part was played. He turned to Arch Delong and said: "Give me a wet bar towel, Arch."

Dabbing the wet towel against his mouth, Buzz moved up toward the door end of the bar and stood there, staring out the dusty, cobwebbed window. DeLong spun a full glass up to Buzz's elbow and said quietly. "It'll do you good right now, Buzz."

Harvey Overgaard said, his voice running clear all over the room: "I can stand a man's black temper just so far. Then I get fed up."

Harvey waited for his words to be challenged and, when they were not, walked out. Kent Masterson just sat quietly at the card table, watching Boone Logan with unreadable eyes.

Boone was like a man all alone in a solitary world. He seemed to hear nothing, see nothing, his eyes fixed on emptiness. There was something almost like a pathetic bewilderment cloaking him. Hoddy had turned back to the bar again, was lying half over it, his head rolling loosely.

Boone started for the door, moving mechanically. He came even with Buzz, hesitated, started to put a hand out. Buzz was still staring through the window, that wet towel against his lips. Boone made a queer sound in his throat and left the place at a rush. A moment later his horse was racing down the street.

Kent Masterson got up, went over beside Hoddy. "A strong man," he said, "never can understand weakness in others. Give me a hand, Arch. The kid is about ready for that bunk in your back room."

There were four of Purse Fallon's Broken Arrow riders at the loading corral, with Hump Styre in charge. When Styre saw Boone Logan come spurring down from town toward the landing, he said to the others: "Here comes the tough member of the Logan family. He won't bluff out as easy as his brother did. Spread out a little and keep on your toes. Let me do the talking."

From downriver sounded the blast of a riverboat whistle, its throaty hoarseness thinned by space. The sound of it cut through Boone Logan's dark tumult of mind and heart, and, when he reined in before the loading corral, his first glance was not at Hump Styre and the others, but at the stack and top hamper of the riverboat, *Mohave*, beating up against the copper-brown, sullen, never-ending current of the river.

When a break in the tangled growth along the river's edge enabled Logan to get a clear view of all the boat, he saw the towing hawser looping down from the hog post to the cattle barge astern. Then Logan looked at Hump Styre and said harshly: "Open the gates and get them out of here!"

"Don't know why we should," retorted Styre. "First come, first served, Logan."

"If it was legitimate, yes," said Logan. "But just as a means of pulling a fast one, no."

"We're waiting for that new boat, the *Pathfinder*," Styre argued. "She's going to move these cattle upriver for us."

"That's what the holding corrals were built for, to hold a jag of cattle while waiting. That's the *Mohave* coming in for a landing and Matt Corbee is taking C Cross cows upriver. We need this corral to load. So get your stuff clear."

The *Mohave* came steadily on, slanting in from midstream toward the landing. The sonorous blast of her whistles echoed again on the heels of Logan's last words.

When those echoes had rolled away to nothingness, Hump Styre said: "It happens that these corrals are one thing along the river that doesn't belong to the C Cross. They were built by the folks in Castella for the use of any and all cow outfits, not for your special convenience and use. We got here first . . . we stay here. That's just the way things are."

Logan said: "One mistake Purse Fallon keeps making over and over again. Trying to block C Cross business by some stupid stall that doesn't fool anybody. I've heard talk that there's to be a new boat on the river . . . this *Pathfinder*. So far, I haven't seen it. For all I know it may be a week or a month before such a boat comes along. In the meantime, there's the *Mohave*, coming in for a landing, and towing a barge for C Cross cattle. And we're going to load that barge, out of this corral, today. So clear it. I'm not telling you again."

In a way, there was a tough streak in Hump Styre, particularly when he had three others to back his hand. He shook his head and said: "Not today, Logan."

Logan was in full character with his next move. Without further word or warning, Logan came out of his saddle in a diving lunge, so fast that even Hump Styre, anticipating some sort of a blow-up, got a fateful half second behind. Hump tried to dodge and drag a gun at the same instant and was unable to finish on either count. Logan's down-whipping left hand caught Styre's right wrist, blocking Styre's draw, while the point of Logan's driving shoulder smashed fully into Styre's chest, knocking him back. Logan's full weight and the power of his lunge belted Styre into the ground and the shock made Styre go momentarily flaccid. Logan ripped the gun from Hump's fingers, and, when Logan bounded erect, that weapon and his own were stabbing, level and ready, at Styre's three companions. "Up!" rapped Logan. "Up . . . quick!"

These three were new Broken Arrow hands. They'd heard about Boone Logan, heard plenty, but had never seen him before. If, privately, they had been inclined to scoff a little at what they had heard, they knew now that such scoffing had been a mistake. They had just seen Hump Styre put out of action in one flashing explosion of power. And now Logan, a gun in each hand, was moving out on them, bleakly savage and dangerous. Their hands went up.

"Over against the fence, facing it!" ordered Logan.

They obeyed, and Logan, moving down behind them, stripped away their guns, tossing the weapons far out to one side. "Now," he said, "you'll open the gates and clear this corral. Put your cows in the holding corrals, or let them run to hell and gone into the brush, I don't care which. Only, get them out of here!"

II

They had no choice now. They got their horses that had been tied to the corral fence. They opened the gates, rode in among the cattle, started hazing them into the clear. Most of the Broken Arrow cows were wild, leggy brutes, cactus cattle, in truth, and they needed little urging once they glimpsed the clear area beyond the gates. They raced through, pushing and bawling, and soon the corral was empty except for the hovering haze of gray dust.

Hump Styre was on his feet, steadying himself against the corral fence. The normal, forward hunch of his high shoulders, which had given him his nickname, was accentuated and he held one hand pressed to his chest. Pallor stained his bony face and his eyes were glazed with pain. He said, thickly: "You'll never have a chance to break me up again, Logan. You and me will have a settlement."

Hump climbed shakily into his saddle and headed uptown, his three companions following. The fact that they had not tried to put the stock into the holding corrals convinced Logan of the correctness of his deduction, that the whole thing had been merely another of Purse Fallon's schemes to block and annoy C Cross business. The Broken Arrow cattle soon scattered and disappeared into the brush of the river bottom.

Logan got his own horse and spurred rapidly out across the flats until he sighted a mounted figure, watching. Standing high in his saddle, Logan waved his hat until that mounted figure answered in kind. Then Logan went back to the landing.

The *Mohave* was tied up by this time, a squat, dumpy, but staunch little craft. The barge, towing from the hog post, was in position under the chute of the loading corral, but the heavy gangplank had not been run out to the chute. So Logan left his horse to go aboard the *Mohave* and see about that. A lighter gangplank from the lower, forward cargo deck of the *Mohave* was just being run out by a couple of Cocopah Indian deck hands, and, as soon as it was soundly in place, Logan crossed it.

He climbed a ladder to the cabin deck, looking for Captain Matt Corbee and was just in time to see Corbee come out of one of the *Mohave*'s half dozen little deck cabins, lugging a couple of hefty traveling bags. Logan opened his mouth to speak to Corbee, then stopped dead still. For right behind Corbee was a slight silver-haired figure with deeply seamed face and faded, tired eyes. Logan gulped and exclaimed: "Buck! Buck Channing!"

"Hello, Boone," said Buck Channing. "Glad to see you, boy!"

Logan, gripping Buck Channing's hand, fumbled a little trying to find words that would cover the stunning shock of Buck Channing's appearance. For the Buck Channing who had left the river range close to a year ago had been leathery and tough and hardy. But now he was thin and white, with no fiber at all in the grip of his hand. He seemed to have aged twenty years in one, and the discovery bewildered as well as shocked Boone Logan.

Logan got a grip on himself finally and blurted: "Man, am I glad to see you. I've been getting your letters saying you'd be back, one of these days. But it's been a long time, Buck, a long time."

"I came as soon as those damned doctors would let me," said Channing. "Don't think I ain't been pawing the ground to get here, Boone. I have, plenty. And does it seem good."

There was a stir of movement behind Channing, and he turned, saying simply: "Here she is, Boone . . . my girl, Carol. Honey, step out here and meet the best damned foreman who ever donned a spur."

She looked, thought Logan, just like that picture of her that hung on the wall above Buck Channing's old desk, back in the home ranch house up in the Tejon Mountains. Just as handsome, only more so, for the picture did not do justice to her rich coloring. She was slightly taller than average, with fair hair and clear hazel eyes, which met and held Logan's glance with a steadiness that was almost a challenge. It was improbable that she sensed Logan's thoughts, yet she flushed slightly and said, almost too brightly: "So this is that legendary figure, Mister Boone Logan. In a way, I'm disappointed. I expected to see a man at least nine feet high . . . a sort of Paul Bunyan in chaps."

Buck Channing said: "You can blame that on me, Boone. I guess I've done a heap of bragging about you."

Logan said: "A man is only as high as his hat, Miss Channing. Sorry."

Silently Logan told himself that this was her doing. This incredible change and decline in Buck Channing. She'd kept him there in the East, which wasn't old Buck's kind of range at all. Yeah, she'd kept him there, letting him eat his heart out yearning to get back to the open country, the country that had made him a big man and a strong one. She had let him fade away to this, and couldn't have given a damn, else she'd have come along out with him to the old home ranch long ago. And it meant that she was selfish and self-centered and ruthless, just like her mother had been—the woman who couldn't take it, who'd run out on old Buck away back in his youth, taking with her the baby daughter that Buck worshiped.

Then, after word had come long years later that the selfish woman had died, Buck had gone East to bring his daughter back and give her all the starved affection in his fine old heart, to lay at her feet the fruits and riches of the great cattle business he had built up here along the Colorado River. And she hadn't cared enough to give old Buck an even break. She had let him slide as far down as this!

Logan looked at Carol Channing again, and at the look in his eyes she caught her breath and went a trifle pale.

Buck Channing, looking inland, saw none of this. He pointed to the herd of cattle that was plodding in toward the river and the landing.

"Ours, Boone?" he asked.

"Yeah, Buck, ours. Bunch of feeders we've been holding on the Indio Mountain range. Going to barge them up to Sweetgrass for a month, and then deliver them to the reservation."

"First glimpse I got of the landing, I thought there was a jag of stock already in the loading corral, but it didn't look very familiar," said Channing.

"There was," said Logan succinctly. "Broken Arrow stuff. They moved out."

"Ha!" exclaimed Channing. "Ha! Same old Boone Logan, I see. Fallon been making much of that kind of trouble?"

"Some. I aim to have a real talk with him next time we meet up."

"We'll be getting along uptown," said Channing. "I'll want my old rooms in the River View Hotel. Come night, I'm going to sit at the window and listen to the old town and watch it come awake. I'm hoping some saddle-pounding son will make it his night to howl and liven things up. I am," he ended a trifle wistfully, "hungry for old sights and old sounds."

There was a lot more luggage than what Captain Matt Corbee had been carrying, and Logan helped him get it down to the lower deck, where a couple of Cocopah boys lugged it out onto the landing. Corbee, watching his chance, murmured to Logan: "Old Buck's gone a long way down, Boone. Almost scares me to look at him."

Logan nodded. "I'm hoping that getting him back to the home ranch will bring him along again, Matt. And, say, you might have the loading gangplank run out from the barge. Then the boys can start pushing the cattle aboard as soon as they get here."

"Can do," said Corbee, and called an order to his Indian deck hands.

Over on the landing, Buck Channing was shaking hands with Kent Masterson and introducing him to the girl. Masterson, in that easy, poised way of his, was laughing and talking to her, and she was smiling at him. Then, as the old cattleman and his daughter went up the slope to town, Masterson came aboard the *Mohave*.

"Got all my supplies. Matt?" he asked.

Captain Corbee waved a hand at the pile of merchandise stacked on the cargo deck and said: "Most of that is yours, Kent. I'll have the boys get at the unloading right away."

Kent Masterson was thirty-five but looked nearly ten years younger because of his slightly florid coloring and the sense of fresh vigor about him. He was sparely built and the cavalry training he had had while riding with Crook on the trail of the Apaches still showed in the way he handled himself. He possessed virile good looks and a shrewd mind for business. Now, as Boone Logan went ashore, Masterson followed him and dropped a hand on Logan's arm.

He said dryly: "I'm hoping not to get what Buzz McClure did, but as a friend I've got to speak out, Boone. I've a proposition to make you . . . about Hoddy. Now wait a minute . . . let me finish. Hoddy is fed up with punching cattle. I know, from what he's said to me at different times, that he'd like nothing better than to run one of my pack strings into the back country. That's the kid of it, Boone. Restless, wanting to be on the move, see new country, new people. How about it? I'll give him the job if it is all right with you."

For a little time there, the dark bleakness had all but vanished from Boone Logan's eyes. Now much of it came back. But he answered quietly enough. "I hate to admit failing in anything, Kent. But it looks like I've failed with Hoddy. I've done the best I know how with the kid. Probably my own fault that things haven't worked out. The C Cross is a religion with me and I've tried to jam it down Hoddy's throat. Maybe, as you say, a change of scenery, a different kind of a job might snap him out of it. It's damn' decent of you to offer. If you can interest him, it's all right with me."

"Fine! When he sobers up, I'll have a talk with him."

Logan went back to his horse and helped put the oncoming herd into the loading corral, and from there through the chute, across the big gangplank, and onto the barge. The last was considerable of a chore, for the cattle were fresh from wild range. When it was done, Shane O'Leary came over to Logan.

"Where's Buzz McClure?" he asked bluntly.

"Uptown, cursing me for a pig-headed fool, which I deserve," said Logan.

"He's not . . . quitting?"

"Not if I can help it."

"I was just wondering," said Shane quietly. "Because if he was, I'd be asking for my time, too."

Logan was gravely thoughtful as he rode slowly back uptown. He left his horse at Speck Tomlin's livery corral and told Speck: "Buck's back. He'll probably be wanting to head out for the ranch first thing in the morning. I'll want a team and that two-seater buckboard of yours, Speck. Slick it up a bit, will you?"

Logan stopped in at the Oro Fino, which was empty at the moment. From behind the bar Arch DeLong said: "Hoddy's doing all right in the back room, Boone. I'll keep an eye on him until he sleeps it off. I tried to get the bottle away from him two or three times."

Logan nodded. "I know. Not your fault, Arch. Where's Buzz?"

"Went out some time ago, right after you left for the landing."

Heading for the River View Hotel, Logan saw Buck Channing shaking hands with Harvey Overgaard in the doorway of Overgaard's general store. The cattleman was making the rounds, apparently, renewing old friendships.

As he went into the hotel, Logan heard a quick burst of feminine laughter in the hotel parlor, and, glancing in there, he saw Kent Masterson talking to Carol Channing. Masterson looked very handsome, his tawny head bent slightly as he looked down at the laughing girl. Logan went into the hotel bar without noticing them.

Buzz McClure was in a chair in the far corner, slouched far down, his hat pulled low, his eyes brooding. Logan pulled a chair up beside him, and said gravely: "I'm right down on my belly to you, fellow. I don't deserve a thing from you, haven't the right to ask a thing. If it'll square things, take a swing at me. Take a dozen. Yeah, I'm right down on my knees."

Buzz drew a deep breath and said quietly: "You don't need to be, Boone. Far as I'm concerned, it never happened. We'll go right on along from here."

Logan dropped a hand on Buzz's arm. "You're a better man than I'll ever be, by head and shoulders. I've been hating hell out of myself for the past couple of hours. About Hoddy . . . ," and Logan went on to tell of Kent Masterson's suggestion and his acceptance of it.

"That's fine. It should help. You know, Boone, for

you and me all things sort of begin and end with the C Cross. Hoddy never did feel that way. Chances are, running a pack string for Masterson will be right up Hoddy's alley. You can buy me one drink. Then I'll be getting down to the *Mohave*, to go on up to Sweetgrass along with Shane and the other boys in the outfit."

The afternoon ran out and the sun went down across the river, giving to the sullen, silt-charged waters a few moments of glory by turning them into a sliding sheet of burnished gold. Then dusk hung, hot and blue and breathless. But with complete dark a faint breeze sprang off the river, bringing a grateful sense of coolness.

Logan ate supper with Buck and Carol Channing at the cattleman's request. Just as they were about to start, Kent Masterson came up to their end of the long table in the hotel dining room and said laughingly: "I can see all kind of heavy business in the air between you and Logan, Buck. So I'm making free to entertain Miss Carol, if she's willing."

The girl spoke swiftly: "Gladly. All the way out here I heard nothing from Dad but talk about cows and range, hides and tallow, beef and prices. You'll be very welcome, Mister Masterson, if you promise not to mention a single word about cattle."

"Huh," grunted Channing. "Well, in that case, I reckon you're just what the doctor ordered, Kent. Sit in, and welcome."

Masterson's judgment of what was in Buck Channing's mind was highly accurate. Channing had a thousand questions to ask.

The old cattleman was hungry to get in full touch

again with all aspects of the cattle empire he had left so fully to the handling and management of Boone Logan. The talk brought back some semblance of the old fire to Buck Channing's eyes, but to Logan this merely emphasized how far the cattleman had slipped, and, in the occasional glances that Logan flashed at the girl, that bleak resentment stood out.

Only once did Carol Channing catch such a glance, and, when she did, that same quick widening of her eyes took place, backed by something like puzzled bewilderment. But immediately she mastered herself and turned even more graciously toward Kent Masterson.

It was easy to see that Masterson's interest in Carol Channing was growing with every moment, with evidence of reciprocity on the girl's part. Which was not hard to understand. Kent Masterson was good to look at, a decisive, forceful man, a good talker, and possessed, when he wanted to turn it on, of a bright and winning sense of humor. They made a fine-looking pair together.

Logan and Buck Channing were still talking C Cross interests when Masterson and the girl finished eating and went out together. At length Buck Channing yawned and said: "I'm going to have a cigar, and then turn in, Boone. We'll leave for the ranch early in the morning?"

Logan nodded. "I've already lined up a team and buckboard from Speck Tomlin. I'll be ready, Buck."

Channing went into the bar for his cigar. Logan went out on the hotel porch, pausing there to build a cigarette. In the darkness of the far end of the porch he heard Kent Masterson's humorous drawl and the music of Carol Channing's laughter. For there was music in the sound. This daughter of Buck Channing's was lovely to look at and lovely to listen to, mused Logan. But just the same, it was going to be hard to forgive the low physical estate to which her selfishness had brought Buck Channing.

Logan swept a match across his jean-clad leg and, when it burst into flame, cupped it in his hands and lifted it toward his slightly bent head. Even as he touched the flame to the tip of his cigarette, Logan caught the faint sound of expelled breath out there in the blackness of the street, a "Hah!" of savage satisfaction.

Logan's reaction was instantaneous. He spun the match away from him to his right, in a tiny, curving, down-dropping arc of crimson, while throwing himself to the left, in one explosive leap.

III

A spurt of gun flame seared the street's blackness and the rolling *boom* of report spread tumbling echoes. Boone Logan, halfway through his leap, felt the very breath of the slug that hurtled past him to *thud* heavily into the front of the hotel. Off balance when he landed, Logan went to his knees, but with a twist and a slither he was off the hotel porch into the street, dragging out a gun as he went. He had kept his eyes glued to that part of the night's blackness where the spurt of gun flame had blossomed. Now, low crouched, he raced for the spot, throwing a shot as he went.

He heard the hard, grinding curse of a man's

disappointment, the pound of running boot heels. He threw a shot at the sound, drew a slug in return that gouged into the street, spattering his boots with dust. The exchange of shots gave Logan an inkling as to the angle of the other's retreat and he closed in fast.

A narrow alley ran between the Oro Fino and Harvey Overgaard's store and it was for this refuge the fellow was making. Logan saw that his quarry would cross briefly at the outer edge of the light flare from Overgaard's store window, so he slowed and was set for the chance.

It was just a flicker of shadowy movement when it came, but Logan sent in his shot, holding low. The spat of hurtling lead, a strangled curse of desperation, told him he had hit. Then a gun blazed, wicked and wild, from low down against the earth. Feet spread, holding lower and lower, Logan emptied the final two shots of his weapon fairly into those snarling, crimson gun flashes.

The night seemed to close up in a vacuum of silence. Then men were running up and down the street, shouting their alarm. From behind, at the hotel, Kent Masterson was calling: "Boone! You all right?"

"All right," Logan answered harshly.

He punched out reeking empties and slipped fresh loads into his gun, then prowled ahead. A man charged out of Overgaard's store and, running along the street, tripped and fell flat on his face with a yelp of dismay. Floundering around in getting to his feet, he made a discovery and bawled it at the top of his lungs.

"Man down over here. Man down!"

Logan pushed into the swiftly gathering group.

Somebody scratched a match and bent low with it. "Styre," they said. "Hump Styre."

"That was my hunch," growled Logan. "He tried for me first when I stood on the hotel porch, lighting a cigarette."

Down the street there was a rush of movement, the *clatter* of departing hoofs. Logan bent a practiced ear, nodded, and murmured: "Three of them. The rest of the Broken Arrow crowd pulling out."

Somebody in the crowd asked: "Why should he have been after your hide, Logan?"

"Ask Purse Fallon," answered Logan. "He knows."

Over on the hotel porch lifted Buck Channing's voice: "Boone . . . Boone Logan!"

Holstering his gun, Logan went over that way. Channing was there to grab him by the arm as he climbed the low steps. "Boone, you're not hit?"

"Not a scratch."

"Who was it?"

"Hump Styre. You wouldn't know him. Came in while you were away. One of Fallon's crowd."

"Is he dead?"

"As he'll ever be."

"I was hoping for some of the old-time excitement, but nothing like this," said Channing, pulling Logan into the hotel with him. "What set it off?"

Kent Masterson was there and he said: "Styre asked for it. He cut down on Boone from the dark, when Boone went to light a smoke. Carol . . . Miss Channing and I were sitting on the porch and saw the whole thing."

"Yes," said the girl, her voice thin and shaken. "The whole terrible, savage thing."

She was standing just beyond Kent Masterson,

her face pale, her eyes wide and stricken. She was looking at Logan as if he were something that had just crawled out of a jungle. She added: "Your advance notices, Dad, were not nearly lurid enough."

Buck Channing swung his head and said, almost sharply: "What would you have had Boone do, child? Stand there and let this Styre *hombre* smoke him down? You should know better than that."

"I only know I heard and saw a man done to death ruthlessly," the girl retorted. "I can still smell gunsmoke."

Buck Channing said, a little wearily, as though thinking a long way back: "There are some things women can't seem to understand."

The first gray, thin light of dawn was seeping through the window of the back room of the Oro Fino. Hoddy Logan, sitting hunched on the edge of the bunk, was building a smoke with shaky fingers when the door of the room opened and Boone Logan came in. Hoddy threw him a single glance from swollen, bloodshot eyes, then went on fumbling his cigarette into shape. The old sullenness pulled at his lips.

"How'd you like to run a pack string for Kent Masterson, kid?" asked Boone quietly.

Hoddy went very still, before mumbling: "Still trying to arrange my life for me, are you?"

"No. It's Kent's idea, not mine. He talked to me about it yesterday, wondering if you'd be interested. I thought I'd ask you."

Hoddy considered for a moment. "I'd like it a hell of a lot better than chousing C Cross cows the rest of my life."

"Well, that's fine. Drop in on Kent and tell him so. He'll put you on. Do you want me to send your gear in from the ranch, or will you be out to get it?"

"I'll come out and get it. Why the sudden change of heart, where I'm concerned?"

Boone reached for his makings. "Put it that I finally realized I was pushing up the wrong trail where you figured. And losing my sense of proportion. I thought I was doing the right thing by you. I know now that I wasn't. I'm sorry for a lot of things, kid."

"You needn't be. Only mistake you made was in rating my possibilities too high. Like those Broken Arrow cows being in the loading corral. They slipped them in there during the night. And I wasn't big enough man to run them out, which Hump Styre and his gang knew, and which I knew. A man can't kid himself about such things, and I quit trying to kid myself a long time ago."

"Forget it. We got our cows loaded on the barge, so no harm was done. Well, I got to be getting along. How you fixed for money?"

"I got enough to get by on. Thanks just the same."

Boone put out his hand. "Good luck, kid. I ask only one thing. Which is, if you ever need me, you'll yell."

Hoddy stood up as he took Boone's hand. He said gravely: "I wish I had more of you in my make-up, and less of myself. That's the honest truth, Boone."

Boone dropped his free hand on Hoddy's shoulder, squeezed it. "I'm going to quit worrying about you, kid, for you're a Logan, too. Good luck."

Hoddy dropped back on the edge of the bunk and sat there for some time after Boone had gone.

He licked his parched lips several times and reached down for the bottle that stood on the floor beside the bunk. He held it up against the light of the window, gauged its contents. Slowly he lowered the bottle to the floor again, got his hat, beat it into shape, and went out into the barroom, where a blear-eyed ancient was swamping out.

Hoddy went along behind Arch DeLong's bar to the water bucket, picked it up, and drank, long and deep. He put his hat on the bar, leaned over, and poured the balance of the bucket's contents over his head, mopped his drenched hair and face with a bar towel, dropped $1 in the empty till, and went out, his head up, his step brisk.

Standing over in the doorway of the hotel, Boone Logan saw Hoddy come out of the Oro Fino, marked his bearing, let out a deep sigh of relief, then went in to get breakfast.

Half an hour later, Boone drove Speck Tomlin's two-seater buckboard up to the hotel and began stowing luggage in the back of it. Buck Channing and his daughter Carol came out. The girl took the back seat, Buck Channing the front. Boone Logan got in beside Buck Channing and had just picked up the reins when hoofs rattled and three riders came along the street.

They were fresh from the desert and the dust of it lay on horses and riders in a gray mantle. At sight of them, Logan handed the reins to Buck Channing and said curtly: "Drive along, Buck, and wait for me at the edge of town."

"And leave you to argue alone with Purse Fallon and a couple of his plug-uglies?" growled Channing. "The devil I will! You stay right here." And Channing grabbed Boone by the arm just as his foreman prepared to drop down to the street again.

Purse Fallon spied the buckboard and its occupants immediately, swung his head, and said something to his two companions, which caused them to swing their horses in to a hitch rail where they dismounted and tied. Fallon came on alone, a burly man sitting his saddle with a thrusting, forward lean to his heavy shoulders. His face was flat and broad, his lips long and thin, his eyes black and bold and arrogant on either side of a nose dented and spread by some ancient injury. Under his thrust-back hat his hair showed black and tightly curly.

He reined in right alongside the buckboard, his bold glance running slowly over its occupants. "This is good," he said, his voice holding a queer, hollow, booming resonance. "Got you both together, Channing, you and this bucko foreman of yours. So I can make my say and there'll be no chance for misunderstanding. To you, Channing, I say this. Call him off, while there's still time. Logan, I mean. This river range is getting just about fed up with him. He's pushing you and your C Cross layout so far out on the limb it is beginning to crack. Me, I've had a big bellyful of him, and that goes for a lot of others. So I say again, call him off . . . or take the consequences."

A glint of the old-time fire shone in Buck Channing's eyes. "He's my foreman, Fallon, and he suits me. He must be successfully blocking some of your rascally schemes, to have you worked up into this kind of a froth. These consequences you speak of, Fallon, are just what?"

"What Logan has been handing out to others, only

twice as tough. Other people have rights along this river besides the C Cross. Logan doesn't seem to think so. You better convince him that he's wrong, Channing, or things are going to get rough."

"What rights of yours has Boone trampled on, Fallon?"

"For a recent example, running my cattle out of the loading corral at the landing yesterday. Those corrals were built by the citizens of Castella, for the use of everybody, not for the use of the C Cross alone. The rule for the use of those corrals is first come, first served. Logan put over a fast one there."

So far, Boone Logan had not said a word, but he was watching Purse Fallon like a hawk, and his eyes had become dark and smoky. Now he spoke coldly: "Let me correct you on the rule for the use of those corrals, Fallon. That rule is . . . you don't put cattle in the holding corrals unless you've got a barge tied up for actual loading. Then you are to load and clear the loading corral as quickly as possible, making room for the next fellow. Styre and the others had the loading corral full of cows, with no barge to load to and no chance of getting one. It was all simply a deal to block us from loading the herd we brought down from the Indios. Well, the deal didn't work, and it won't, if you try it again."

Fallon shifted a trifle in his saddle, leaning a trifle farther forward. "Glad you mentioned Hump Styre, Logan. I was going to remind you about Styre."

Buck Channing's grasp on Boone Logan's arm had relaxed slightly. Now, swift and smooth, Logan slipped from the buckboard, swung off to one side, watching Fallon with cold intensity. He rasped: "Well, what about Styre?"

Buck Channing swore softly and helplessly. Carol Channing, a silent, big-eyed spectator to it all, sat, tense and straight, in the back seat, her face pale. For now, hovering over the street was that same bleak tension that had been there the night before when guns had blazed red and a man had died violently.

Boone Logan said again: "Well . . . what about Styre?"

Purse Fallon's black eyes filmed warily. "Why," he said almost mildly, "I'm not going to forget about Hump . . . not for a minute, Logan." Fallon swung his head and looked at Buck Channing. "I'm warning you for the last time, Channing. Call off this bucko foreman of yours, or don't kick when the ride turns rough."

With that, Fallon spun his horse and rode back to join his companions. Logan stepped into the buckboard, took the reins from Channing, kicked off the brake, and let the broncos run. Fallon had his back turned as they passed.

The C Cross ranch headquarters stood at the lip of a timbered bench on the west slope of the Tejon Mountains. It was north of Castella some fifteen miles and about eight miles back from the river. Sitting a tall horse in front of the ranch house, a man could look through a gap in the timber and glimpse the river, rolling tawny brown beyond the stretch of sage desert that lay between it and the base of the Tejons. From the porch of the ranch house it was possible to glimpse the same vista.

A small corner room of the south wing of the ranch house, with an outer as well as an inner door, served as an office, and from this nerve center the wide-spread affairs of the C Cross were conducted. On one wall was spread a large map of the country and on it, blocked in red, were the range areas where C Cross cattle ran. Small pieces of paper were pinned over each of these areas and on these slips were listed the number of cattle and the names of the riders guarding them for each particular patch of range. Thus, almost at a glance, it was possible to get the picture of the physical state of affairs of the C Cross. Boone Logan was just affixing two corrected slips, one at Indio Mountains, the other at Sweetgrass, along the river, showing the transfer of 200 head from the former to the latter place, when Buck and Carol Channing came in.

"Just making Carol acquainted with her new home, Boone," said the cattleman.

The girl had changed from her traveling clothes into a dress of soft blue material. It made her look younger, more girlish, with a fresher, warmer beauty. And abruptly Boone Logan saw her less with the eyes of blame for Buck Channing's shocking physical decline, and more in appreciation of her own undoubted charms. She noted the look, and a faint flush touched her cheek.

Buck Channing was looking at the map. "I like that," he said abruptly. "There it is, the whole thing at one glance. Quite a change from the old days when I used to keep my tallies on a piece of wrapping paper stuck in a shirt pocket. We'll have a lot to talk over later today."

Logan shook his head. "I got riding to do, Buck. Pete Fine is in reporting slow-elking trouble at Glass Springs. And according to Andy March there's been a couple of long-range shots taken at him and Steve Scarlett at Black Buttes. So I'll be drifting inside half an hour." He indicated a couple of leather-bound notebooks on the desk. "You go through those, Buck, and you'll find all the details in pretty good shape."

Channing squinted at the map, tracing with a thin forefinger. "Indio Mountains a couple of days ago, then to Castella. Now home, but heading for Glass Springs and Black Buttes. Kind of wearing out your saddle, ain't you, boy?"

Logan shrugged his big shoulders. "A man looks after his job, or he doesn't. I was born to ride, and I'm not kicking."

"Soon as I get so I can pound leather again, I'll take some of the weight off your back," declared Channing. "Though I must say I can't see where that weight is bending you over any. But then, you always was a bobcat for punishment."

Hoofs sounded outside, and the girl, glancing through the window, gave a little exclamation of pleasure. "It's Kent ... Mister Masterson, Dad." And she hurried out.

Watching through the window, Buck Channing saw Carol greet Masterson with a warm smile of welcome. He said slowly: "Masterson seems quite taken with Carol, and she with him, Boone."

"She could go a lot further and do worse," said Logan quietly. "Kent is a shrewd *hombre* at business and his trading and pack outfits are reaching deeper into the back country all the time. I can remember when he started with two pack bronc's, a saddle horse, and a twenty-dollar gold piece. Now he's got a dozen pack strings working all the time and figures on putting out more. Hoddy is going to run one for him."

"I've been meaning to ask you about Hoddy.

Hadn't seen the kid around. What's the matter? I'd always looked on Hoddy as being as much a part of the C Cross as you, Boone."

Logan shrugged again. "He just hasn't got cattle in his blood like you and me, Buck. He's been restless, dissatisfied. Kent Masterson made the proposition of letting Hoddy go to work for him. It struck me as a pretty good proposition. Well, Pete Fine is waiting for me. You take it easy, Buck. Things are rolling pretty good, all in all."

When Logan went out, Kent Masterson, standing on the porch steps with Carol Channing, called over to him: "Hoddy is pulling out in the morning on the Ash Creek-Fort Macon run, Boone. Thought you'd like to know."

Logan threw an arm up in acknowledgment. "Thanks a heap, Kent. I won't forget this."

From the porch, Kent Masterson and Carol watched Boone Logan and Pete Fine ride off, leading a pack horse loaded with grub. Masterson said slowly: "There goes a strange man. Boone Logan, I mean."

The girl tossed her head slightly. "Merely to call him strange is being somewhat generous, I think."

Masterson flashed her a quick look. "Don't like him, eh?"

"I don't think like or dislike enters into it at all," said Carol, abruptly thoughtful. "Rather say that he frightens me, as though I can see utter savagery very close to the surface in him. It is like being around a charge of dynamite, waiting for it to explode."

Masterson laughed softly. "Boone takes a little getting used to, for a fact. He's a strong man in all ways, and unable to show much understanding for anyone who isn't. Like with his brother Hoddy." And Masterson went on to explain. "Then," he added, "there is Boone's black temper. When and if Boone Logan and his world ever come crashing down, it will be his temper that does it. On the other hand, in the opposite mood he can be as gentle as a woman. It seems that you either like Boone Logan a lot, or you dislike him with equal intensity. But you can't ever ignore him. He's made himself a big man along this river range . . . plenty big."

"Dad," admitted the girl, "swears by him. But I, unless I change my point of view radically, am liable to swear at him. I never met a man I felt so instinctively antagonistic toward."

"That," said Masterson, "is sure a misfortune for Boone Logan."

Buck Channing, who had moved around inside the house toward the porch, arrived there just in time to hear the girl's last remark and shook his head gloomily, as though he had heard something he did not like.

IV

One week elapsed before Logan rode up to the home C Cross corrals again. His mood was a scrambled one. At Ash Creek he had met with Hoddy and the pack train. Hoddy was brighter and more cheerful than he'd been for a long, long time, and that made Boone feel very good indeed. But the other troubles he had found at Glass

Springs and Black Buttes were real and part of a pattern of attack against the C Cross that was becoming slowly clearer with every passing day.

One of Speck Tomlin's buckboards stood over at the hitch rail running between two sugar pines near the ranch house, its team shot-hipped and dozing. Logan wondered about that as he beat the worst of the dust from himself and went over to the office door. The door was open and inside were Buck Channing and Captain Corbee of the *Mohave*. Logan shot a quick look at Corbee.

"Nothing went wrong on the trip up to Sweetgrass?"

"Not a thing," answered Corbee. "What made you think there might have been?"

"They're nibbling and gouging at us in other places, Matt, and you don't ride up this way very often. So, putting both angles together. . . ." Logan shrugged, pulled up a chair, and dropped into it a little wearily.

"They? Who are they?"

Logan shrugged again. "Haven't got that answer yet. But I've quit kidding myself that this and that just sort of happen. I'm convinced there is a real plan beginning to work against us, with some central mind calling the shots."

Buck Channing leaned forward in his chair. "Maybe . . . Purse Fallon?"

"Maybe. But I'm a long way from sure. Certainly Fallon is after us, and it might be him. And I'm not underrating him. Yet I think I know how Purse's mind works. He's the sort to bull his way along, raise hell in general, and let the chips fall. And for that very reason I doubt he'd have the patience and savvy to gnaw us down gradual. And that seems to be what's in the wind now."

"We're a big outfit and there's always been a certain amount of small fry willing and eager to take a bite out of a big outfit when the chance offers," said Buck Channing. "From the very first we've had that sort of thing to contend with, Boone."

"Know what you mean." Logan nodded. "But this is different. For what would it gain any small fry to do some long-range sniping at our boys at Black Buttes? And the slow-elking at Glass Springs is a little too big for small fry to handle. They got away with ten head the last time they hit. Rustled them off the fringe of the herd at night, drove them back into the desert, butchered them quiet, and took the meat away on pack horses."

"Indians maybe," suggested Channing.

Logan shook his head. "If it had been one critter or even two, I might figure that. But not ten at a clatter. And then, coming in past Dead Horse, early this morning, somebody cut down on me with a Winchester from that red rim to the north. Made a pretty good shot at that range, too. The slug gouged a chunk out of my saddle horn. Aimed about a foot too far, else they'd have cut me in half. No, Buck, it begins to shape up as a long-range plan to cut us down, then bust us complete."

"Damn," growled Channing. "And me not worth a thin snort in the way of being able to help. Yesterday I tried a saddle for the first time. Carol and I went for a ride. And I couldn't take it, Boone. I was afraid to let the bronco get off a walk. Even just a walk seemed to shake me to pieces. Right now I'm so lamed up I can hardly wiggle. Guess that sawbones who kept me in that cussed hospital so long knew what he was talking about, all right."

Logan looked at him keenly. "You mentioned that hospital business once before, Buck. How come?"

Channing shrugged. "One of those things, I guess. A man goes just so far in this world before he begins to bust up. With me it came about two weeks after I got back to where Carol and her mother had lived. Carol was crazy to get out here to the ranch, and, of course, I wasn't hanging back on the lead rope myself. We were all set to start and then I just sort of began coming apart at the seams. They ended up by putting me in that there hospital, and there I stayed, month after month. Thought I never would get out."

"You say that Carol was anxious to get out here?"

"Anxious! She was pawing the ground. Shucks, if I'd held together, we'd have been out here inside of six weeks after I left. She sure was a powerful comfort to me, while I was laid up. With me all the time."

Logan bent his head over the making of a cigarette, his fatigue-sunken eyes thoughtful. Matt Corbee said: "Going to tell him of the deal we cooked up, Buck?"

"You tell him," said Channing.

"Well," said Corbee, "it's like this, Boone. Buck here has just bought himself a boat . . . the *Mohave*. And he's hiring me and the crew to run her for him. Yes, sir, the old *Mohave* is part of the C Cross now. She's through tramping up and down the river from Yuma to Gold Run, hauling supplies and freight for a bunch of senseless yaps. From here on out the *Mohave* handles just C Cross business, exclusive, and no other."

"What about the freight and supplies for all the river towns?" asked Logan, his mood quickening. "Ain't you kind of leaving the boys flat, Matt?"

"No, by gravy!" exclaimed Corbee. "It's them that have left me flat. That new boat, the *Pathfinder*, has made her first run, Boone. And offering freight rates I can't touch and still keep operating. And what did the merchants and traders and others along the river do . . . men I been taking care of all these years? Why, they forgot about Matt Corbee and the old *Mohave* and jumped like hungry fish for the bait the *Pathfinder*'s offered. Says they to me . . . 'You'll have to meet the *Pathfinder*'s freight rates, Corbee, or else. Business, you know.' So I says for them to go ahead and be damned. I never did gouge anybody on my rates and I could have, plenty, if I'd been that breed of cat, back when the *Mohave* was the only boat on the river. I tangled in one of these freight-rate rows once before, up on the Sacramento River trade, and I come close to losing my shirt. So, never again for Matt Corbee."

Logan looked at Buck Channing. "You've been going through stuff in the desk," he accused. "You found that letter I wrote and never got up enough nerve to send to you while you were away."

"Cussed right, I did," said Channing. "And thought so much of your idea, boy, that, when Matt here came out to tell us he was going to have to fold up, and so couldn't haul our cows any more, I hit him with the proposition of selling the *Mohave* to us and coming along on the deal to run her for us. Suited Matt, so the deal is closed. And now every chunk of river range from here to hell and gone is open to our cows."

Logan's eyes were shining. "In my original idea

I was thinking of a boat smaller than the *Mohave*, that wouldn't cost so much. But if your bankroll can stand the strain, Buck, the *Mohave* is perfect. We can do a mite of fixing on her and haul cows on her as well as in a tow barge. Just about double the number of critters per trip. Now we can bite into all that rich open river meadow range on the other side of the river as well as on this. We can forget about the hard to reach and guard back-country range, and keep our herds all along the river where the grass is better and we can guard them easier. We'll be more compact and stronger."

"The more I think about it, the better I like the idea," declared Channing. "It's a deal that calls for a little celebration. During my prowling about the house I found a bottle I put away before I went East. Relax, gents, while I go get it."

They had their drink, and then Matt Corbee made ready to head back to Castella. Boone Logan went out with him to the buckboard. "I'll ride in to town tomorrow, Matt. We'll go over the *Mohave* and see what fixing has to be done, so she'll haul cattle as well as tow them. I'm mighty happy about this, Matt."

"So am I," said Corbee simply. "Means I'm all through arguing and bargaining and jawing with penny-pinching *hombres* in every rat hole of a town between Yuma and the big cañon up above. Be seeing you, Boone."

The buckboard rattled away and Logan was heading for the bunkhouse when, from the timbered slope beyond the headquarters, two riders came jogging—Carol Channing and Kent Masterson. Masterson's cavalry training made him perfectly at home in the saddle. It was the girl who surprised Logan. Evidently she had done considerable riding in the East. At any rate, she sat her saddle well, swaying with slim, lithe grace to each curvet of the spirited pony she was up on. Her fair, bared head shone in the sunlight and her cheeks were warmly colored from the action of the ride. She was laughing gaily at some remark Masterson had made. When they drew up at the corrals, Logan went over to them.

"I'll take care of your bronc', Miss Channing," he said.

She hesitated slightly, then nodded. "Thank you." She dismounted and tossed him the reins.

To Masterson, Logan said: "Bumped into Hoddy at Ash Creek, Kent. He seemed happy as a jay bird. I'm thanking you again for that, fellow."

"Don't thank me, Boone. I'm sure I got a good man in the kid. Wasn't that Matt Corbee who just rattled off in that buckboard?"

"Yeah. He's a C Cross man now."

"A C Cross man? What do you mean?"

Logan, busy stripping the gear from the girl's pony, explained briefly of the deal that had been put through for the *Mohave*. Masterson sobered, his eyes narrowing slightly. "But where does that leave me and my trading business, Boone? I got to have supplies brought up from Yuma. Dog-gone it, man, such a deal cuts my feet right out from under me."

"No it doesn't. That new boat, the *Pathfinder*, is running now, and hauling freight at rates that Matt Corbee can't touch and stay in business. So when Buck Channing made Corbee an offer for the *Mohave*, he jumped at it."

Masterson was still grave, his face almost hard. He said: "That means I got to get back to town in a hurry and get my business affairs straightened out with this *Pathfinder* crowd. Carol, you'll excuse me?"

"Of course," answered the girl. "Thanks for coming out, Kent. I enjoyed our ride."

Masterson merely nodded and without another word spurred off, so abruptly that Logan looked after him in some wonder. The girl said: "You and Dad and Matt Corbee might have given Kent a little advance notice. This does leave him caught short."

"The deal," Logan told her quietly, "was all settled when I came in from the back country an hour ago. And it was the first inkling I had that anything of the sort was in your father's mind. It may be a little tough on Kent for a time, but it is a great thing for the C Cross. And for that, of course, I'm mighty happy."

The girl seemed to be studying him. "Just why are you so devoted to the C Cross? I understand that the C Cross is virtually a religion with you, a feeling reaching far beyond normal loyalty to your job."

"The C Cross," said Logan, "has been mighty good to me. But mainly it has been the man, your father. There we were, my brother Hoddy and me . . . orphan kids. I was sixteen, Hoddy three years younger. We were down and out, with no reasonably open trail ahead of us. We'd hit up every outfit between here and Yuma for jobs. Every one of them turned us down flat. Too young, they said. Which was pretty tough to take at that age, and when you hadn't had a square meal in months. And then we met up with Buck Channing. Well, he not only gave us jobs that kids could do . . . he gave us a home. He was kind and like a father to us. He saved us from plenty, for, about the time we met up with him, we were beginning to play with the idea of pulling a hold-up somewhere, just to get enough money to eat. Yeah, Buck Channing saved us from going completely wild. He gave us a home and a future. I don't think you can understand what that meant to a kid who had never had either. Came a day when Buck made me foreman of his ranch. If I lived a million years, I'd never be able to repay your dad for what he did for me and Hoddy. Maybe that answers your question."

There was an intensity of feeling in Logan's tone before he finished that had the girl a trifle wide of eye. "You . . . you have made a lot of enemies for the C Cross. Do you think that is doing Dad any good?"

"The C Cross," Logan told her, "is a big, rich outfit. And this country is wild, with more than its share of *hombres* who would like nothing better than to work on the wealth of the C Cross. You don't discourage men of that sort by yelling boo at them. It takes considerable stronger action. And after that they hate you as a matter of course. We've never bothered anybody who didn't start trouble first, Miss Channing. I hope you'll give me credit for never doing anything that would harm your father or his ranch. You believe that, don't you?"

The directness of his glance was disconcerting and there was no equivocating. The color in the girl's face deepened slightly. But she met his look and said: "I believe you. I might question your methods, but not your purpose."

She turned away then, but paused as Logan said: "Wait! I have a confession to make. I had some unjust thoughts about you, and I want to apologize."

"Unjust thoughts. In what way?"

"About your father. I was hit hard when I first saw Buck down on the *Mohave* the other day. He had gone away a lusty, vigorous man. He came back just a shadow of his old self. And I blamed you for that. I thought that it was because you had kept him overlong in the East, away from the ranch and the life he loved. I know better now. I should have known better at the time. I'm sorry, and I apologize."

She did not flare in anger as he thought she would. She merely said: "So that was the cause for the strange look in your eyes, as though you hated me. Not that it mattered particularly one way or the other. Yet I did wonder why that should be. At least it is further proof of your fidelity to Dad and his interests."

She went off then, quickly, to the ranch house. And Logan, watching her go, lithe, quick stepping, as slimly graceful as a wind-swept reed, abruptly realized that something new and compelling had come into his life. He knew he could no longer look at Carol Channing indifferently.

V

For the better part of two weeks Boone Logan fairly lived in his saddle. He went on to the reservation with the Sweetgrass herd, sent the receipts and other papers in to the home ranch by Buzz McClure, then rode a great rough half circle that touched at Skeleton Basin, at Black Buttes, at Glass Springs, and finally into the Indio Mountain range again. And from each of these ranges, when he left, long lines of C Cross cattle began plodding out the sear, dusty miles, centering toward Castella or the home ranch headquarters. At point of these herds, along the flanks, and back in the dusty drag, riders talked and speculated over the big change the outfit was making.

Logan, saddle-leaned almost to gauntness, gray with the dust of hundreds of miles of desert, pounded up to the home corrals in the late afternoon of a savagely hot day. He unsaddled and corralled his fagged-out mount, and then went directly up to the office. He was reaching for the door when Carol Channing came around the corner of the house. She was trim and chic in a riding outfit Logan had not seen before and he stood silently for a moment, looking at her.

She colored slightly at the intensity of his glance, but her face was troubled and her tone a trifle curt when she spoke. "If you're looking for Dad, he's not here. He's in town."

"Something wrong?"

"Not with Dad particularly, but in other ways, yes."

"What?"

"That idea of yours which influenced him to buy the *Mohave*. The whole river country has risen up against him on account of that. A lot of them did not care for us before. Now they'll all hate us, and I don't know as I blame them." Her eyes were flaming as she finished, her tone bitter.

Logan reached for his makings. "Go on," he said. "Don't stop now. What's the rest of the story?"

"Why, simply that everyone along the river is being left high and dry for supplies, what with the *Mohave* being taken off its regular run."

"That," said Logan slowly, "doesn't exactly add up. There's the new boat, the *Pathfinder*. If the *Mohave* could handle the supply question before, the *Pathfinder* should be able to do a still better job, being bigger and faster."

"But the people who own the *Pathfinder* have set out to rob everybody on the river!" cried the girl. "They've boosted freight rates out of all reason. For the past three days merchants and traders from miles up and down the river have been coming here to see Dad, demanding that the *Mohave* go back on regular schedule. Kent will have to go out of business, give up his pack trains, unless something is done to bring those *Pathfinder* people to their senses. And the only way to do that, Kent says, is for the *Mohave* to resume her regular run in competition and at the old freight rates. They've been after Dad until they've virtually forced him to go to Castella and talk the thing over with Captain Corbee."

Logan finished spinning his cigarette into shape, lighted it, and inhaled deeply. Then the fatigue lines about his lips smoothed out and he began to grin, then chuckle, then laugh aloud. The girl's flush deepened and so did her anger.

"I fail to see anything funny about it," she charged furiously.

"I do." Logan grinned. "If there is anything I can get a chuckle out of, it is to see a cheapskate and a penny pincher get pinched. Oh, I don't mean Kent Masterson. This is a little tough on Kent, I agree, but we'll probably be able to give Kent a lift over the rough spots. But the others . . . let them suffer."

Carol fairly stamped her foot. "I don't understand

a man like you," she fumed. "I swear I don't. How can you laugh and say let them suffer. . . ."

"Wait a minute," broke in Logan. "There are things maybe you don't know. Like this. If all those yelping merchants and traders along the river had stuck by Matt Corbee, the *Mohave* would still be paddling her way up and down, same as always. But what did they do when the *Pathfinder* people came along, hanging out the bait of lower freight rates than Matt could afford to meet? Why they just gobbled up the bait, hook, line, and sinker. And what did they tell old Matt? Why, that he would have to meet or better the *Pathfinder* rates if he wanted to keep their business. Which Matt couldn't do and still pay operating expenses." Boone Logan took a deep breath and then, holding the girl's gaze, continued: "Matt told them that and all he got was a shrug off. Matt wasn't going to ruin himself completely in a freight-rate war. So he just stepped out and sold the *Mohave* to your Dad. And now that the word has gone out and the *Pathfinder* people know that they have the river to themselves, they are out to make the cheapskates pay and pay and pay. And, lovely lady, I can't say I'm not getting a laugh out of it, because I am. And I'm heading for town *pronto,* to see that they don't talk Buck Channing into giving in to their hypocritical yaps and yelps."

"Good!" sputtered the angry girl. "About your going in to town, I mean. That's what I've been waiting around here for . . . hoping that you would show up, so I could head you for town and see that you use your influence on Dad and get him to agree to putting the *Mohave* back on her regular run. You can do more with him about such things than any-one else. I heard him tell them all flatly out here that he wouldn't agree to anything until he had talked with you. And you're going in and tell him to put the *Mohave* back on her old schedule."

Logan had grown grave again. Now he shook his head. "I'm sorry, but I'm not going to tell him that. On the contrary, I'm going to tell him to let them stew. It's their juice and they asked for it."

She stepped a little closer to him, very straight, her face going a little pale. "You wouldn't do that . . . even if I asked it as a favor?"

With his habitual cloak of stern gravity, the signs of fatigue pulled at Logan's face again. He straightened, as though in sudden decision. "I'm going to tell you something, Carol Channing. I've never known anyone like you. Just now, when you came around the corner of the house, it was like a cool, sweet breeze. And I realized all of a sudden that the reason I pounded out the circle of our camps and ranges as hard as I did, was so I could get back home here . . . and see you again . . . and hear your voice, maybe when there was laughter and happiness in it. I think I would ride a thou-sand miles, just for one minute of that. Which ought to tell you something."

He broke off, to take a final drag at his cigarette, before flipping the butt aside. The girl's eyes were wide as she stared at him, and the pallor of her face had become deeper.

"Now," went on Logan, his tone almost harsh, "you know how I feel. Which should tell you that nearly anything in this world you asked of me I'd do, and gladly. Except make a play that would hurt the C Cross, which in the long run would be hurting you. No, I won't do that, even if you ask it. And it would be hurting the C Cross and your interests badly, if the *Mohave* went back on the regular river run again. So that isn't going to happen. Now, I'm heading for town and I'm not letting your father down!"

As Logan headed once more for the corrals, the girl darted into the house. By the time he had caught up a fresh mount and was saddling it, she was there beside him, with hat and a light jacket. "Will you catch up a pony for me, please?" she asked.

Silently Logan did so, and presently they were lining out for town, side-by-side. By the time they got down out of the Tejons and started out across the desert, the sun was setting, and by the time they reached town the first pale stars were budding. Then, for the first time since leaving the ranch, Carol spoke.

"I'm asking you once more, Boone Logan, to tell Dad to put the *Mohave* back on her regular run. Isn't . . . isn't my judgment worth anything? I don't want us to be hated more than we are."

Logan jerked his head toward a star. "If you were to ask me to get that star for you, I'd break my neck trying. But about this other . . . no . . . for we can't afford it. And don't let how others feel worry you. Those that hate us have done so for a long, long time, and would keep on even if we did give in to them. And while, right now, they are yapping for us to help them, if the shoe was on the other foot, they wouldn't give us a kind word. I'm reminding you, that I know this river, this country, and the people in it. As yet, you don't. In time you will, and then you'll understand."

The girl's voice was almost tearful. "I . . . I want Dad to have friends in his old age, not enemies. Why can't you see that?"

"Far back as I can remember, which is considerable, Buck Channing has had his friends and his enemies. They'll stay that way, regardless. Nothing we can do now will change that."

"You . . ." she choked—"you are impossible, Boone Logan."

The dusk was too thick for her to note how he flinched at these words, note how the settled bleakness of his face pulled tighter and tighter. He said gravely: "I'm sorry."

Castella was livelier than Logan had seen the place for a long time. Strange buckboards and strange saddle mounts lined the hitch rails. Activity seemed to center about the River View Hotel. Men were gathered in little groups on the hotel porch, talking and arguing. Voices were strident and angry, and feeling was running high.

Logan found a gap at a hitch rail, reined in there, with the girl beside him. As Logan was tying the horses, he said: "Suppose you run along over to Overgaard's store and wait for your dad and me there."

"No! I'm going to be right at your heels. And I'm going to let these men know that there is one member of the C Cross who is in sympathy with their problem. And neither you nor Dad can keep me from it."

Logan caught her by the elbows and lifted her effortlessly until her startled eyes were on a level with his own where he held her, shaking her gently. "If you," he growled, "were just a few years younger, I'd suggest that your Dad cut himself a good stout willow switch and take you out behind the woodshed. Or let me take over the chore myself. It would be a pleasure. But, if you must, come along."

He headed for the hotel at a long-legged prowl so that the girl had almost to run to keep up with him. Lights were on in the building, and, as Logan and Carol came into the yellow flare shining from the open door, a man yelled: "There he is! There's the guy really responsible."

There was a rush to meet him and men were all around him and the girl, arguing, gesticulating, throwing angry accusations. It was a demonstration that frightened the girl and unconsciously she pressed closer to Logan, and laid a hand on his arm. Logan dropped his own hand over her fearful one, bent his head, and said: "Don't let this worry you, Carol. All noise, like a flock of yelping coyotes." And then, shielding the girl with an arm, he swung his big shoulders to open the way through the crowd for them.

A man he shouldered aside cursed angrily, and then, for the first time, the crowd heard Logan's voice. "Lay off that kind of talk! There's a lady here. Lay off, I say, or I'll jam a fist down your throat."

Before the cold whip of Logan's tone and words, the crowd hesitated, gave back, and the next moment Logan swept the girl safely through the door. In there, backed into a corner along with Matt Corbee, was Buck Channing. The cattleman looked harassed and weary and, at sight of Logan's fatigue-drawn, sun-blackened face, threw up a glad and welcoming hand.

"Boone! Come over here, boy, and give me a leg

up with these yapping *hombres!*" As Logan and the girl reached his side, Buck Channing put an arm about his daughter and said to Logan: "Damn it, boy, they've been spurring me raw. You'd think I'd robbed a bank of something, because I bought up the *Mohave*. You know what all the yelping is about?"

"Yeah, I know, Buck. Carol told me. And if you're waiting for my opinion, it is short and quick. Don't give an inch. Let them holler. They've asked for this."

"Right!" barked Matt Corbee. "They were ready to cut me right off at the pockets. Now they're getting some of their own medicine, they're squealing like pigs under a gate."

Buck Channing passed a weary hand before his eyes. "One minute I feel that way myself, the next I'm not so sure," he mumbled. "Don't know what's the matter with me . . . except I'm not the man I used to be. If I was, I'd make up my mind one way or the other and that would be that."

The girl said swiftly: "I feel like I did from the first, Dad. These men have rights. We don't want them all against the C Cross. I . . . I don't agree with Boone Logan . . . not at all!"

Buck Channing made that same weary gesture, looked at Logan, and said simply: "Boone, I don't know . . . I just don't know."

Logan said grimly: "Buck, did I ever let you down?"

"No, boy, you never did."

"Then don't let me down. I've already started our backcountry herds for the river. The first of them will be dragging in within a couple of days. And we've got to move them to pastures along the river by boat and barge. We've busted up our back-country camps. We're moving to new fields. If we stop now, we're going to be wide open to more different kinds of trouble than we've ever bumped into before. You've got to back me in this, Buck, all the way . . . or. . . ." Logan's shrug and the dark grimness about his mouth were very expressive.

Carol Channing saw the decision forming in her father's eyes and she made one more try to head it off. "Dad, he'll lead you into. . . ."

"No, child, he won't." Channing's voice was suddenly sure and stern. "Boone, knows what he's doing. He's never been wrong before, and he isn't now. Boy, you handle this thing. And whatever you say goes!"

There were men who had been listening to this interplay of words. Now one of them said harshly: "That settles it. It looks like Logan will never give us a break."

VI

Logan turned on the speaker, his eyes gone smoky. "I've got a fair memory, Chalfant. And I'm not forgetting that day last spring when one of the C Cross chuck wagons, out on a big circle, ran short of grub and pulled up at your store at Bull-frog to lay in a supply. Boley Smith, running the wagon, didn't have any money in his jeans at the time, and you refused flat to let him have the supplies on tick, making some wisecrack to the effect that any time the C Cross got anything out of your store they'd have to lay down the cash. Well, that meant a long, out of the way trip for Boley before he could get the grub he wanted. Now, the C Cross never failed to pay a bill yet, so we'll pay you off right now. Even if we did put the *Mohave* back on her regular run, there would be no supplies landed for you. Chew on that, and, if you choke, it's your hard luck."

The word spread swiftly. Men came crowding in from outdoors, to argue, plead, even to threaten. Boone Logan let them get it out of their systems, and, when they began quieting down, he ran his glance over the lot of them.

"For a long time Matt Corbee and the old *Mohave* hauled freight and supplies to you *hombres*," he said harshly. "For a long time Matt had the river to himself. He could have gouged you on rates and made you like it. But he never did. He was fair. Then comes a new boat, the *Pathfinder*. The people running it dangled some slick bait in front of you. If you'd had any brains at all, you'd have seen what was in the wind. Even if you didn't have brains enough to see that, you might have considered the decent break Matt Corbee had always given you and stuck by him out of sheer gratitude alone. But did you? No! To hell with Matt and the *Mohave*! Here was a chance for you to make a few more dollars profit. And what became of Matt Corbee you didn't care one good damn.

"But you walked into something like a flock of dumb, blind sheep. Instead of making more profit, you're going to have to pay through the nose. And so you all come screaming to the C Cross to get you off the hook. Well, C Cross has other business to attend to . . . its own business. It has its own use for the *Mohave* and that use isn't hauling supplies for you dimwits. That's the whole story. Now don't bother us any more." Logan turned to Buck Channing. "Let's get out of here, Buck. Come on!"

Laying the weight of his big shoulders on the crowd, Logan opened a way for Buck Channing, the girl, and Matt Corbee. They got into a hallway and Logan turned into the first vacant room he came to. When the others came in, he closed and locked the door.

Buck Channing dropped on the end of the bed, but his eyes were shining. "Boy, you told them! And you were right, all the way."

Logan turned to Matt Corbee. "I guess you heard some of the threats I heard, Matt. Most of them empty talk, of course, but a few fools might try something. Best thing you can do is slip out the back way, get down to the *Mohave*, and set up a watch on her. I'll be down to help you out later."

Said Matt: "Should they try anything against the old *Mohave*, I'll blow them loose from their belt buckles with that old Greener buckshot thrower of mine. See you later, Boone."

Corbee unlocked the door and went out. Logan closed the door, leaned against it, and bent a weary look on Carol. "I wish you wouldn't waste your sympathy on that crowd," he told her. "There wasn't a one of them who ever did or ever would turn a finger to help the C Cross. To the contrary, a lot of them have tried to kick a spoke out of our wheel at one time or another."

"Every man out there will leave here hating us," flared the girl. "That doesn't bother you, of course. For you love conflict, animosity. You fatten on it. Why, clear down at Yuma, when Dad and I were waiting for the *Mohave* to show up and were in an eating house, there were two men at a nearby table and we overheard their talk. They were cursing someone . . . and that someone was none other than you, Boone Logan."

Logan smiled mirthlessly. "Considering time and distance, which would have put those two at Yuma about then, let's see if I can describe them. They were both lanky gents, one with a scar running from his temple to the corner of his chin on the left side of his face. That would be Scar Ringe. The other was badly pockmarked . . . by name, Touch Teliferro. Right?"

Wonderingly the girl nodded.

Buck Channing said: "That's the pair of them, Boone."

"I consider it an honor to be cursed by such as them," said Logan dryly. "Slow-elkers and petty-larceny coyotes, both. They got out of this upriver country just ahead of a lynch rope that the boys and I were waving at them."

A step sounded in the hall outside, and then there was a knock on the door. Logan stepped aside, opened the door slightly, took a look, and swung the portal wide. "Hello, Kent. Come on in."

Kent Masterson's usual air of gay good humor was not in evidence. He faced Logan and said abruptly: "Knowing you as well as I do, Logan, I don't suppose there is any use banking on you to change your mind about the *Mohave*. Yet where does that leave me? I never shortchanged on Matt Corbee."

Logan dropped a hand on Masterson's shoulder. "You may have to scratch gravel for a little while, Kent. But we'll see that your warehouse is kept full . . . at the old rates."

Masterson shrugged Logan's hand aside impatiently, took a short turn up and down the room, then faced Logan again. "I never question the right of any man to be faithful to his hire. But that man can push the interests of his outfit so far and hard that he's liable to end up doing his hire more harm than good. Ever think of things that way?"

Logan studied Masterson gravely, his eyes narrowing slightly. "Go on," he said. "Say the rest of what you're thinking."

"I will," rapped Masterson. "I don't suppose you've ever stopped to consider how far you've strained the patience of your friends at one time or another. Well, you have, plenty. You bull your way straight through to your objective, and, if anybody gets trampled in the process, that's their hard luck, it seems. You've built up the power and holdings of the C Cross . . . there's no denying that. But you haven't made any friends for the outfit along the way. Now you've pulled this *Mohave* deal. I grant you it's going to benefit the C Cross temporarily. But in the long run it's going to hurt more than help, for the C Cross is going to be hated from one end of this river to the other. And nothing ever lasted long in this world with enough people hating it."

"I'd say that depended a lot on what breed of cats did the hating," murmured Logan quietly.

Masterson made a violent gesture. "You're as bad as the river. You get hold of something and you never give up. There's no way but your way, is there?"

Logan's voice went a trifle thin and cold. "C Cross interests have been my interests for a long, long time, Kent. I can't see your right to challenge them."

"You keep on brewing animosities toward the C Cross and it will take a better talker than you are to prove to me where that's helping the interests of Buck and Carol Channing!" flared Masterson.

"I'm satisfied with Boone's ways, Masterson," said Buck Channing dryly. "And you wouldn't accuse me of being careless with Carol's interest, would you?"

Before Masterson could answer that one, another knock sounded at the door, and, when Logan opened it, a Cocopah Indian stood there. "Cap Corbee," said the Indian, "he say you better come . . . plenty *pronto.*"

Logan threw a quick look at Channing. "I suggest that you and Carol take rooms right here, Buck, and keep out of sight until morning. I'll see you then." Then he was gone after the flitting Indian.

A crowd was gathering at the landing where the *Mohave* was tied up. Logan, coming up through the dark, heard all kinds of wild talk, some of it advocating taking over the boat by force. There was no way of reaching the *Mohave* except straight through the crowd and it was characteristic of Logan that he went that way, straight through. A shout went up the moment he was recognized.

"Here he is! Now's a good time to find out just who's running things along this river . . . Logan or the rest of us!"

The shouter grabbed at Logan, and Logan knocked him winding with a flailing sweep of his fist. It took the crowd a moment to understand and Logan was almost to the gangplank before they came at him in a massed rush.

Feet spread, Logan squared to meet them, smashing out with both fists, which held them momentarily. But as the pressure piled up, Logan whipped out a gun and lashed out with it, twice, landing solidly both times, the recipients of the blows going down in sprawled heaps.

Then it was Logan's voice that hit them, so hard and ruthless it was almost a snarl: "Back up! Back up, damn you, or I let lead through somebody!"

From the upper deck of the *Mohave* came a yell from Matt Corbee. "If Boone Logan shoots, I follow suit. And I got plenty buckshot here to spray around. Break it up, you crazy fools, break it up!"

This double threat stopped them, and Logan backed across the gangplank. The crowd jeered, cursed, yelled threats, but had no stomach for attack in the face of guns held by two determined men. For a while the crowd stayed there, taking out their feelings in talk, and then began to break up and drift off uptown again. Soon the landing lay dark and deserted.

"Hated to bother you, Boone," Corbee told him. "I wasn't afraid for myself, but they could have done the old *Mohave* some damage, so I sent for you, knowing they'd go plenty slow with you around."

"That's all right, Matt. Glad you did. Wish we had a couple of the boys here to help us stand guard. For we'll have to make a night of it."

"I will, but you won't," declared Corbee. "You've been going like hell and you're all fagged out. I could see that, up at the hotel. Now me, I've done little but lay around and sleep for the past week, so I'm making a night of it at guard and you're going into my cabin and get some rest. Don't worry. If any sign of trouble shows again, I'll give you a yell. Now get in there and hit that bunk."

"You make a picture I can't resist," said Logan.

He was asleep almost before he got his boots off.

The sun rose on a quiet Castella. Many of the disappointed traders and merchants had pulled out during the night, with the rest leaving early in the morning, for distances were long in this country, between different landings and towns along the river.

The whine of saw and the clatter of hammers greeted Boone Logan when he awakened to find Corbee directing several Cocopah deck hands at enclosing the forward cargo deck of the *Mohave* with stout railings.

"We'll be ready for them, soon as the cattle get here, Boone," said Corbee. "Have a good sleep?"

"Never better. You get some yourself."

"Later on I'll grab a little shut-eye."

Logan climbed the low slope to town and went directly to the hotel to see Buck Channing and Carol just emerging from breakfast. Channing smiled grimly. The cattleman did not look any younger, but the glint in his eye hinted of older and more vigorous days.

"First thing this morning I took a look and the *Mohave* seemed quite all right, Boone. The trouble wasn't too bad?"

"Mostly talk and noise as usual. They were trying a big bluff and it didn't work. Now, it seems, they've pulled out and can do their yelping at the *Pathfinder* people, which is where they should have gone in the first place." Logan looked at the girl and smiled gravely. "Surprised to find the world still in one piece, maybe?"

She tilted her chin at him. "It could have been very serious," she said coldly. "I didn't enjoy it, and none of us will relish the fruits of it."

"You don't," said Logan succinctly, "move a bedded herd just because the coyotes yelp all night. For, always, come sunup, the coyotes are gone. They may yelp another night, but what of it?"

"Do you rate everyone a coyote who doesn't agree with you?" demanded the girl icily.

Logan chuckled. "Gosh, no. I just tag them by their yelps. You heading for home, Buck? Well, then, I'll be out to the ranch a little later."

Logan had breakfast, then went over to Kent Masterson's warehouse. He found Masterson there, busy checking out supplies for a pack train just about to leave. Logan prowled about, taking note of the piles of merchandise and supplies. When the pack train plodded away, the lead mule's bell *tinkling*, Logan went over to Masterson.

"You got a good month's supplies here, Kent," said Logan bluntly. "So why were you moaning last night? I told you we'd see that you didn't suffer."

Masterson was cool, a barrier in his eyes Logan had never seen there before. "It was the principle of the thing I didn't like. Everything for the C Cross . . . everything . . . and to hell with the rest."

"Did the C Cross ever hurt you, personally, in any way?"

"No."

"Then what in hell are you hollering about?" Logan's tone had frost in it. "If you built yourself up to being the biggest trader along the river, as a friend I'd be glad of your success. But last night you were ready to take the other side against me. Get this right, Kent. Corbee and the *Mohave* were through with the river trade before Buck Channing ever had any idea of buying the boat. Matt went through one freight-rate war up on the Sacramento, and it like to ruined him. He wasn't going to go through another. So when the *Pathfinder* people began cutting under him and the fools along the river fell for the bait, Matt made up his mind to quit. And he had quit before Buck bought him out with the idea of using the *Mohave* in our own business alone."

"If C Cross hadn't bought the boat, Corbee would have gone back on his regular run when the folks along the river asked him to."

"Think so? Go ask Matt and find out. I'm telling you he was done . . . all through. Didn't hear Matt urging Buck Channing to put the boat back on the run last night, did you?"

"It was you who swayed the balance. Had you kept out of it, Channing would have listened to reason."

The look and attitude of Masterson gave Logan a queer feeling, as though something worthwhile was slipping away between them—the old friendship maybe. His mood broke, his eyes warmed, and he dropped a hand on Masterson's arm.

"What the hell. There's no sense to this argument between us two. Come on over to the Oro Fino, Kent, and I'll buy you a drink."

Masterson pulled his arm away, the barrier in his eyes going higher and stronger. "No! That day in the Oro Fino, when you slugged Buzz McClure because he stood between you and your brother when you were all set to work Hoddy over, Harvey Overgaard said something. In case you didn't hear it, I'll tell you what it was. Harvey said . . . 'I can stand a man's black temper only so far . . . then I get fed up.' Well, I can stand a man taking in all the center of the street only so far . . . then *I* get fed up. I'm fed up now."

Boone Logan stood very, very still, the new warmth in his eyes fading away behind a cloak of inscrutability. Two or three times he started to speak, but each time his lips clamped grimly before a word was uttered. Then, with a certain bitterness pulling at his face, he shrugged slightly and turned away.

"All right," he murmured, "if that's the way you feel about it. Sorry."

VII

The nearer of the back-country C Cross herds were beginning to arrive at Castella. As fast as they did so, they were loaded onto the barge and into the enclosure on the *Mohave*'s forward cargo deck, and by that means went upriver to newer and more lusty range. Twenty miles up from Castella and on the west bank of the river were vast, sprawling flats, lush with grass fed by river seepage, walled off from any other economical access than by riverboat by incredible miles of empty, sun-blasted desert. It was virgin range, rich range.

This was the largest single area, but for fifty miles on either side of the river smaller but equally rich stretches of grazing country opened up here and there. C Cross cattle began grazing over all of it.

Back and forth forged the *Mohave* and her tow barge. In the dust of the loading and holding corrals at Castella Landing, C Cross cowboys yipped and sweated, and with each load of cattle taking off for new pastures, some of those riders and their horses went along.

The word of the C Cross' new venture spread and cowmen from harsh, distant inland ranges began drifting into Castella to see first-hand what was going on. Among them was Purse Fallon. Comment varied. Most of the cattlemen were envious, but not hostile. A small group, led by Purse Fallon, set up some hostile talk, complaining that C Cross was hogging all the best range in the country. But as one old-timer put it: "That river range has been laying there empty from the beginning of things. Nobody up to now had brains and guts enough to figure how to use it. If Channing is faster in the head than the rest of us, that's our fault, not his."

To which Buzz McClure, who happened to be in the Oro Fino at the time, washing some of the dust of the loading corral out of his throat, replied: "It was Boone Logan's idea, not Channing's. The smartest cowman ever to hit this river, Boone is. And nobody is quicker to admit that than Buck Channing himself."

Purse Fallon looked Buzz over with a sneer. "Some gents are sure hounds for punishment. If anybody ever sunk his fist into my face, I'd have his heart for it, if it was the last act of my life."

Buzz colored slightly. "Lots of things you and I see from different angles, Fallon."

Boone Logan worked harder than any man in the C Cross outfit and those who knew him best wondered at his mood. Always grimly intent, he was more so now.

Several times Buck Channing drove the buckboard to town to see how things were going, and one day, noting Logan's intensity, he said: "Don't drive yourself so hard, boy. We got all summer to do this job."

"Maybe," answered Logan. "But I'll feel better when our last cow is loaded and moved upriver. Ever strike you how wide open we are, spread to hell and gone this way? Fallon is missing a golden opportunity if he doesn't hit one of our herds coming in. He could do us a lot of harm. I can't savvy why he hasn't taken a cut at us."

"Maybe he's small potatoes, after all, with a bark bigger than his bite."

Logan built a smoke. "Carol's all right? I notice she hasn't been to town with you lately."

Buck Channing scowled. "She's all right. Seems satisfied to hang around the ranch. Maybe that's because Kent Masterson is out there so much."

Logan looked at the river with shadowed eyes and said nothing more.

The *Mohave* pulled out with another load and she was not an hour gone when the *Pathfinder* came forging upriver, to tie up at the landing. A big pile of supplies were unloaded, and Logan, glimpsing one of the tags, saw that it was consigned to Kent Masterson. Logan thought, a trifle sardonically, that for all his uproar, Masterson evidently figured to stay in business.

Abruptly Logan decided to take a trip to the ranch. He did not try and make excuses to himself as to why. He was simply hungry for the sight of Carol Channing, and for the sound of her voice.

The big part of the transfer job was done. Only one herd remained, that from Skeleton Basin, and, as it had the longest trail in, it was still a couple of days away. Logan drew Buzz McClure aside: "I'm going out to the ranch, Buzz. Stingy Dale and the other boys won't be in from Skeleton Basin before tomorrow night at the earliest. So you do a chore of loafing. Hang around the different gathering places. Do a lot of listening and looking. Things have been going altogether too smooth and quiet for us. And I'm not kidding myself that all those who've been scratching us before have suddenly forgotten they still have claws. Probably you won't hear a thing. But you might."

Buzz nodded. "I'll look . . . and listen," he said briefly.

Logan, short of tobacco, stopped at Overgaard's store to get some. Overgaard, setting out Logan's change, said gruffly: "Buzz McClure doesn't seem to be holding any grudge, Boone, so I don't know why I should. It's easy to criticize, isn't it?"

Some of Logan's gray mood dropped away from him. "Thanks, Harvey. This means a lot to me. Buzz, he's the salt of the earth. A better man than I'll ever be. I don't mind telling you now that I went right down on my face in front of Buzz, for hitting him. And the good old rascal just said to forget it, that, as far as he was concerned, it hadn't happened. I was pretty upset at the time, but that still was no excuse for me doing what I did. I'll never get away from despising myself."

Logan paused in the doorway of the store to spin up a smoke. Kent Masterson came riding into town. His horse was lathered and Masterson's face was set. He looked neither right or left as he passed the store. Logan, wondering, went out to his own pony, headed for home.

It was good to be back at the quiet of ranch headquarters, under the green timber. Big timber had a way of hushing things, of muting sounds. Logan had a shave, a hot bath, and change of clothes, which relaxed him to a sense of comforting weariness. He went up to the ranch house and into the office. He fiddled around there for a time, but knew his need was not in this room. So he went deeper into the ranch house and found Carol curled up in a big chair in the living room. She had been reading, but laid the book aside when Logan came in.

"Dad's not here," she said. "You must have seen him in town."

"I did," Logan told her. "It's not him I want to see, but you ... just as you are ... sitting there. Don't move. Just let me look at you a little while."

She colored slightly, watching him with some uncertainty. His cleanly shaven face had a dark mahogany shine to it that brought out the faint suggestion of gauntness his features always held in repose. He looked what he was—a big, strong, competent man whose youth was shackled by responsibility and purpose beyond his years.

Quite on impulse, Carol unconsciously quoted Masterson: "You are a strange man, Boone Logan. Whether a person liked you or hated you, he could never ignore you."

"I'm wishing right now I was a different kind of a man than I am," he told her. "So that I might win a smile from you, or the sound of your laughter. That's all I want now."

"Goodness! You make me feel important. When did you eat last?"

"I don't know. Sometime earlier today, I guess. Lately I haven't paid much attention. Why?"

"I was considering getting supper. Would you care to eat with me?"

"Would I! Lord!"

"Very well. Come along to the kitchen. But keep out of my way."

He tipped a chair back against the wall, watching her. In her cool, starched apron she made a picture. Logan told her so. And that won the smile he was looking for.

She made hot biscuits, fried thick slices of ham, broke eggs into a pan. When they sat down opposite each other, Logan said: "In a cook shack or a hash house, ham and eggs are just grub. Like this . . . they're something a man would push a mountain to get at."

She laughed softly. "Poor man! You certainly are in a desperate mood. It is good to hear someone appreciate my cooking. Dad never says anything about it, one way or the other."

It was a good meal. The best, Logan thought, he'd ever had in his life. Not just the food, but her. She was in a strange new mood that was light, cheerful, and friendlier than she'd ever been before. It was as though some invisible barrier that had always been between them had been pushed aside.

Logan said gravely: "There are some moments in a man's life that he never forgets, and the more of them he has to remember, the wealthier he is.

I'm a rich man this instant. A lovely woman, a perfect moment."

She cupped her chin in her hands, her elbows on the table, studying him. "I want you to grant me a favor, Boone Logan."

He said slowly: "I hope I can grant it. Don't ask me something I can't do, please."

She knew what he was thinking. "It has nothing to do with that old boat all the fussing was about. It is about you. Don't ever be any different than you are. Be just . . . Boone Logan. It becomes you tremendously."

"That," said Logan, startled, "sets me to fighting my head. Not so awful long ago you were rawhiding me for being. . . ."

"Just Boone Logan. I know. That was then. This is now, and in the future. Now there will be no more personalities. You can dry the dishes for me, then run along. I've things to do."

They were halfway through the dishes when a buckboard rattled up outside and Buck Channing came in. He stared, then exclaimed: "I'll be darned! This is something like. If it had been Kent Masterson instead of you, I'd have thrown him out. I thought that jigger was a friend of yours, boy?"

"He is," said Logan. "A little peeved up now. But he'll get over it. Every man has a right to get peckish now and then. I've made a fool of myself that way more than once. So I can't deny Kent the same right."

The old cattleman snorted. "You are a durned sight more generous than he is." He turned to Carol. "Sorry to make you dirty up dishes again, lass, but I'm hungry."

Logan looked down at the girl and grinned.

"Somebody else is peckish, I'd say. I'm drifting before he starts in on me. Thanks . . . for everything."

The moment Logan was out of the house, Carol Channing turned on her father. "What's this about Kent Masterson, Dad?"

"He's making talk in town against Boone Logan," growled the cattleman. "Not good talk, either. I thought Buzz McClure was going to punch his head for him, and I was hoping Buzz would. I don't want you to think I'm butting in, or trying to run your life, Carol, but I'm afraid I'm not going to be exactly cordial to Kent Masterson when he shows around these premises in the future."

"He was out here today," said the girl quietly. "He asked me to marry him."

Buck Channing went very still, searching his daughter's face with a strained glance. "Yeah? And you told him . . . ?"

"That I was sorry, but it was of no use. In other words . . . no."

Buck Channing let out a joyous roar, hugged his daughter mightily. "Bless you, child! I'm not sorry. I'm tickled plumb out of my boots. Ah, you're a smart little rascal. You saw through him, didn't you?"

"I think I did," admitted the girl slowly.

Aside from a couple of old-timers who were always kept close to the home ranch to take care of various chores, Boone Logan had the big bunkhouse to himself. It had been a long time, he realized, since he had spent a quiet evening in the bunkhouse with the boys. It was good to sit at the battered old card and reading table and play a few hands of solo in relaxed content. And after that to turn in on his familiar old bunk.

He lay for a while in thought, there in the soft dark. And his thoughts were all of that girl up in the ranch house. He could not figure out her sudden change of front. Always, until today, there had been that subtle atmosphere of antagonism between them. Now, for some reason he could not fathom, it had been whisked aside and the result was comforting and warming. But she still had him fighting smoke in some ways. That favor she had asked, that he always be the Boone Logan of old, certainly had him back on his heels.

He awoke in the late, chill dark, for the elevation of the headquarters, up here in the Tejons, was enough to lift it above the warm mugginess of the summer nights along the river. It was the sound of racing hoofs that brought him awake—racing hoofs pounding in across the benchland right up to the very door of the bunkhouse.

Logan was up and to the bunkhouse door as those hoofs came to a flying halt. He sent his voice reaching across the dark. "Yeah . . . what's up? This is Logan."

"Tippy Foss, Boone! They've hit the Skeleton Basin herd and stampeded it. Scattered it to hell and gone!"

"Did Stingy Dale . . . ?"

"Stingy is dead. Al Claverly is shot up bad and Bill Kolchack and Andy Ferriss are taking care of him. We were bedded for the night at Stony Flat. That's where it happened."

Logan's voice went cold and crisp. "Catch up a fresh bronc' for yourself, Tippy, and one for me. Be with you in a minute."

By this time the two old-timers were awake, and,

as Logan lighted the lamp on the bunkhouse table, they lifted sleepy heads from their blankets. "What's up, Boone?"

He told them curtly as he dressed swiftly: "You two hook a team to the spring wagon. Pile a good pad of hay and some blankets in the back. Take along a five-gallon can of water. Then head out for Stony Flat. And hook a team up to the old man's buckboard, while you're about it. Take your shooting irons along to Stony Flat, just in case. Fly to it, boys!"

There was a light going in the ranch house when Logan got up there and the door opened quickly to Logan's knock. Buck Channing held the lamp, peering out at Logan. Behind him stood the girl, wrapped from chin to toe in a dressing robe. "What is it, boy?" demanded Channing.

Logan saw the girl's eyes widen, her face pale as he told the dire news. "I hate to ask it of you, Buck," he ended, "but I told Jerry and Río to hook up your buckboard. If you'd line out to town and get Doc Newcomb headed out for Stony Flat, it might mean the difference for Al Claverly."

"Hell's gates, boy, of course I'll go! They killed Stingy Dale, you say? Why, damn their eyes, if they want it this tough, that's the way they'll get it. See you at Stony Flat, Boone."

The wide-eyed girl knew she would never forget the picture of Boone Logan that she glimpsed as he turned away into the night's blackness, tall and darkly ominous, the butt of a big gun flaring at either hip.

VIII

Gray dawn lay over Stony Flat and the surrounding desert. Gray were the feelings of Boone Logan and his men as they stood watch over the blanket-covered figures of a dead comrade and a badly wounded one. Jerry Boland and Río Shore had broken all records getting out there in the spring wagon. Now they were brewing hot coffee over a tiny fire of sage twigs. Tippy Foss, looking out to the west in the growing light, said: "Here comes the buckboard, Boone. That's the old man driving and he's got two people with him."

The third person was Carol Channing, sitting between her father and Doc Newcomb. The buckboard team was foaming as Buck Channing set the brake and skidded everything to a halt. "I didn't let any grass grow," growled Channing. "We got here in time?"

Logan nodded. "Al's a stout lad. Do your best by him, Doc."

Doc Newcomb, satchel in hand, hurried over to Al Claverly. Carol Channing went with him. "Didn't have a chance at keeping her home," Buck Channing told Logan. "Any idea who pulled this little trick?"

"Yeah, Purse Fallon and his crowd. They left one casualty behind. A dead bronc', and the saddle on it is that flossy rig Dude Orinda was so proud of. Orinda is one of Fallon's gang. After the first surprise rush, our boys did a lot of good shooting. They got this bronc' down and were making things so hot that Orinda couldn't chance coming back after his prize saddle. He must have doubled up with somebody else and just kept on going."

"We bumped into some of the cattle on the way out," said Channing. "If it was the herd they wanted, they didn't get all of it by a hell of a lot."

"That's what I can't figure." Logan nodded. "The cattle are all around here. They didn't run far, being pretty well fagged from the drive in from Skeleton Basin. And even if Fallon's gang had tried to run off with it, or any sizable part of it, they must have known they couldn't move the cattle far enough and fast enough to keep ahead of the inevitable pursuit. On the face of it, it's the most wanton, harebrained deal in the book, like a kid throwing rocks at the windows of the house of somebody he didn't like."

"On the face of it, yeah," growled Channing. "But it must go deeper than that, Boone. Grown men, even a flock of rascals, don't pull a deal like this just for fun or orneriness. There is some kind of a plan, some kind of a scheme behind it. So we'll go slow and use our heads."

Doc Newcomb was neither optimistic nor pessimistic when they loaded Al Claverly gently into the back of the spring wagon. "Fifty-fifty," said Doc laconically. "We'll know for sure by this time tomorrow. An easy ride from here to town will help a lot."

Río Shore took the reins. "I'll keep it easy, Doc. Come along and see."

Buck Channing turned to the buckboard. "Come along, child," he told the girl. "We'll follow them in." He looked at Logan. "Stingy?"

"We'll bury him under the timber back of the

home ranch, where some of our other boys are,"
said Logan. "Send Río back with the spring wagon."

Channing climbed into the buckboard. Logan
caught the girl by the elbows, tossed her lightly up,
stood for a moment with a hand on her arm. "No
man," he said gently, "can do better than go down
fighting for the things he believes in and likes best.
Stingy won't be forgotten, or unavenged."

Sudden tears misted Carol's eyes and she was
biting her lips as Buck Channing swung the buckboard around.

Much was done before the day was over with.
Hard riding got most of the herd bunched and
moving again for, as Logan had said, most of the
cattle had not run far. Buzz McClure came out from
town when Río returned with the spring wagon,
and Buzz was in charge of the herd the balance of
the way in to Castella.

In the gentle dusk, under the brooding, silent
timber above headquarters, they held a simple cer-
emony and laid Stingy Dale away. Buck Channing
and Carol were there with the rest, and on the way
back to the house Carol fell in step with Boone
Logan.

"I'm beginning to understand," she said simply.
"An outfit is something more than merely a means
of earning a living. It is a creation built by toil and
hardship and unselfish effort. It is something to
find pride in, to defend at all costs, to live for . . .
and die for, if need be. We . . . we take care of our
own, don't we, Boone?"

"Yes," he said quietly. "We take care of our own."

Logan prepared immediately for town, catching

up a fresh horse. He was startled when Buck Channing asked Río Shore and Jerry Boland to hitch a fresh team to the buckboard. "I want to have a look at that new river range we're going on to," explained the cattleman. "Carol and I are going to take a little boat ride with Matt Corbee."

Before leaving, Logan drew Río and Jerry aside. "Do your sleeping in relays for a while, boys. I don't think they'd dare, but they might have ideas against the home layout. So keep your guns handy at all times."

In town, Logan's first call was at Doc Newcomb's. Doc said: "I got the bullet. That was what had me worried. I feel better about things now,"

Buck Channing and Carol came over. "Carol's bound she's going to help you keep watch through the night, Doc," explained Channing.

Logan said softly: "Good girl."

Logan prowled the town from end to end but could locate no sign of Purse Fallon or any of his men. He took a look in the Oro Fino and was just about to leave when Arch DeLong called him over to the bar, handed him a folded, slightly crumpled paper. "Do me a favor, will you, Boone? Drop over to Masterson's office and give this to him. He must have lost it when he was in here yesterday evening. I found it laying on the floor. He hasn't been in since and I couldn't get clear long enough to deliver it myself. It's a freight bill for stuff brought up to him on the *Pathfinder*. He might be hunting his head off for the damn' thing."

Logan straightened out the paper, ran an eye over it. He nodded and was about to refold it, when his eyes narrowed and he took another look, a more careful one. He flashed a glance at DeLong, saw that Arch was busy polishing glasses, apparently having forgotten about the whole thing already.

"Sure, Arch, I'll deliver it," said Logan. He pocketed the paper and went out.

Kent Masterson's warehouse was locked and dark, and there was no sign of life anywhere. Then, as Logan was about to head for the center of town, he heard the mellow tinkling bell of a lead mule of a pack train, coming in to the corrals. There was the murmur of a voice urging on a lagging pack animal. It was Hoddy's voice.

Logan went down to the corrals as the weary pack train came to a halt. He called: "Hi, kid!"

"Boone!" answered Hoddy. "Just the person I want to see."

Logan knew a swift gust of warm pleasure. This sounded like the Hoddy of older days. He went over to where Hoddy was just dismounting. "What's on your mind, Hoddy?"

The stars were bright and brilliant, but Logan couldn't make out the expression on Hoddy's face. Hoddy was building a smoke and Boone emulated him, waiting. Hoddy began slowly: "For quite a little spell I was the biggest damn' fool in the world, but in the past couple of weeks I've done more clear thinking than ever before. Slogging along alone behind a pack train, spending nights alone under the stars, seems to have sort of loosened up the processes of that buckshot I call my brain. And I've had one hell of a good look at myself. Likewise and besides, I've arrived at the truth of the old saying that blood is thicker than water. Boone, you look out for Kent Masterson. He's no damn' good!"

Boone was very still. Then he said: "Go on, kid. I'm powerful interested."

"Months ago Masterson started working on me, and I can't understand why I didn't blow his crooked heart out, then and there. It must have been the liquor I always had in me. He was smooth, just dropping a word here and a word there, making me feel sorry for myself, and I was then, plenty . . . damn' fool that I was. It shaped up that I was wasting my time riding for the old C Cross, that there was only one Logan who'd ever get places with the old outfit, and that was you. He said the C Cross wasn't going to last, that he'd had word the old man was plenty sick in the East and probably wouldn't live. He said that when the old man did die, the C Cross would go to pieces, and where would that leave me? He said that when the breakup began, smart men would be able to grab off some of those pieces. I . . . I listened to that guff, Boone, and didn't knock his teeth out. I reckon you'll hate me forever for that."

"No, kid, I'd never hate you for anything. Go on."

"Well, it all shaped up that, if I'd break loose from the C Cross and go to work for him, he'd see that I was in a position to cash in when the C Cross fell apart. The fact that I'd listened as long as I had, with him slyly tearing you apart, got me. That was the reason I kept hitting the booze harder and harder. Then, after that final mess in the Oro Fino, when I'd slept off that final jag, and you came into the back room for that little talk . . . and you were so damn' decent . . . that's when I first began to come alive. You got to believe me, Boone, that was when I began to wake up."

"I believe you, kid."

Hoddy drew a deep breath as though in relief. "I figured it this way. Masterson had some kind of a scheme against you and the C Cross. If I'd told you all this at the time, you'd probably have figured most of it just a product of an imagination drove loco by the liquor I'd been sopping up. I had to get more definite proof. And how better to get it than appear to fall in with Masterson's scheming, and how better to do that than to run a pack string for him for a while? Today I saw something I think just about cinches it. I saw him and Purse Fallon riding together as friendly as you please."

"Ah," breathed Boone. "Where and how?"

"Over on the old Custer trail, about ten miles south of Stony Flat. The trail runs through a dry wash there. It was pretty hot and I'd halted the string for a little breather. There was a big rock up on the bank of the wash that threw some shade and I was hunkered under it, having a smoke. Who should I see heading past, about a hundred and fifty yards out, but Masterson and Fallon and half a dozen others. Two of them were doubled up on one horse. Masterson and Fallon were riding a little ahead of the rest, friendly as you please. I stayed right where I was and let them get plenty well out of that part of the country before I started the string on for town. Which is why I'm late getting in. So there it is, Boone."

Boone helped Hoddy unsaddle the pack string and turn the weary mules into the corral. While they worked, they talked, and when, half an hour later, Boone headed for the landing where the *Mohave* was tied up waiting for the arrival of the Skeleton Basin herd early next morning, many things had been arranged.

On the *Mohave* Boone found Buck Channing and Matt Corbee having a friendly drink in Corbee's little cabin. Corbee jumped to get another glass, but Logan shook his head and laid the freight bill Arch DeLong had given him in front of Corbee.

"If you'd ever have hauled freight at that rate, Matt, what would have happened to you?"

Corbee looked the bill over, swore hugely. "I'd've gone busted. That's just about cost, Boone. What the hell is this . . . the *Pathfinder* hauling freight for Kent Masterson at cost? I knew they were doing it downriver to put me out of business, but I thought they jumped their rates before they got this far up, and so set all the wise *hombres* screaming bloody murder."

"Look at the date," said Boone. "This bill is for that freight the *Pathfinder* delivered to Masterson on the morning after the big ruckus over the *Mohave* going off her regular run. In other words, while traders downriver were being robbed on rates, Masterson was getting his freight hauled for cost."

"But . . . but he was squawking just as loud as anybody else," sputtered Corbee.

"For two reasons, maybe," said Boone. "One to make it look good, the other because it was hurting him in a way you'd never dream."

Buck Channing said: "What you driving at, boy? Tell us the rest."

Boone Logan shook his head. "Later, when I get all the pieces fitted together."

"Anyhow," grumbled the cattleman, "I told you out home last night that I'd had a big plenty of Kent Masterson. And I'm sure glad that smart youngster of mine has, too. Masterson had gall

enough to ask Carol to marry him, and she, bless
her heart, turned him down flat. Matt, that's pretty
smooth liquor. How about another finger or two?"

The *Mohave* with the push of the river current behind her was eating up the last ten miles of her return trip to Castella. She had delivered the last of
the Skeleton Basin herd to new range upriver. The
transfer of the C Cross herds to the distance-
locked grass along the river bottoms was complete
and the outfit had entered a brand new phase of
existence, and from all discernible angles a pros-
perous one. Standing on the texas deck above the
thrashing buckets of the paddle wheel, Boone Logan knew a satisfying sense of achievement. With
him were Buck and Carol Channing.

"A few years ago," said Channing, "if anybody
had told me I'd be handling cows the way we been
doing, I'd've damned him as being too crazy to let
run loose. But it looks awful good to me now."

"We'll be sending Matt Corbee on a trip down to
Yuma," said Logan. "We need quite a jag of lumber
to build cabins for the boys with the herds. By next
spring that new railroad will be in as far as Yuma.
And we'll lay C Cross cattle smack at the yards,
without them having to walk off an ounce of fat
along some barren desert trail. The *Mohave* will
more than earn her keep, Buck."

Carol stole a glance up at this big foreman of her
father's outfit. His eyes were narrowed, looking a
long way, as though peering deep into the future
and planning moves still months away. There was
in him, she thought, the fabric of greatness, the
ability to envision, to plan and dare, and the grim,
unshakeable determination to make his dreams

come true. He was of the breed of men who had opened up all the frontiers of the world, used the old accepted means while they were good, then discarded them for something new and better when the time and place warranted.

The mellow blast of the *Mohave's* whistle signaled that Castella was in sight from the pilot house, so they went up there and stood beside it while Captain Corbee put the *Mohave* through a wide, easy turn and came back up against the current to her berth at the landing. A tall, bony-faced man, a stranger, was waiting there and the *Mohave's* engines had hardly stopped when he was aboard and hurrying up to them.

He introduced himself abruptly. "Captain Josh Sumner of the *Pathfinder*, looking for the skipper of this craft."

"Right here," said Corbee, stepping out of the pilot house. "What can I do for you?"

"You might drop downstream about eight miles and pull me off a sandbar."

"What? You mean the *Pathfinder* is aground?"

"That's right. We got out of the channel a little and hung up hard and fast. It happened just before daylight."

"Mister," said Matt Corbee, "when you've been on this river as long as I have, you'll learn one thing . . . to do your running in daylight and tie up for the nights. You're lucky just to have hit a sand bank, instead of tearing your bottom out on a snag."

"I tried to tell . . . er . . . the bosses that, but they said to take her through. Too much time wasted otherwise, so they said. And I'm only working for them."

Matt Corbee turned to Buck Channing. "This is your boat, Buck. It's up to you."

Channing shrugged. "I doubt they'd do as much for us," he growled. "But. . . ."

"Wait a minute, Buck," cut in Boone Logan. "No rush about this thing. Just who are these bosses, Captain Sumner?"

Sumner looked uncomfortable. "Does that matter?"

"It matters plenty," said Logan crisply. "We have to know just who owns the *Pathfinder* before we drag her clear."

"Well," growled Sumner, "in that case they are Jack Ahrens of Yuma, and Kent Masterson of Castella."

"Ah!" exclaimed Logan. "In that case, we'll have to have a little talk with Mister Masterson. We'll go uptown and find him."

Channing was dumbfounded and could only sputter and rumble, while Corbee was in almost the same condition. Carol caught Logan's arm. "Boone, what are you going to do?"

Logan smiled down at her. "Don't worry. Just sort of adjust freight rates along the river. Tell you all about it when we get back."

IX

Kent Masterson was in his office at his warehouse. At sight of them, particularly Sumner, he jumped to his feet. "Sumner," he barked harshly, "what are you doing here?"

"Lining up help to get the *Pathfinder* off a sandbar. We're hard and fast about eight miles downstream. I had a couple of the crew row me up this far in the small boat. From the looks of things, these fellows are going to set a price for pulling us clear."

"They'll not bargain with me," rapped Masterson. "We'll get the *Pathfinder* clear by other methods. I thought you knew your business, Sumner. What kind of a river man do you call yourself?"

"I told you it was taking big risks to run at night on this river," defended Sumner. "I warned you and Ahrens this might happen, but you wouldn't listen."

"I know this river," put in Matt Corbee. "Low water season on hand right now. Tomorrow there'll be less water under the *Pathfinder* than there is now. Next week there'll be still less. More sand and mud will be piling up around the *Pathfinder* all the time. You get her clear now, and in a hurry, or you never will. This old devil river gets it's teeth into something, it don't let go without one hell of a fight. But . . . it's your boat." He shrugged.

That Matt Corbee was speaking the truth, Kent Masterson knew fully well. His face was drawn and beaked with cornered fury, but he gave in to the inevitable. "All right, Channing," he snarled. "What's your price?"

"You can dicker with Boone here," growled the cattleman. "His judgment is pretty sound."

Open hate was in Masterson's eyes as he met Logan's cold glance. "Name it," he spat.

"It isn't much, Kent," drawled Logan. "Just a guarantee of fair play, that's all. You'll write it out and sign it . . . a guarantee of fair freight rates to other traders and merchants along the river . . . rates no higher than those Matt Corbee charged when he was running the *Mohave* on the old route. That's our price, Kent."

"It'll be a cold day when I let you tell me how to run my business!" exploded Masterson.

"Then," murmured Logan, "there isn't a thing we can do for you. Come on, Buck, Matt."

They started to leave when Masterson, in a strangled voice, said hoarsely: "Wait!"

He dropped down to his desk, seized paper and pen, and wrote. When he finished, he pushed the paper across to Logan, who read it carefully, nodded, folded it, and handed it to Buck Channing.

"Put it away where it'll be safe, Buck."

"I'll do that," growled Channing. "And you'll live up to it, Masterson or I'll see to it that you're off this river if it takes every red cent I got to my name . . . and I got several. I'll put the *Mohave* back on her old run and, by gravy, I'll haul freight free if I have to, to put a crimp in you and this Ahrens jigger. You want a fight and you'll get one that they can date time from. Chew on that, Masterson, for it's cold turkey."

The *Pathfinder* lay with her bow upstream. Looking at the steady sweep of the river current along her hull gave the queer sense that she was still plowing along. But she wasn't. Her paddle wheel was idle and closer inspection showed that the forward third of her was lifted upward at a slant.

Matt Corbee, at the wheel of the *Mohave*, said to Josh Sumner: "You bend the heaviest hawser you have to your hog post. Let the other end of it down in your small boat. I'll come around below you and pick it up and tie fast. When we're ready, I'll give you a whistle signal. You give the *Pathfinder* all she's got, full astern. With that, and the old *Mohave* laying into the pull, I think we can do the business."

Captain Sumner went across to the *Pathfinder* in his small boat while the *Mohave* went downstream, swung around, and came beating back up, feeling her way cautiously, with Cocopah Indian deck hands out on the bow working sounding poles. Beside the *Mohave*'s pilot house, Logan, Carol, and her father stood, interested spectators.

They saw the big hawser fastened to the *Pathfinder*'s hog post, saw the small boat come down with the other end, which was picked up and looped about a bitt on the bow of the *Mohave*. Matt Corbee cut his engines and let the *Mohave* drift until the hawser came taut. Then he reached for his whistle cord and sent three sharp *toots* echoing.

They saw the wheel of the *Pathfinder* begin to turn, slowly at first, then faster and faster until everything was a welter of foam. Then the *Mohave*'s wheel began to pound, full astern. The tug of war was on.

The river fought back, trying to hold what it had gotten a grip on. The hawser *twanged* and *hummed* like a giant violin string and a faint haze lay along it as moisture sprayed from it, squeezed out by the press of hard-tightened fibers.

The girl dropped a hand on Logan's arm and said, awe in her voice: "Man against the elements. The oldest battle in the world, Boone. The river . . . doesn't want to give up, does it?"

"Tough old scoundrel, for a fact, this river," said Logan. "But we're whipping it. Things are moving."

They were, and suddenly the *Pathfinder* came clear with a rush. Instantly Matt Corbee threw his wheel hard over and the *Mohave* swung nimbly clear of the bigger boat as it came surging down. Alert deck hands freed the hawser from the bitt and Corbee gave a triumphant blast of his whistle as the *Pathfinder* slid by and her captain waved his thanks.

Buck Channing felt of a paper in his pocket and muttered to himself: "Masterson better keep his written word, or so help me I'll have his hide."

Back at Castella, the *Mohave* still and securely berthed, Logan saw Buck and Carol to their buckboard. "I'll be out later on," he said. "Some things I have to take care of."

Buck Channing looked at him keenly, trying to read more into the words than had been spoken. But Logan's face was smiling and inscrutable.

Logan watched the buckboard out of sight, then headed for the Oro Fino, where Buzz McClure was playing solitaire. At sight of Logan, Buzz stacked the cards. "All set?" he murmured.

"All set. Where's Hoddy?"

"Over at Mig Ariel's saddle shop getting a spur strap fixed. Either there or at Masterson's pack mule corrals, where he said he'd wait for us. You figure to put Masterson on the griddle first?"

"That's right. And through him find out where we can locate Purse Fallon, Dude Orinda, and the rest of Fallon's gang. Stingy Dale and Al Claverly won't rest easy until we even up for them. And that's what I aim to do."

"Al's doing all right. I dropped in at Doc Newcomb's this morning and Al was able to talk to me a little. He says he was sure it was Purse Fallon himself who got Stingy."

They left the Oro Fino, heading for Kent Masterson's warehouse that stood at the east edge of town. They were in the open, before it, when the first shot rolled a heavy echo and Buzz McClure went down in a heap, one leg knocked clean from under him.

Only the desert-bred instinct of split-second alertness saved Boone Logan from quick annihilation then and there. That instinct carried him in a flashing leap to one side and just clear of a lashing hail of lead. He saw them, one at either corner of the warehouse and another in the doorway of the place, and Boone thought with savage anger: *I walked right into it and they got Buzz . . . good old Buzz!*

But they'd gotten only a leg of Buzz, and from his sprawled position on the ground he was in action with quick-striking fury. Buzz got that one at the left-hand corner of the warehouse, got him dead center and heart high. It was Dude Orinda and he came clear of the corner, walking away up on his toes before pitching on his face.

Boone Logan hammered that open doorway with both guns, feeling that there lay the greatest danger. But it came close to costing him dearly, for the one at the right-hand corner of the warehouse, although missing twice, got a third shot home.

The shock of the bullet staggered Logan, but he kept his feet and lashed back. His slug brought a burst of splinters from the corner of the building, glanced, and took hold, and the fellow came clear in a queer, squatting blind spin, clawing at his throat. Logan hit him again and dropped him.

Logan yelled thickly: "Hammer that door, Buzz . . . I'm going in!"

He went forward at a lurching run, fighting off

the numbing pain within him, dragging desperately at failing strength. Buzz, cursing bitterly, did the best he could until his gun snapped empty.

Logan got within twenty feet of the door and knew he couldn't make it. That damned slug he'd taken. . . . He stumbled and went to his knees, and Purse Fallon, teeth bared in a wicked, gloating snarl, leaped clear of the door to savor in full this final triumphant enactment of long-simmering hate.

The muzzle of one of Boone Logan's guns was jammed against the earth as he used it to hold himself up. He saw Purse Fallon through a strange, thickening fog. And it took all the strength he possessed to tip the other gun up and let loose a final shot. Then he collapsed, flat on his face, and the lead Fallon had intended for his heart whistled just above him, struck the earth beyond his sprawled feet, and whined away in ricochet.

As for Fallon, there was a queer, frozen look on his face. He leaned back against the wall of the warehouse, his feet spread widely, but his knees were buckling and his shoulders were sliding down the wall. Abruptly his head rolled loosely and he went all the way down, his teeth still bared in that set, obscene snarl.

Kent Masterson stepped out of that doorway. He had a sawed-off shotgun and now he lifted it deliberately, pulling down on Boone Logan's prone figure. His eyes were raw with hate. And that was when Hoddy Logan came around the corner of the warehouse at a run, a ready gun in his fist. He never hesitated. Inside of three running strides he had emptied the weapon, the last shot letting go when the muzzle of the weapon was less than a foot from Kent Masterson's crumpling figure.

A man darted out of the warehouse, whimpering with terror, shooting wildly as he raced for the far corner of the place. Hoddy Logan caught up Masterson's sawed-off shotgun and let go with both barrels, and the fleeing renegade went off his feet as though struck by a mighty gust of wind.

Hoddy dropped the reeking weapon, darted over to the still figure of his brother, and dropped down on his knees. His voice held a hurt, little-boy note in it as he gulped: "Boone . . . Boone, old fellow. . . ."

X

The cool, balsam-laden breath of green timber lay in the room like a healing benediction. Boone Logan, gaunt, thin, and hollow-eyed, was content to lean back against cushioning pillows and just breathe deeply of that well-loved air. For he could breathe deeply now, without pain. For a long time he hadn't been able to. The pain hadn't really begun to leave him until they'd brought him out from town in the spring wagon. That, he thought, must have been a long time ago, all right. There was a gap in things, somehow, that he hadn't been able to get straight. But it was too much effort to try and figure it right now. It was much better just to lie here, breathe that good air, and sleep. . . .

But a fellow couldn't sleep all the time, not when the stirring of the old wells of energy began coming back. He was glad of the day when Hoddy came in with hot water and other implements and shaved the bristly growth from his face.

"I feel better now, kid," Boone had murmured.

"You look better, I'll tell the world." Hoddy had

grinned. "I can recognize you again now that you're out from behind all that brush."

Then Buzz had come in, awkward on crutches, to cuss Boone affectionately. And it was Buzz who had given him all the story of those few wild moments so many weeks before.

Of course Carol Channing had been in and out all the time. Quiet, deft, swift, and light-footed as a shadow, but never saying much or giving Boone a chance to say much to her. It had brought him huge content just to have her around.

Gruff old Buck Channing had hung around, too, until now he came in and pulled a chair up beside the bed, saying: "Carol's finally allowed me to chew the rag with you a while, boy. That girl's a corker. She's been running me and the rest of the boys like nobody's business."

"How're things along our river range?" Boone asked.

"Finer than frog hair and all quiet everywhere, since that clean-up you and Hoddy and Buzz put on. Which is what I want to talk about. I'm still fighting my head trying to figure out some of the angles . . . Masterson in particular. What set him off, anyhow?"

"I've done a lot of thinking on that, Buck. I think I got most of the answer. It goes a long way back. There was ambition in Kent Masterson, unbalanced ambition, which ran him from a square-shooter into a crooked one, and a schemer. He wanted to be big himself, and envied bigness in others, and his ambition got away from him."

"Go on . . . go on," growled Channing. "That still isn't telling me why he took a stand against us, trying to make us put the *Mohave* back on her regular run while all the time he was half owner of the *Pathfinder* and getting his freight hauled in at cost."

Logan smiled slightly. "He took that stand to cover up and at the same time play both ends against the middle. What he was after was to drive all the other traders off the river, and hog all the business himself. He and his Yuma partner would boost the rates enough to bust the other traders and packers, and take over everything themselves."

"I can see that. It makes sense," admitted Channing. "But why all the sudden hullabaloo about putting the *Mohave* back in business again, after driving her off the river? That's what hits me as being so damned loony."

"Because," said Boone slowly, "Masterson had another big ambition . . . which was to get hold of the C Cross. He had his plans all set and was organized with Purse Fallon and Fallon's crowd to begin taking the C Cross to the cleaners. And then, out of a clear sky, here we buy up the *Mohave*, move our herds out of the back-country range where they could be worked on, and up to the new river range where they are almost untouchable. The day Masterson got the news of our new schedule of operation he looked like he'd been kicked in the belly by a mule. I wondered why then. I know now. It meant that all his fine scheming with Fallon had gone up in smoke. His only chance to keep us from making the move was to get the *Mohave* back on her old run, so he tied in with the other traders who were up here howling. And when that got him nowhere, then he began showing his fangs, for the first time."

"I'm getting it, at last," Channing admitted. "They did take one crack at us, didn't they . . . out at

Stony Flats, against our Skeleton Basin herd? Even then, they didn't run off with any of our cows."

"They weren't intending to run off with any cows. All they were after was to make us sore so we'd go after them and walk into something. We never did until that day of the big shoot-out. Fallon and his crowd had been holing up in Masterson's warehouse, waiting for the big chance. They thought they had me and Buzz cold . . . and they did for that matter, but they muffed it."

"Masterson," snorted the old cattleman, "sure had his nerve, thinking he could ever get control of the C Cross. To have any chance at all for that, boy, both you and me would have to be six feet under."

"That's what he was figuring on, Buck. Somehow he got word that you were plenty sick in the East, and he gambled you never would get back here. And me . . . well, I could always be lured into a corner and smoked down."

"How do you know he knew I was sick?"

Boone shrugged. "Hoddy found that out."

"*Humph!* And when I didn't die," snorted Channing, "when I showed up out here again with a kick or two still left in the old carcass, that damned whelp set out to try and marry into the C Cross."

"That's not fair to Carol," rapped Logan curtly. "She is fine enough to set any man to counting stars. Just for herself, without any ranch thrown in."

"Oh, I didn't mean it that way, damn it! But it still burns me that such a whelp figured he had a chance to marry my girl. He sure played it deep, Boone."

Logan nodded, a trifle somberly. "At one time I would have staked my life on Kent Masterson. I figured him one of my best friends. He stood up for me in more than one open argument." Logan shook his head. "Sometimes I just can't understand."

"I know how you feel," agreed Channing. "Still, they do say you got to play a fish, if he's a big one, before you can land him. And I'm not calling you a fish, either, boy."

Boone grinned. "I know what you mean, Buck."

The door opened and Carol came in bearing a tray of food. "All right, Dad, you've had your session of talk. Now get out of here."

"You see, Boone?" said Channing, heading for the door. "I told you she was getting bossy as hell." But the old fellow was grinning.

She put the tray on the bedside table and began punching pillows into shape, propping Logan a little higher and straighter. Her face was close above him. Swiftly Logan put up his hands, framed her face, pulled her down, and kissed her.

Her startled lips lingered on his, breathlessly. Then she pulled away, straightened, and eyed him reprovingly. "That," she stated severely, "was taking unfair advantage, and I ought to smack you good for it, Boone Logan." But her eyes glowed.

Logan chuckled. "You don't dare smack me, because I'm just a poor, weak man."

Her lips quirked and a dimple showed. "This," she said, "might as well be settled now as later."

She leaned over swiftly and kissed him, dodged his reaching hands, and turned to the tray. "We'll just let things rest right there," she told him over her shoulder. "I don't intend to be proposed to by a human scarecrow so weak I don't dare smack him when I get mad." Her eyes were very tender when she looked at him again.

Said Logan blissfully: "That sure is a powerful incentive to get well fast. Just watch my smoke."

She turned to face him fully again. "In your way, you have a silver tongue, Boone Logan. I guess it's just no use. . . ."

Then she was down on her knees beside the bed, drawing his head into her arms.

ABOUT THE AUTHOR

L. P. Holmes was the author of a number of out-standing Western novels. Born in a snowed-in log cabin in the heart of the Rockies near Brecken-ridge, Colorado, Holmes moved with his family when very young to northern California and it was there that his father and older brothers built the ranch house where Holmes grew up and where, in later life, he would live again. He published his first story—"The Passing of the Ghost"—in *Action Stories* (9/25). He was paid ½¢ a word and received a check for $40. "Yeah . . . forty bucks," he said later. "Don't laugh. In those far-off days . . . a pair of young parents with a three-year-old son could buy a lot of groceries on forty bucks." He went on to contribute nearly 600 stories of varying lengths to the magazine market as well as to write over fifty Western novels under his own name and the by-line Matt Stuart. For many years of his life, Holmes would write in the mornings and spend his after-noons calling on a group of friends in town, among them the blind Western author, Charles H. Snow, who Lew Holmes always called "Judge" Snow (because he was Napa's Justice of the Peace in

1920–1924) and who frequently makes an appearance in later novels as a local justice in Holmes's imaginary Western communities. Holmes's Golden Age as an author was from 1948 through 1960. During these years he produced such notable novels as *Desert Rails, Black Sage, Summer Range, Dead Man's Saddle,* and *Somewhere They Die* for which he received the Spur Award from the Western Writers of America. In these novels one finds the themes so basic to his Western fiction: the loyalty which unites one man to another, the pride one must take in his work and a job well done, the innate generosity of most of the people who live in Holmes's ambient Western communities, and the vital relationship between a man and a woman in making a better life.